WALK THROUGH THE VALLEY

THE HILL TRIBE

KEPHRA RUBIN

Walk through the Valley: The Hill Tribe
By Kephra Rubin
Copyright ©2011-2014. All Rights Reserved
Images © 2011-2014 Kephra Rubin

No part of this book may be reproduced in any form, by any means, or incorporated into any work or collection without written permission of the copyright owner.

You helped me rise from ash and see the light, long after the sun had set.

More of this is true
than you're meant to believe.

"The way they came out of the fog... it was like they crawled right out of the ground. I took aim, but when I fired, my target didn't go down. He reacted. I swear I hit him. I shot him again and again. He reacted every time as if he'd been hit, but he wouldn't die. Why won't you die? I screamed. They just kept coming."
-Anonymous Vietnam Veteran

CHAPTER 1
KAPAOW

"I think they're starting to piece it together now," Kapaow remarked.

"Sure, but are they any closer to *believing?*" Kim countered.

"Believing what? That there is a species of creature whose presence we can barely detect? That they rule the world by affecting our minds, amplifying our fears while obliterating our desire for freedom? That, when needed, they can use any weak mind or empty soul to do their bidding and change the tides of this eternal battle in their favor again and again? You *know* what's really going on in the world and you talk to me like I'm crazy for not just coming out and telling them. Kim, these soldiers wouldn't even abandon us. They'd just smile and giggle at our childish, silly tribal view of the world. There's two wars going on right now: the battle out here that we can see, and the battle within us. These creatures don't win the outer battles because they are powerful. They are powerful because, time and time again, we allow them to win the *inner* battles. I have to help them fight their inner battles. *Then* we can win our war and gain our people's freedom from oppression."

"I know, I know, but it is hard to believe. It is hard to have resolve when I have seen these people come and go. My mother has seen them go, and my grandmother all the same. They all say they want to make a difference, but once they realize it isn't going to be easy, they give up, and they use 'following orders' as a way to justify it. I just think we need to take matters into our own hands and stop looking for outside help."

"Over a thousand years ago we tried that and failed. We should have kept trying, learned from our mistakes, been smarter with the battles we chose. There's a lot that should have been done, Kim. It's too late now. We are paying for the submissions of our ancestors. We can't get out of this alone. The world is too crazy now. *They* have their hold on more minds than we care to count. It's like they've made us invisible."

The two paused as they considered the concept of being unseen, even as they cried out for help.

"Did you hear it last night? The Tree Fairies are in rare form as of late."

"Call them whatever you want with me, but never call them Tree Fairies to the Americans, okay? *Promise* me," Kapaow insisted. He could not stress this enough.

"Why? That's what they are." Kim was aghast at his reaction, as if calling a goat a goat was now suddenly ridiculous.

"I was talking with Ghost Doc, feeling him out... he's the most open minded, after all."

"Of course."

"I led the conversation towards the unknown and the idea of fairies in the forest. He said not very long ago, Americans knew that fairies were evil. But somehow, within just a few decades, everyone forgot. They actually believe fairies are good. Ghost Doc thinks it is insane because all ancient tales ended with horrible things happening to the characters at the hand of fairies. He said that, almost overnight, it all changed. If you say Tree Fairy to them, they will laugh at you."

Kim gasped. "If the warnings they tell their children at night have lost all effectiveness, perhaps the Tree Fairies really have taken over the entire world!"

"No!" Kapaow became a body of fury at her comment. "They do not rule *us!* They *never* will! We are not alone, Kim. There are others who resist their influence. You *have* to believe that."

"I do believe it. I just don't know if it matters. They are so powerful. Did you hear it last night? It was... *them.* I know it was. You can always hear the difference between combat and someone being torn apart by them. I heard gunshots, so someone died. Then the fairies raised the body of the fallen, I know because I heard the screams of disbelief... and then I heard the screams of agony. The Tree Fairies are so sadistic, the way they torture their victims. They enjoy it all, don't they? The suffering, the control, the power–they love it all, and they're getting closer to us."

"I know." Kapaow nodded.

"We're running out of time."

"I *know,*" Kapaow growled. "I swear they were at that last scuffle."

"We should leave, set up a new village again."

Kapaow ignored her. "Have you been meditating? You need to keep your head clear."

"I *know,* Kapaow."

"Well, you sound very negative and helpless is my only point. Perhaps they've been here longer than we realized, chipping away at you."

"Oh, like you're so much better? What are you really doing anyway? *Waiting.* That's all you've been doing is waiting for them to see. Go to the shore and fish if that's all you're going to do!" Kim yelled.

"Hey! I'm doing more than you'll ever be able to comprehend. Watching them, waiting to see who's thinking about what, making sure Ghost is near Bleak when he needs to be, pushing Chinny towards Sinner at the right times, back and forth, crissing and crossing them to make sure they see what they need to see. I know what I'm doing."

"You sound like one of *them*, you master manipulator, you."

Kapaow slapped her across the face. She touched where he had struck her and looked at him with wide eyes, in total shock at his behavior. That was not like Kapaow. He stopped himself. It was scary how much effort it took to not slap her again. It was them, amplifying his anger, his fear, trying to twist his mind so that those most important to him became his enemies. He pulled her close and hugged her hard, kissed her forehead and quieted her. He looked around the forest.

I know you're here. You're probably watching.

No, he chastised himself. *Do not so much as think in their direction.*

Who knew what they were capable of? This all may be an attempt at learning more of the plan. He closed his eyes and felt for Kim's soul, letting hers intermingle with his own. She was his blood. He loved her. Nothing would change that.

"I am sorry, Kim. I promise you, this will work"

"If it doesn't?"

"Then I will try and learn from my mistakes instead of repeating them."

They held each other in silence, and Kapaow began to feel better. *They* must have attempted to influence them, but it did not work. Now *they* had given up on influencing Kim and Kapaow. Their love was too strong, their minds too clear, their fear too well conquered to allow themselves to be whipped into a frenzy. They had beaten *them.* This was how Kapaow knew it was possible to win. Small victories could lead to larger ones.

"I feel better, thank you," Kim said, then after a moment she pulled away. "Was that *them?*"

"I think so, but we beat them, didn't we?"

"Yes, and that's wonderful… but where did they go?"

The thought hadn't occurred to Kapaow. Where *did* they go? Kapaow took her by the hand and began to run.

"We have to get back to the others."

CHAPTER 2
CHINNY

"Left side!"

It had started out as a routine check, business as usual. They came upon a bloke that just didn't seem right. He didn't smile, which on its own wasn't enough, but he didn't make eye contact either. The rest of the people seemed tense, like they knew something. A lot of Viet Cong would muscle their way into villages and force the people to hide them. Once things got a little too close, the bloke ran, and they followed him right into a trap

Now they were being flanked. Chinny wanted his team to open fire, but they still had no clear targets. If only they could retreat and draw out their enemy to separate them from the civilians.

"AAAHH!!!" A woman took a round through her back, which exited her clavicle bone and burst from beneath her skin. She wasn't dead and would likely survive, but the wound was horrid: bits torn to shreds, with bone sticking out.

"TWO O'CLOCK!" Chinny screamed at the sight of a gun barrel poking around a corner.

Crack-Crack-Crack

Chinny eased his finger against the trigger of his rifle in risk repetition.

"GO!" Sinner screamed. Chinny pushed forward as Sinner fired his shotgun.

BOOM! CH-CHK BOOM!

Pellets fired from a shotgun tend to spread out. Not just in a circular pattern, but also front to back. The string of pellets zipping by created the effect of a burst fully automatic fire from the point of view of the enemy. It put the pressure on while allowing them a moment to move. Another target presented itself. Chinny watched Sinner pull the trigger once, but hit the target nine times as the buckshot spread and impacted every major organ.

"It much like team!" Kapaow's innocent voice was a stark contrast to his vicious abilities as a warrior.

"What?" Chinny had no idea what the bloke was talking about.

"It not so hard, much like team!"

Chinny almost stopped firing. What the bloody hell was this fool talking about? He fired a few more times before realizing what he was talking about. It was a tired discussion, certainly not one worth engaging in now.

"Not this shite again, Kapaow—move!" Chinny growled.

"AMBUSH!" Ghost screamed.

It was a poorly orchestrated one, but sure enough, plenty of blokes were exposing themselves. Perhaps they had delayed a bit while working up the courage to attack. Things were working up into a frenzy.

Kapaow fired and reloaded his grenade launcher so fast it almost sounded semi-automatic. "Yes, *this* shit!" Kapaow yelled back.

KA-PAOW! KA-PAOWKAPAOW! The grenade rounds detonated.

"Not now!" Chinny didn't care if Kapaow heard him as he yelled while firing his rifle.

"Now only time you talk!" Kapaow replied, referencing the fact that they only ever had something that resembled a meaningful conversation when their lives were on the line.

"Yeah, because it's so hard to fucking ignore ya, ya twat!"

"Who push you? Only me, Chinny!"

"I don't need a bloody girlfriend," Chinny grumbled, "I need covering fire! COVERING FIRE!" he screamed.

"Need soon! What if I die, Chinny? What if you die? What if too late? Then you die bad. Must die good, Chinny. Happy!" Kapaow reasoned as Chinny moved away. "Not too late!"

Chinny was suddenly reminded of his rugby days as some twat smashed into him from the side. His head hit the ground the hardest. The impact made a ringing sound in his ears and a sick feeling in his stomach. He struggled for his wits, but found himself pausing.

He was looking at a bush with arms: *No, you bloody fool, it's a man, shoot him!* The man wore a suit made of local grasses. Chinny took a punch to the face. This did little other than royally piss him off. He struggled for his rifle, which had fallen just out of reach.

He felt dirty, scaly hands wrapping around his neck as he reached for his sidearm, which was blocked by the bastard's legs. *Blood hell!* He snapped his hand up as quickly as he could and drew his knife from its sheath. He swung the blade and felt it dig its way through flesh, grinding through the joint where the jaw hinged. He twisted and felt it pop. He stabbed twice more into his lungs, pushing him off. He drew his pistol, and turned to fire five rounds at a charging attacker attempting to club him with his rifle. The bloke took a face dive right into the dirt. Chinny turned back and fired a bullet through the skull of the other one; better to end it for him instead of let him bleed out through his lungs. Choking to death on blood was likely worse than drowning. Drowning was one thing he'd never wish on his enemy.

"CLEAR!" Bleak yelled. Everyone checked their sectors and called out all-clear.

"Clear!" Chinny added.

Chinny was knocked to the ground again. *Bloody fuckin' hell, twice in one day?* This time he went straight for his knife and stabbed. *What the hell?* It was the bloke he'd already shot five times. Chinny stabbed again. How was this even possible?

Cr-cr-cr-cr-cr-cr-cr-cr-CRACK!

One long stream of bullets gnawed away at the man until his head was gone and Chinny was covered in blood. He wiped the filth from his face, his vision blurring. Once the blurs became clear, he saw Kapaow standing over him, his hand outstretched, a smile on his face. Chinny took his hand and was hoisted to his feet. He looked down at the body.

"Bloody disgusting save ya got there, mate." He patted Kapaow on the back.

"Maybe Mai?"

"What?"

"Mai, she pretty, yes?"

"Oh, *bloody hell,* Kapaow."

"We should probably call this in," Bleak said.

"Okay..." Chinny replied, slightly annoyed. "So call it in."

"Right."

Chinny glared at the body again. Five shots to the chest and the bloody bastard was still able to get up and knock him on his arse. "All in a day's work," he said to no one in particular.

"Yeah. Great job, great pay. Great benefits, too," Ghost quipped as he came up alongside Chinny to check him for wounds.

"Let's get this shite cleaned up quick as we can, yeah? Important business back at the village."

Business he rather regretted.

CHAPTER 3
CHINNY

It was something a person could only do once in their life, and yet they'd never remember doing it. At least, he didn't think so. The sight of it was something he could never get used to. Sure, after a while he'd learned to choke back his disgust for the sake of being polite. He never could tell which dug through his teeth more: the sight of the blood or the sound of the screams. As much as he tried to avoid the thought, some part of him couldn't help but wonder: What *did* it feel like?

He tried to imagine himself choking on his own fluids, surrounded by people trying to help but only adding to his terror. He tried to feel the light scorching his eyes. He actually shivered as the air that should have felt warm was icy-cold as it climbed down his throat. How that mysterious, godly hand hovered above, ready to judge, to smite. To feel doomed, not knowing what would happen next.

Smack!

Chinny wondered: what *was* it like to be born?

"WAAAAAAhhhhh …AAAAHHhhhhhh …" The sound of a baby crying marked yet another life delivered to this world by hands trained to kill.

"Okay, we got a breath! Bleak, hand me that—"

"That's nasty, that is *always* just… nasss..."

"Bleak—"

" …teeeeee—"

"Bleak, hand me the towel already, come on," Ghost Doc said, half laughing, half frustrated, and far from shy around blood.

"Go Doc, best doc! Numbah one." Ling Pao, or Kapaow as the boys had started calling him for his skill with explosives, was the father. He chanted his approval of Ghost Doc's delivering capabilities in rather broken English.

"I ain't handin' you shit, ya dig? There ain't words for how… *nnnasty...*" Bleak was far more squeamish around babies than corpses.

"Pretty baby, Bleek-ah too bleak," Kapaow said, reaching out to physically turn Bleak's frown upside down.

"Quit it, Kapaow."

9

"Stop being such a Melvin and wrap this…" Ghost mocked. "Yes. *Thank you,* Kapaow At least *somebody* can keep his wits about him. Sheesh, man, it's a darn baby." Ghost cuddled the baby for a moment before handing him over to Kapaow's beaming wife.

"Whatever. I'll get you a damn towel," Bleak shot back.

"*Kapaow* took care of that. Why don't you go get Mamma Ling some tea instead?" Ghost responded, obviously continuing to toy with Bleak.

"Oh? Why? Cuz I'm black? I'm supposed to go get some tea cuz I'm black?"

"Fine, get her some milk."

"That's not my point… nevuh mind man, ol' jivin' ass turkey."

"Go Doc, we name him Go Doc!" Kapaow was happy, and Chinny tried to smile for him.

Truth be told, Chinny had seen more dreadful things in a day than most men witnessed in a lifetime. Regardless of how many bullet holes, intestines, shite and piss he'd dealt with, it was the goopy, gloppy, shriveled body of a little ankle biter covered in slime and blood that was more unsettling. *Come watch,* they say. *See something you've been chasing for years stretch out to the size of a melon.*

It was the same story as usual with Bleak, or Carl Green as his mum might say. He was always carrying on about something that wasn't right or shouldn't be. Only to turn around, built like a brick shit house the way he was, and do the right thing in the end. Which at the time was milking a goat.

"Come on, Bleak, ya bloody milko. What's the holdup then? This sheila's gettin' thirsty, yeah?" Chinny called out.

"The fuck you just say to me? I know you're not talkin' that Aussie jibba jabba to *me.*"

"Ha, ha. Hurry up with the milk, Mister Green. This woman just did an amazing thing. She's gonna need her strength." Chinny exaggerated his artificial joy for the sake of Kapaow.

"Yeah, yeah," Bleak grumbled as he brought the milk over. "Drink this, Mama Ling," he said sweetly.

Chinny scanned the tree line and then his men. Bleak was an imposing figure. It was odd to watch him give Kapaow a big, warm hug. He watched as the two shook hands. In contrast to Bleak's hand, Kapaow's was crinkled and scarred, like the crinkly mess left from frying an egg white.

Ghost Doc's brass bracelet jingled when he again checked Kapaow's… what was it? *Oh, yes, another son.* It matched

Kapaow's bracelet almost perfectly. The villagers had slaughtered a chicken in celebration of Ghost receiving the bracelet. Everyone danced into the night. It was quite a ceremony. The wearer was to never take it off, a condition Ghost Doc was sure to heed. For a moment, Chinny took his eyes off the tree line, off his men, off the situation, and examined his own bare wrists.

"Chinny! Chinny, come! Come." Kapaow was almost skipping.

"All right, all right. I'm on it then, yeah? No need to yabber on about it like some bloody sheepshagger."

"Yes, Chinny. Chinny, you bless him. Go Doc. You bless." Kapaow's smile was ear-to-ear. Chinny wasn't technically the bloke in charge, but he somehow became the village shaman or some galah nonsense, blessing *every* baby that popped out. In spite of his many blessings, he still didn't have a bracelet of his own. Not that he wanted one.

"This boy is loved by all present and by those no longer here. We will protect this boy with our lives, and if necessary, give our lives in doing so. May God deem us worthy of seeing this boy become a man. Cheers." He felt a knot of awkwardness in his stomach. He said the same bloody thing every time.

He looked at the boy, so void of hate, anger, or misery. So perfect, so very unlike him. Kapaow came up beside him, always quick to give a hug. Chinny put his hands up to stop him—no... there was no one beside him. Who had he felt at his side a second ago? He looked around and saw Kapaow hugging Bleak and Ghost Doc. Chinny was alone, but he swore someone was standing next to him... strange.

There was no one close by and no one looked at him as he scanned the village. *Hmmm... strange.* He looked back at the baby. His stomach tightened, his chest feeling a bit of pain. He always thought he'd be a father someday. *Oh well.*

"Thank uh, thank uh. Thank Chinny, thank Chinny!"

The small statured man ran over and lifted him off the ground before Chinny had a chance to put his hands up in protest. He heaved his body up and down in celebratory splendor. Kapaow was a Montagnard, or a Yard, for short. Yards were *extremely* strong for their size, as was evidenced by Chinny's inability to break free from Kapaow's grasp.

Bleak was slapping his knees and laughing to the point of coughing. The air filled with the decayed smiles of people who lacked proper oral hygiene. Ghost Doc had been working on getting toothbrushes and the like sent in, but for many, the damage was already done. It was all quite charming.

12 | KEPHRA RUBIN

The radio came to life. *"The Chink baby get borned yet 'er what, Chinny? I'm gettin' pretty tired of runnin' with the gook pack through the damn forest."* Chinny could feel his I.Q. drop.

"Say again, Sinner? I don't believe I read you clearly."

"Oh, don't start that shit, Chinny. Come on buddy, it's freakin' hotter n' sweat under a fat lady's titties out here."

"Still not reading you." Chinny was inclined to let him roast.

"Dang it... Chinny, did Kapaow's child get borned yet? If so, me and the men would like to return to base and have a look-see."

"Right-oh. RTB on the double."

"Thank the lord. Uncle Sam find out where all the dead bodies went yet?"

"Last week's C-Rations," Chinny quipped.

"Ha ha, thought they tasted better."

"Double time. They're gonna let *you* gut the boar."

"Who says zipper heads ain't nice? Goin' have me some pulled pork tonight, boy."

"Sinner," Chinny chided with his jaws clamped down.

"Oh, please. You know they love me." Sinner got the last word, as he often did.

Chinny held his head, fighting back the headache he got anytime Sinner spoke. He was a good soldier, Chinny reminded himself. He took a deep breath, scanning the tree line and for the first time in a long time. He took a moment to appreciate the scenery.

The silence of the air was a rare beauty. In the distance, one could detect the faintest chatter of the jungle: bugs and birds and faint echoes of assorted animals. It was so quiet he almost couldn't hear any gunfire in the distance over the laughter. Perhaps the jungle was happy, too.

Chinny shifted in place, his knees creaking. At home, he was still a boy. In the 'Nam, at the age of 27, he was an old man.

Sinner rounded the corner a while later with a troop of Yards in tow. He had them singing a song about someone's overweight mother having sex with her skinny husband and putting him in the emergency room... again. The Yards tried to sing along, butchering the English language. Bleak made a crack about Sinner lacking lyrical skill and Ghost Doc shushed them all. One big happy family. Chinny checked the tree line.

"Sin, make sure you hydrate these guys and pop some salts and stretch," Ghost paused in frustration. "Beeefore you sit down and have alcohol, which you're doing right *now*, even though you know you're going to get cramps later. Groovy man," Ghost Doc, aka mother hen, warned.

"Now what in the hell is 'groovy' s'pposed ta mean?"

"Groovy, boss, great ... sarcastically in this case."

"Oh, fox shit in a hen house, Ghost. Where the hell'd you hear that?"

"What? Everybody's saying it."

"Doc, come on now. A man has needs, and my main squeeze is right in this here flask. Ooohweee!" Sinner coughed profusely as he gulped down the fermented concoction made by the Yards.

It was Chinny's idea to conceal the drink's recipe from Sinner. Luckily there was always an excuse to send him out on water detail right around the time the women chewed and spit the brew into containers for fermenting. It was a difficult scenario. No drugs, no smoking, no alcohol: those were Chinny's rules. The villagers viewed the fermented herbal brew as a bonding ritual, denial of which would have driven a wedge between them and slowed progress. So he allowed it, but made sure to keep a watchful eye so it never got out of hand.

"Now dat is sum gooooood shine." Sinner turned to Bleak. "Ya feel me, Spook?"

"Fuck you, honkey," Bleak punched Sinner in the arm.

"Ow! Dangit! What'd you do that for?"

"Fuck you."

"Guys, you need to hydrate. See everyone else drinking *water?*" Ghost demanded again.

"Oh, fuck those zipper heads They can't even brush they teeth right."

"Brother, you got like six teeth between you and yo grandmamma. Don't even," Bleak retorted. Sinner had a full set, but the two were always going back and forth.

The Yanks were amusing in general, though he'd rather fall on a pike than work with most of them. The Americans as a whole had only begun to trickle in, and already they were too loud, too smelly, and too careless on even the most basic patrols. In spite of having to police noise levels from time to time, he figured he had the best Yanks available.

There was some uneasiness about how Bleak had been given his rank. Some thought perhaps he'd been caught in bed with a higher up's wife or some other mess and the promotion was a roundabout way of getting him killed. What about the rest of the team? Was the group some kind of rubbish bin for all the muck? Their mission did feel somewhat removed from the rest of the

Montagnard initiative. Perhaps it was more about some sort of political maneuvering he didn't care to understand. Either way, Bleak had started out rather cocky. Even worse, though, as time went on he grew more and more fearful, perhaps even slightly paranoid. Most frustrating of all was how little the lad saw of his own potential.

"AWWW yeah. Here it is baby. We gon' boogie tonight!" Bleak had fetched his drum, a gift from the Yards.

He thumped and danced, singing songs Chinny didn't know and arguing with Sinner about which one to play next. Chinny started to laugh … and then …

A memory killed the smile.

CHAPTER 4
CHINNY

Chinny remembered the way the rain made the bodies sink into the mud, the way the sun later hardened them in place. He remembered how it took a good portion of the day to dig them all out. Mostly Yard children, babies. The ears were missing from every corpse.

He mulled over the images in his mind. He had seen so much, certain memories pushed others out of the way. He was like a cup with too much brew; all the good things kept spilling out to make room for the bad. Yet, he couldn't face the bad day-in and day-out. His mind was becoming a black place. His memories were covered up with black to prevent reliving those wretched experiences. Every once in a while, though, the memories would tear their way to the front of his mind, begging for attention, begging not to be forgotten. The slash marks, the lumpy gashes where their little ears had been taken as trophies. Someone needed to stay with them, to not get on with life like it never happened. Someone needed to remember them.

Chinny glanced over and saw Kapaow laughing, urging Chinny to join them. In the here and now, the village was facing an impending genocide, yet they danced and sang songs to the rhythm of Bleak's drum. It was so easy for them, so easy it made Chinny angry, and his anger became something he tried to bury as well. What would he do if they were all slaughtered, their ears torn from their flesh? Where would he put all of them inside of his mind? What would spill out? What would he lose to make room for them?

No, ya bloody twat. Just leave it all behind. Finish the job and be done with it. Forget all this shite as soon as you leave this godforsaken place.

Chinny put it all away and looked over the team. Ghost Doc pretended to play the guitar, surprisingly well. He adjusted the tuning knobs, pausing to flick a make-believe cigarette he placed in his mouth and let dangle from his lips. He leaned in and slammed his hand across the strings, letting the sound vibrato. Sinner vocalized the sounds.

15

The Yards loved them all for different reasons. What escaped him was what the Yard women saw in Sinner, of all people. No doubt there would be a brass bracelet on his wrist soon enough, one big happy family. Chinny sighed to alleviate the knot in his gut. Hopefully he'd be redeployed by then.

They were all lucky. Out in the bush with good people, doing good things. They hadn't been attacked in quite a while. The word must have been out that the team of foreigners led by an Aussie were here for the good of the people. That was how Australia handled things. Steal the hearts, capture the minds, and the rest would follow. Not quite as glamorous as bombing everything, but far more effective. This little sanctuary they had built was proof of that.

He stared down at the dirt, pretending to move to the rhythm like everyone else, occasionally cracking a smile or sending a few signals to a lady he'd never follow up with. He wondered what such a friendly people could have possibly done to have so much taken away.

"Hey, Chin?" The drumming grew louder as Bleak approached. "The guys on guard want to party. Whatchu think?"

"What do *you* think?"

"No big deal, right?"

"No big deal?" Chinny questioned.

"Yeah?"

"Asking or telling?" Chinny asked.

"Ain't shit happen around here in like forever, right?" Bleak smiled.

"Best to leave 'em on watch, lad. Ya never know. You should know this."

"Hey, man… yeah… no… I know…" Bleak nodded, a tad disappointed as he walked back to the party.

Cadeo, one of the orphans of the village, came over. *Oh, bloody hell.* The ankle biter had a big smile on his face. Chinny took a deep breath and did the best he could to smile back. *Are my knees up for this?* His heart started to pump harder than it did during the last gunfight he'd been in. *Why can't they all just stick to themselves? Do the work, shut up, and go home when it's done?*

"Supah Mang!" Cadeo said with a huge smile and his fists pressed up to the sky.

"Ha ha, ya want another go of the old Superman, aye? Right, then. Up ya go." He hoisted Cadeo up onto a bench they'd made together.

It was a shabby structure, indeed. It had a slight tilt to it, such that you could never rest the Hong fruit brought over by Kapaow's friend from Dalat without the damn things rolling off. About the only thing it *was* good for was climbing on top of and jumping off into Chinny's arms.

"Wow! That was a good one!" Chinny lied. *Just keep making nice.*

"I go far?"

"Yes, you did!" He did actually jump pretty far that time. "You think you can jump farther?"

"Nooo ..."

"I'll catch ya, don't worry." Chinny took three steps back, a little over a meter away.

"No, too far."

"Come on, mate, you can do it. I'll catch ya. I promise." Chinny smiled. Truth be told, he really did think the little bugger could make it.

"You catch me, yes?" Cadeo wiggled and focused on Chinny's hands as he mustered up the will to jump.

"I promise. I always keep my promises." Chinny reached out as far as he could.

Cadeo jumped. Chinny wasn't sure he'd actually do it. Not only did he jump, he flattened himself out, parallel to the ground, Superman style. Chinny reached out as far as he could without moving his feet. The boy collided with Chinny, who took him up in his arms as securely as he could. He spun around a little to dampen some of the force ...and perhaps because Cadeo loved to get dizzy. *Kids.* He placed Cadeo steady on the ground and couldn't help but crack a smile as the boy jumped up and down and declared himself Superman.

This all felt so familiar, but Chinny couldn't place it. It was like he'd done it before... maybe not. What was it, then? A faint suspicion in the back of his mind. Something called to him, tried to remind him. It was like staring at redacted paperwork and trying to figure out what words hid behind the black lines. Perhaps some buried things didn't want attention, at least not yet. Everything always seemed so long ago out in the bush. A day was a week, a week a month, a month a year. Lifetimes ago, something beckoned to him. Try as he might, he couldn't place it. The harder he tried, the more sick he felt in his stomach.

"Okay, that's enough for today, mate. My knees are killing me. Go harass Sinner."

"Supah Mang, Supah Mang," Cadeo chanted and smiled as he skipped away.

Thank God. As usual, Chinny waited until everyone was fired up from the party before wandering away. He could hear Sinner telling the boy to go away. Chinny loved sending Cadeo over to him, since he so quickly got under the man's skin. He watched the men and women huddled in a mass, dancing and swaying, and took it as his cue to disappear. It was something he was very good at.

The leaves rustled in a gentle breeze. He tried to move with every thump of Bleak's drum. That was the key to stealth: searching for opportunities to mask the noises one made. He also liked to move in the same manner as some animals. Humans had a certain rhythm to how they moved. Right now, Chinny was sneaking away like a goat. He searched for a spot where Kapaow probably wouldn't find him. Sitting down behind a tree, he let out a long sigh of relief. Finally, some alone time.

Pap ... pap ... pap

Only a few minutes had passed before the sound of a man's footsteps rustled through the jungle. *So much for quiet time.* The man walked a little to the left and paused, a little to the right and paused. What would be a good excuse for not joining the party? The footsteps drew closer, to the left, then the right. He knew it was rude, but he had a right to be alone if he chose. Now the man was moving in a circle.

"I'm over here, Kapaow," Chinny sighed. No sense in delaying the inevitable.

Kapaow held two small cups of brew and handed one to Chinny before sitting next to him. Together they stared out into the wilderness. The quiet of it all made Chinny uncomfortable. Kapaow sipped his brew and remained focused on the jungle. Chinny wondered when Kapaow would try to drag him to the party as he always did. Maybe Chinny'd complain about his knee.

Kapaow patted him on his thigh a couple of times and stood up, took a sip of brew and smiled, then patted him on his shoulder. After a sigh, he walked away. His pace quickened into a light jog and he returned to his wife in the center of the dancing circle. Chinny's stomach turned over.

Why hadn't Kapaow invited him over? Maybe Chinny would have accepted this time. He watched them all dancing and suddenly, he felt a fool. *It's all for the best, mate. No sense giving a shite about something that's just gonna be taken away.* He sagged back into his hiding place. A small leaf flapped in the wind, struggling to stay attached. A couple of the men on guard put down their tools of destruction in favor of happier gestures. When was the last time Chinny danced, anyway? He was probably awful.

He yawned. Perhaps the heat, a bit of exhaustion, came to them all. Perhaps Ghost Doc was correct in asking them to hydrate more frequently. Good water discipline was essential. He might have found himself a bit lacking in that regard, at least tonight.

Ghost Doc and Kapaow held hands over Mamma Ling, dancing in a circle around her. Chinny wasn't looking, but he knew what it sounded like when they did that dance. His eyes searched for the darkest hole in the jungle. The liquor was strong and his cup took a while to be emptied. It was dark now, but the party raged on. Chinny's eyes relaxed and the night shifted back and forth, growing and shrinking to-and-fro and molding itself into shapes. Like watching the clouds, he used his imagination to find things in the shapes. He saw what could have looked somewhat like a roo, hopping about with a joey in its pouch. In truth, he didn't see them much back home. Sinner loved to make the assumption, though.

He saw his wife at home, her delicate blonde hair glistening in a ray of sunlight. That was how he first noticed her. The light shined off it in such a way—amazing. He was rushing to get somewhere, but all it took was a glint and his heart skipped. Try as he might, it was his only memory of her. What did her face look like? It'd been years.

He tried to think back and remember whether his eyes had always seen flickering little colors hiding in the blackness, perhaps similar to the way a man only heard a ringing in his ears when it was silent. Or was this some new degradation of his health? The shifting night looked like different paint blots of black mixed with a dash of other colors.

At that moment, the blots appeared to form into the faintest of outlines. His stomach felt a bit queasy. It almost looked like a face. It moved around, swayed, and surveyed the village. It was very round, almost like an infant's face. As he began to see the outlines of tiny features, he felt downright ill. It was almost like the face had finally decided to stare at Chinny. The drums fell silent. He was all alone.

The sound of air passing through his throat made scratchy muffled noises in his ears. He breathed faster when the face's eyes seemed to open wider and wider. His teeth ground like two porcelain cups skidding across each other. It was so faint, so minute, yet he swore, *somehow*, that the eyes appeared somewhat blue. He couldn't breathe. He needed to stand.

It must be the humidity. Always so humid out here. Breathe, Chinny. Just relax.

He chucked his empty cup into the darkness and shook his head to break his trance. Whether it was the alcohol or something else, he preferred to blame the alcohol. His eyes felt heavy, the awful tasting booze taking its toll. The airy sound of white noise in the distance faded. Chinny looked up at the stars, away from the dark void, and into one that had a little shimmer.

Look away, Chinny. Think of good things.

His men finally getting a well-deserved night of joy after quite some time of heavy construction and boring but potentially dangerous patrols. Or the hospital that they built, despite the engineers who were supposed to help never showing. *Lazy bastards.* They could have checked into it, but the radio equipment was sketchy at best in this particular area of Yard territory. Every now and again some group of fools would fly in a helicopter looking to flash their title, say something useless, and leave without contributing anything to the cause.

Positive thoughts, mate. Let it go.

The intel, the most precious part of it all, was quite useful. The locals were finally starting to trust them. Things *had* changed. The Aussie approach to warfare was working. He was proud of the men. They adapted and were eager to learn. Even the fact that Sinner, the most difficult to be proud of, was dancing with the Yards at this very moment was a reward in itself. He peeked through the foliage and managed to find the man. He was slapping his knee and clapping, and definitely drunk.

Things really were better. Maybe this whole mess could be settled using the hearts and minds method. Maybe someday they wouldn't need to fire a shot to make a change. Sinner stopped slapping his knee long enough to put a flower in Ho Ti Hwon's hair. She'd probably show her gratitude later. Sinner turned and looked out into the jungle. His smile went away. Sinner froze in the crowd like a statue.

Damn it all.

Chinny's knees were weak, his heart light and fluttering like one might feel staring over the edge of a mile high cliff. Immediately, Chinny looked to Kapaow. In his mind Chinny begged, *not tonight.* Then Sinner and Kapaow stared at each other, and that was it. Bleak stopped dancing. A cold look crossed his face.

Chinny sighed and, slower than what was appropriate, drew his pistol. He flicked off the safety and the entire party came to a ragged halt. Sinner cupped his hand around his mouth and screamed to Chinny. Chinny didn't react right away, but he heard him.

"CONTACT!"

CHAPTER 5
SINNER

Sinner took a dive at the nearest weapon, wishing it was his Lady Antoinette but instead getting one of those Tyco Toy plastic crap M16s. The thing about diving for a rifle was a man had to do it drunk. That way he couldn't feel the jagged rocks diggin' into his spine when he did some stupid roll maneuver, nor could he feel it when he jammed his fuckin' finger in the trigger guard. He never used to do dumb monkey-moves like that. Them stupid yellow niggers were rubbing off on him.

Quick as could be he was up on his feet, safety off, barking at the dark like a dog from Hell looking for souls to take home to papa. Each bullet exited the barrel at roughly three thousand feet per second with some damn thirteen hundred foot-pounds of force.

Yeah, how's God's wrath feel, Charlie? Still want to slit Yard babies' throats?

The one-in-fourteen inch twist rate of the barrel didn't really stabilize the tiny bullet all that much, but Mister Eugene Stoner intended it that way when he designed it. A lazy bullet was a tumbling bullet just as soon as it hit flesh and turned a pathetic little poodle shooter into a Goddamn meat axe ready to sever the heads of them baby killers out in those woods.

"TASTE IT, MUTHAFUCKAS!" he screamed into the wind, to the enemies that hid within the dark. No one came into his house uninvited and expected to get anything less than full bore. Before the Dinks in the trees even had time to react, one of 'em was already screaming in agony. Sinner adjusted his fire.

Forgive me, Father, for I have sinned. Forgive me—as I sin again. Forgive me still… as I have no intentions of stopping. These mother fuckers gotta die.

Sinner didn't like full-auto fire, and instead placed paired shots out whenever he saw a flicker or possible threat. He heard the click of the hammer inside the gun fall on an empty chamber and he panicked. Even a piss and vinegar, fire-breathing, red-blooded American could admit when he hadn't completely thought his actions through to the last letter. Where the fuck was his Lady Antoinette? That's what he really needed right about now.

BLAP BLAP BLAP!

Next on scene was a kid whose name he still couldn't pronounce, shooting nice controlled bursts with his AK-47. How come Sinner's piece of shit gun only got a 20-round magazine and the kid got a 30-rounder? *No fair.* More Slopes were screaming in the distance as he searched for a spare magazine, but it was dark and the bonfire only helped a little. His hand smacked something on his rifle as he felt around on the ground for a magazine. He looked, and realized that there was a second magazine taped to the now empty one. He yanked the mag and flipped it over, seating the new mag into the gun. He hit the release lever to send the bolt home... nothing happened.

Dang it, Sinner, you didn't check the chamber before reloading. The gun hadn't run dry. It'd jammed. He ejected the mag and yanked back on the charging handle three times, tilted the gun to let the stuck case fall out, slapped the mag back in, pulled it down to make sure it was seated fully and hit the bolt release again.

CLICK!

Fuckin' piece a sh—

"SIN!" Bleak was so goddamn black, Sinner didn't see him standing right there beside him as he tossed The Lady his way. Lady Antoinette, cuz if them fuckers are hungry, let 'em eat lead. He racked that slide back and forth like a fuckin' trombone and nine roughly 33-caliber balls flew out in a circular pattern with each trigger pull. Again and again he racked the action until he heard that horrible sound.

Click.

When he saw the flash roaring out of Bleak's M14, the blaze lit up the whites of his eyes and the snarl of his teeth. Sinner forgave himself for not seeing Bleak beside him, because surely his mouth was closed a moment ago.

"HA HA HA HA!" Sinner laughed.

"WHAT THE FUCK ARE YOU LAUGHING AT, HONKEY?!"

"I'll tell ya later!"

Bleak's M14 fired all over the damn forest.

Stupid niggers don't understand the basics of physics. Just like them old dumbass bean counters can't grasp the fact that a big fucking bullet fired at a ri-Goddamn-diculous firing rate from a little gun is impossible to control.

The 20-round box magazine was empty faster than a cat could lick its ass and that was the fastest thing on four feet. Sinner doubted if the shit stain had even so much as hit the air.

"Semi-auto fuck face. Calm yourself, boy!"

"DON'T CALL ME BOY!"

Sinner felt something hit his foot; a pouch full of 12-gauge shells. Ghost Doc had dropped the satchel on his way by. The little tulip of a man moved so fast he was like some kinda...well... ghost. A ghost firing and reloading his pistol so fast it sounded like a solid string of fire. He was furiously running about making sure anyone who didn't have a weapon had taken cover. Then he ran back and fetched a few weapons to arm them, only to fight his way through it all over again. The man was crazy.

The rest of the Yards were finally getting to their damn feet. Together they unleashed everything they had. The sea of lead that flowed into the forest was a great start to a fucked up night. No single shot could be heard separate from the next. Surviving this was impossible.

"CEASE FIRE! CEASE FIRE! CEASE FIRE GODDAMNIT! CONSERVE YOUR AMMO!" Chinny screamed at the top of his lungs. "WHAT DO WE SEE?" The Aussie's voice cracked when he screamed again.

"Nothing! That's right cuz me an' The Lady put 'em to pasture, mmmhmmm, that's right. For*give* me father for I have *sinned*." Sinner looked down at one of the Yard women and winked with a smile to match. "That's right, baby."

"Duly noted, Mister Sin, but for the sake of clarity, perhaps we should ensure that contact did indeed occur."

"Huh?"

"With all due respect, I have yet to see any return fire, or initiative fire to begin with."

"Well, that's cuz I'm so fast." Sinner smiled.

"I see ... Bleak! Give us a report."

"I don't know, Chin."

"Ya don't know what you saw? Fuck, they're *your* eyes, mate!"

"I-I don't know. Bad vibe, boss."

"Kapaow?"

"Bad, beddy beddy bad."

"Okay, fan out! You're too close together. Get eyes-on. If there's civilians out there I'm hanging you fucks myself!"

They were all scared shitless. There was no two ways about it. Had Sinner fucked the pig on this whole thing? "This ain't good,

Chinny. I'm telling you, I got a sixth sense about these things," Sinner whispered as loudly as he could.

"I'm not doubting you, mate. Let's just take a breath."

Sinner breathed deep. It was funny, the way time slowed down in a pickle. The rate of fire, the fact that most of them had shot only one mag, two at best–less than a minute had passed since he first initiated Charlie's ass kickin'. It was not at all enough time for Chinny to believe they were safe. Still, the lack of return fire was concerning. Chinny was investigating, gathering intel. He was already a few steps ahead, thinking everything out.

"Hey... monkey face," he whispered to Bleak.

"Fuck you, honkey."

"Thanks for gettin' me The Lady. Musta had one too many tonight, I couldn't find her straightaway, so I dived for that piece of shit M16. Sorry I got caught with my pants down."

"It's cool, cracka. Sorry I's buggin' on the full auto before. Shit just caught me off guard, ya dig?"

"Yeah. I swear you a dark som'bitch, I didn't even see you right there. Shaka Zulu, king of the night people, ha ha." Bleak punched Sinner in the arm. "Ouch! Fuck you do that for?"

"Drop bitches, yeah!" Kapaow whispered excitedly, and held his hand up for a high five.

"Thanks. You saw some shit, too. Right?" Sinner felt good seeing Kapaow nod like his head would spin off its axis.

"Did you even check what was out there before you started shooting?" Chinny yelled. *Awww shit.* Kapaow and Bleak stepped a few feet away from Sinner.

"Oh, real nice, you assholes," Sinner whispered at them. "Yeah, didn't ... didn't you hear me, Chin? I's like... s'like, 'Who goes there?' and shit... Oh fuck. Come on, Chin. You know how it is out here. Fuck you doin' rollin' up on a village in the middle of the night, carryin' a gun you don't want some fun. Feel me?"

"You saw a gun?" Chinny asked, much louder now.

"Just in case, I'll get the non-coms to the rear," Ghost said, walking away from the argument.

Sinner looked at Bleak. The light of the fire still showed Bleak's eyes and teeth more than anything else. There was a twinkle in his eye, like a cross burning in the distance.

Wait a minute ... that's fire! Fire in front of us! SHIT! SHIT! It's a fuck, a fuckin'—

"DOWN!" Sinner screamed, pushing Bleak to the ground and landing on top of him. *It's a fuckin' flame thrower!*

WALK THROUGH THE VALLEY

The heat scorched the hair off his back, but somehow he didn't get badly burned. They knocked each other's teeth as they hit the ground awkwardly in some fairy-ass smooch fest. He could taste copper. If he wasn't about to be spit roasted by a midget in pajamas. He might have lost his dinner.

Clack! Clack! Clack!

Chinny was shooting single shots into the forest, slow and smooth, eyes down the barrel, cool as a glass of lemonade. That man didn't fear death for a second. Chinny was a God Almighty Samurai Warrior welcoming death with open arms.

How's he always so John Wayne all the time? Sinner thought.

Twenty feet away, little Cadeo was firing an AK-47 that stood taller than him when rested on its stock. He shot from the hip into the night, each bullet's recoil jerking the gun back several inches. Sinner felt a strange mix of fear and pride at the sight. If only he could get over there, tell the dumb shit to tuck the stock under his arm to stabilize it. If only he could stop this madness and take the kid for ice cream. *Whatever, the fight's on. Get to shootin' Sinner.*

Sinner heard screams coming from his left. It was Ling Ting, Kapaow's oldest son, covered in flames, still shooting at the enemy. That was why none of the flaming liquid had scorched him; the stream was intended for another target. Had Sinner taken the brunt of the flame instead of hitting the dirt like a bitch, the boy might still be alive. Then again, Bleak would be dead. Sinner looked at Bleak and saw the fire of the boy reflected in his eyes.

"I'm sorry," was all Sinner could say. *Sorry I saved you and not the boy.* Would Bleak forgive him?

BOOM!

The sound of an explosion drew his eyes from Ting. The flame thrower's tank must have been hit. Chinny had advanced again. *Stupid son of a bitch.* He was out in the open. Sinner figured it must have been him that had blown up the torch tank. It lit up the forest like the North Star, setting two more chinkos on fire, making it obvious it was an eight-man team. Now they could see their targets. He crouched and fired, trying to be cool, but it was just so hard. He took aim, barely able to see the sights of his shotgun, and fired on a figure that had little flashes of light popping out near its chest—gunfire.

BOOM chik-chik BOOM ch-chik BOOM ch-chik BOOM ch-ch BOOM ch-ch CLICK!

The click that indicated the gun had run out of shells always seemed louder than the actual shots. Bullets whizzed past. The wet crack of a baseball bat on a melon was the sound of a head exploding just behind Sinner. Blood splattered his face and he wiped his eyes. The first thing he saw when his vision cleared was a piece of skull on the ground, the hair still clinging to it tangled around a flower.

"What the fuck?! What the *fuck*?!" Bleak screamed... but he screamed like someone Sinner had never heard before.

Sinner looked at his eyes, and all he saw was terror. The sight of such fear inspired a lick of it in himself. He started to feel that painful chill down his spine, the shiver of his hairs standing on end. Sure, they were in something terrifying, but nothing ever made Bleak that afraid.

Sinner took aim again and tried to see what had Bleak losing his grip. He couldn't tell. There was just too much shit going on. The trees started to ignite around the enemy as bullets continued to lick at his skin. He fought his fear of death and swallowed it down into a place Chinny had taught him to bury such things, but it seemed to keep clawing back up again.

Then he saw it.

He stopped firing. Some small part in his mind screamed for him to stay in the fight, but he saw it. Bleak's rounds impacted the target. He watched chunks ripping from its body. The target continued to push forward! How was that even possible? When it approached a large patch of fire, Sinner's hands began to shake... Bleak had blown his jaw clean off. Blood was pouring from him. The poor bastard stopped. Such wounds could only result in stopping. Bleak shot him more after reloading.

The bloody mess started to walk forward again. Sinner thought of his grandmother when she'd been sick and near death: how she had become delirious from the fever. She'd had drips of vomit clinging to her face. Her eyes seemed to belong to someone else: a stranger. She smiled a horrid smile, her slimy brown teeth with strings of spit connecting them all together. She reached out for a hug, he stopped then, just like he stopped now. She got up and started to walk toward him, her body so feeble that she moved like a broken animal. He'd backed away then, just like he was backing away now. Her fingers were yellow and cracked, with pieces of digested food stuck to them. She came in to touch his face right as he was pressed up against the wall and had nowhere else to go. How he felt then, that's how he felt right now.

The man wasn't dead. How wasn't he dead? He kept walking toward them, getting closer and closer. His skin was so tattered it started to fall off in chunks. He dropped its weapon, but did not collapse. He reached out for Sinner, his only eye staring at him, chunks of blood and flesh dripping from his hand.

"What the fuck? What the *fuck!*" Sinner screamed.

He reached into Bleak's pistol belt, withdrew the Colt .45, dropped the safety, and fired. Together, they chewed pieces off of him until there was nothing left. They looked at each other, Sinner knew they needed to move.

"Fuck it. Let's go," Sinner demanded, grabbing another magazine from Bleak's belt.

Sinner tripped and fell not three paces out. Lying on his back, his feet flat on the ground to stabilize, he shot the figures *next* to the flaming targets again and again. He'd have no trouble finding the fiery ones later. He unloaded on the rest while the light was still good. He was ready for the reload and dropped the mag after six shots, knowing the seventh had already loaded in the chamber.

He knew he was hitting them. He could see them dropping. They couldn't be getting up again. How could they *all* be as tough as that last guy? It was impossible. There must have been more than he originally thought, because targets continued to present themselves. Bleak had come back and covered him while he got back to his feet.

Click

He reached into Bleak's belt again and withdrew another magazine, slamming it home and hitting the slide release while at the same time starting to squeeze the trigger. The bullet fired just as the slide closed. More wet thwacks were hitting all around him. *Fuck.* He was spending too much time on the pistol and not using it to fight his way back to his main weapon. He started to shoot slower now, one handed. With his other hand, he reached for the ammo satchel. He fumbled around. He couldn't stop shaking.

FUCK! You fat bastard. Don't you start fuckin' up now! Not now! One shell in the tube, another. The next got stuck. He fired the pistol until it went dry before looking down. *Stupid jackass.* The round was backwards! He picked the shotgun up, spun the shell, and fired. Slid the shell in, racked the action and fired again. He grabbed four more shells before properly mounting the shotgun in the pocket of his shoulder and thumbed those rounds in as well.

His chest heaved. His hands were too loose on his gun. He wasn't moving fast enough. He wasn't shooting accurately enough. He wasn't doing his job.

SHUT UP! SHUT UP AND FIGHT! Think slower, man, just like Chinny says. Adrenaline's gonna make you faster than you've ever seen yourself. You're not moving too slow. You're so fast, you're too fast. Think slower, pilgrim.

The shotgun ran dry again.

FUCK! Get up and fight you fat, inbred, worthless bastard. Ain't gon' be no more friends to bury!

Sinner bashed his leg with his fist as he rocked onto his knees and grabbed the AK that Ting had dropped. His skin scorched under the passing bullets that grazed his face. Ling Ting's burning corpse and the campfire must have created a clear outline for the Cong bitches to aim at.

"We're being outlined!" he screamed to Bleak, who knew exactly what to do.

A sharp howl ripped through the air. Sinner got the wind knocked out of him when Bleak tackled him. They hit the dirt just as the smoke-trail flew above them.

"RPG!" Chinny screamed as he lobbed a grenade into the woods.

The rocket-propelled grenade exploded and sent a concussion wave through their bodies. That kangaroo muncher was getting too close to the enemy.

"They should prolly move up!" Bleak yelled.

"So fuckin' tell 'em!" Sinner snapped back.

"Move up! Move up!" Bleak screamed to the Yards.

Sinner tried to stand and fell on his face. Behind him, he heard more wet thwacks. His leg had cramped up. Ghost was gonna have an "I told you so" waiting for that one. He struggled to his feet and limped forward, stumbling on something soft and squishy. He fell again. He was getting frustrated. What the hell had he slipped on? He looked down and saw a little tube of meat or something, maybe a rolled up piece of pig's skin from the barbeque displaced by an RPG. He scrambled to get back up again when it finally dawned on him. Bullets ripped past, dangerously close, but Sinner didn't move.

No. No. It's not that. No, Goddamn it. God, you didn't let that happen.

God *did* let it happen, though, didn't he? He couldn't tell what he'd slipped on at first, but in the firelight, he could now see it in fact a tiny arm. It wasn't that everything had stopped. It was more that everything stopped mattering to Sinner. He just stared at it–a baby's arm.

He sat motionless until his anger overwhelmed his devastation. He wanted to kill them all for what they'd done. He was choking. He was going blind from the water swelling in his eyes as he tried to keep firing. He wanted to pick up the arm, but his hand felt stuck. He tried to let go of the gun, but had to yank hard to break away. He felt an awful pain from letting go. He picked up the tiny purple arm and put it in his cargo pants pocket. It was slippery. Everything started feeling slippery because his hands were bleeding.

"AAAAHHHHHHHHHHH!" he screamed until his throat went hoarse.

He rushed forward, unable to form words anymore. He ripped the AK from his other hand to drop it, then he realized his hands had cooked right to the metal parts of the gun. Ting was still burning.

You picked up a scorching hot gun, ya moron!

He was lucky the bullets in the magazine hadn't exploded and maimed him.

Stupid, Sinner. You should have thought of that.

The enemy must have been coming in waves. It had to be an entire platoon. Every trigger pull was agony, but pain cleansed a sinner's soul. He embraced it. Bleak tossed him a grenade. Sinner laid down covering fire while Bleak pulled the pin and tossed his. Bleak covered Sinner as he did the same. The concussions were only a second or two apart. Then they both unloaded on the enemy. Something hit Sinner right in the eye, maybe a tiny piece of shrapnel, maybe a shard of bone. He didn't have time to check it. He just closed his eye, using the other to aim, and kept on fighting.

THUNK sssssssssssBOOM!

YEEHA!

He wondered where the hell Kapaow had been! Crazy son of a bitch left to go find his Blooper. He launched 40-millimeter grenades into the forest, *Thunk sssssssssssBOOM!* One after the other. The little fucker was fast. Kapaow practiced almost every day, reloading while wearing a cowboy hat, very John Wayne. Each time Kapaow fired, he made some skinny chink go *Kapaow! Ha ha.* For a minute, Sinner couldn't help but remember how long it took him to get Kapaow to stop going into the damn forest armed with only a crossbow.

Bunch of primitive yellow monkey bastards.

Kapaow screamed some kind of gook-ese at the enemy. Sinner couldn't make it all out, but he picked out a few things. *Bac Bac,*

La De, that meant something like, *"Come and get it, we'll shoot you dead."* Kapaow was taunting them. There were no screams. He was getting instant kills. That weapon was a true one-hit wonder. The tree line was speckled with sparks and flashes of enemy fire. The burning bodies weren't lighting up enough of the forest to see just how many there were.

Duh-duh-duh-duh-duh-duh-doom, Duh-duh-duh-duh-duh-doom, duh-duh-duh-duh-duh-duh…

YEEHA! Someone got to the M60! That was going to turn the tides a bit. Whoever had it started out doing pretty good, nice controlled bursts, but was getting a little too excited, shooting in much longer strings. At this point, anything going *boom* was a good thing. Everyone tightened up, staggered formations, closing in on the tree line. No words were needed. Brothers in arms just knew what to do. The unity, the connection. For a second he felt whole.

Heat scorched Sinner's arms as bullets clawed by, some missing his skull by a cunt-hair. Blood sprayed into his last open eye and chunks of bone pelted his face. How could this be happening? *Why* was this happening? They were kicking ass and the enemy just kept on coming. How many did they bring? They came here to build hospitals and teach these pigs how to wash their asses for fuck's sake. He felt a strong hand haul him off the ground. Chinny.

"Come on then, mate. There's work still, yeah?"

Sinner tried to open his eyes, but the sting of blood made it hard to see. Seconds later someone was washing the blood from his eyes.

"Get the fuck out here, damn it!" Sinner didn't want anyone dying because of him.

He opened his eyes and saw the blurry image of bare tits. It was Kim. Ghost Doc was on her tail, firing his pistol while she ran around tending to the wounded. He had been teaching her first aid. It seemed she'd had a pop quiz on her hands.

Kim handed him a rifle. He yanked the action back and a live round popped out. She already had it ready to go for him. He dove into the action like the firefight was Ellen Stratton. No time for thanks.

Sinner was side by side with a dingo muncher, a nigger, and about a hundred assorted gooks, slopes, chinks, dinks, zipper heads and a tree huggin' pansy. His father'd turn over in his grave if he knew.

Good. Fuck that old racist bastard.

As the thunder and lightning, dust and blood of the battle settled to the Earth, all that was left was the sound of women and children crying for their loved ones. Chinny was carrying a boy whose face was unrecognizable through the blood oozing out. Sinner watched as he had many times before, waiting for a tear to shed from Chinny's eye. One never came.

Sinner reached into his pocket and pulled out the baby's arm. Kapaow screamed for his newborn son. He screamed so loud Sinner wasn't sure he'd ever forget the sound. He screamed "GO DOC? GO DOC?" Sinner tried to hide the arm, but his fingers were starting to cramp up. He couldn't get it back into his pocket fast enough.

Kapaow looked down at the little arm in his hand and fell to his knees. He cried and screamed, asking any force that would answer, "*Why?*" There was no answer. Kapaow snatched the little arm from his hand. He punched Sinner's chest with both fists. Sinner didn't fight back, didn't try to stop him, even as he began to welt and bruise. He endured it. Even when the pain made his body want to pull away, he stood fast. There wasn't any amount of pain that could make up for it. Trying to make it right was a losing battle, but a man had to do *something*.

So, he bore the pain.

CHAPTER 6
KAPAOW

Some time had passed since the attack, since he lost his...

Perhaps he'd been avoiding the grieving process, but he had to do it sooner or later. Kapaow looked around to make sure no one was watching. He closed his eyes and touched the ground, calming his mind as best he could. His anger he put aside, along with his pain and many other feelings that blurred his inner vision. He continued to sift until all that was left was a deep, warm sensation with subtle tingling: the Earth's soul. He began to travel in his mind. It was only his imagination, but imagination connecting you to everything. He imagined the presence of it all, from the grass, up through the roots of the trees. He travelled until he felt as much as he could possibly feel. The soul of the entire jungle, the animals within, even the remnants of souls still clinging to the fibers of his clothes.

He drifted until he felt the presence of their home. He travelled through the grass and felt the laughter touching every blade. He journeyed through the soul of the air until it touched the faces of his fellow villagers. He instantly recognized the feeling of his wife and children. The feeling was the only thing that truly filled every part of him from the center of his heart, out through the surface of his skin.

He drifted down and focused intently on the soul of his newborn son, which had become a part of the earth as well. Go Doc, he named him Go Doc, after his friend. He waited, drifting about until he felt his infant son's soul allow him inside. He became his son, felt what he felt. His skin was cold and tender. Everything seemed to abrade and irritate. He was uncomfortable and tired. Yet there was something so magical about it all, so wondrous. He tried to look at things, but the light still hurt his eyes. So he closed them, and he felt for his mother's soul, pressing into her skin to be closer to it. He felt for his father, such a big soul, so powerful. He felt safe, in all of the startling new world. The souls he felt connected to would protect him, he could tell, he knew.

What was that? Something shook him, some kind of pain in his ears. Kapaow knew it was the sound of the attack, but the soul of his son didn't know what it was. He could feel the confusion, the fear and overwhelming agony. because in his boy's mind it could truly be anything. The entire world had decided it didn't like him anymore and he felt pushed away by it.

Lights even brighter burned his eyes. *What's happening?* he cried. *AAAH!* His mother held him so tight it hurt his arms, he had trouble breathing. *Let me breathe! Please!*

Kapaow suffocated as his boy suffocated. He gasped for air as his son did when his mother pulled him away just enough so she could check his face. She looked so scared, what was she afraid of? Kapaow knew, but he began to lose himself in his son's disorientation. *Please keep me safe! Please!*

Kapaow dug his fingers into the Earth as he felt time slow down; his son had felt some sort of hollow feeling. It was like a gap, a vacuum, a point where things broke apart, and he suddenly knew everything in the universe, so much that Kapaow could not comprehend or describe the feeling. He felt the stars, the universe. Then, it all collapsed in on itself, onto him, he felt pain searing through his body now. With enough empathy, a person can feel anything.

Kapaow knew the feeling was shrapnel from an exploding RPG.

His hands shook, his stomach churned. It felt like a hand was inside his body crushing his heart, stabbing through his body. He began to cry.

"Why? *Why?*" He gasped *"Why?"* He screamed. *"WHY?"* He cried so hard he stopped breathing.

"Kapaow! Bloody hell!" Somehow Chinny had found him. "Ya alright, mate? Come on."

Kapaow pushed him away. He needed to finish. He needed to see his son through to the very end. Chinny fought back to his side. "I no can!" Kapaow felt frustrated on top of it all as he struggled to translate his feelings into Chinny's language.

"Can't what, mate? What?"

"Have to feel my son, must feel him die."

"No!" Chinny grabbed him by his shoulders and forced him to look in his eyes. "No. You don't suffer, This isn't your fault, mate. It's theirs. Ya understand me? It's *theirs.* Ya bury that hate. Ya bury it and make it burn. You turn it into a weapon and take it to the people who did this. Bury it, Kapaow."

Kapaow tried to travel back in his mind, to pick up where he left off, to see it through, but he remembered the feeling of the shrapnel. It was too much, too much to go through again. He hugged Chinny, his friend, his brother. Chinny patted him on the back and told him they would get through it.

Chinny pulled away. "Bury it," he said. His attitude was different, like he had locked himself away again. Chinny left him on the ground. Kapaow tried to find his son again, to finish the feeling, but stopped himself.

Bury it.

CHAPTER 7
CHINNY

The screaming had finally subsided with the morning's light.
Their flame throwers and machine guns pierced the night.
Together they stood, did what they could, but still so many died.
Seven dead, fifteen wounded. Why?

Chinny was a terrible poet. He was a terrible mechanic, a terrible cook, and a terrible painter. He couldn't deliver babies. He couldn't stitch a wound straight. He couldn't throw a boomerang no matter how many times Sinner asked. He couldn't whittle the way that Mamma Ling could, outside of figure-four dead falls and other simple mechanisms. She was an artist. He was terrible at public speaking. He couldn't draw and he couldn't sing. Despite his best efforts, he couldn't play an instrument. He wasn't much for math or science or economics. In fact, the only thing his heart didn't falter over was his incompetence when it came to politics, possibly the only shortcoming worth being proud of. It was a long list of shortcomings.

"How's the hands?" Chinny asked, standing over Sinner.

"I'm good to go."

"It's not what I asked, mate."

"Well, it's what I'm tellin' ya, Chin. I'm good to go. I fucked up. I'm sorry," Sinner looked off at nothing, struggling to choke back his tears." But I'm not gettin' benched over some bullshit."

"The thought hadn't crossed my mind…" He paused. "Stand up a tick for me, mate."

"What's your angle, boss?" Sinner asked, a slight quiver of fear in his voice.

"Pick up the rifle."

"Why?"

"Pick it up!"

Arguments were the last thing he needed right now. Sinner grimaced, but he knelt down and moaned, wrapping his hand around the grip of the AK. He exhaled hard, like someone dipping into an ice cold bath. His knees wiggled on the way back up. Their eyes met, and he looked straight into Sinner's pupils.

A man like this couldn't be told. He had to be shown. Sinner already knew he was banged up. The man felt guilty; his upper lip stiff, his mouth thin with remorse. He wanted desperately to make up for not fighting hard enough. One couldn't hope to explain to a man in the bush that he did all he could, that these things happened all the time. That, considering the nature of the attack, they had fared quite well. A man in the bush didn't want to hear any of that. No. A man in the bush wanted to die with the ones he'd failed. Chinny understood.

"Right then. Call's already in for medevac. No worries. You had a good run."

"Uhh…" Kim said, her shy voice quivering, "Toc comes. I am afraid to ask Kapaow to speak with him, but there is no one else."

He scanned the area and saw that Kapaow had indeed made his way back into the village and was now spending time with Ghost. Ghost was a much better match for coping and understood emotions far better.

"I ain't fuckin' goin' anywhere!" Sinner yelled as Chinny walked away. "You hear me?"

The biggest problem holding the Yards back from a proper defense was their lack of cultural cohesiveness. Toc was from a village not far from their own, and yet he spoke in a manner none could understand, except for Kapaow. Sinner looked angry, perhaps still yearning to exchange a few more words. Chinny was relieved to see him back down for now and head to his hooch. He'd accept the reality of things, likely because he was too exhausted to argue.

Chinny approached the grieving father. "Kapaow, I'm sorry, mate. Toc is here." Kapaow said nothing, but went to greet the man. Chinny took a deep breath and hoped his next task didn't cause a fight. "Bleak?" Chinny's heart thumped.

"Right here."

"Go on and get yourself a patrol together. Kapaow, Teng and Zhang, perhaps a couple others. See what ya find, but don't venture off too far." Sinner stopped in his tracks.

Chinny's heart sped up a bit, anticipating the confrontation. Sinner would want to lead the patrol. Sin took a breath and his shoulders heaved up… then lowered back down as he exhaled and continued to stomp off to bed. A pretty young woman covered in dirt and grime to the point she might be confused for an ugly woman followed him in, surely to apply ointments to his minor burns and check his wound dressings. Everyone had their way of coping. Chinny would have Ghost Doc make sure they remained hydrated.

He felt a tickle on his shoulder and half-jumped at the sight of Kim attempting to address a minor wound he'd sustained on his shoulder. She smiled at him; such a sweetheart. He grabbed her hands and pulled them away, pointing to Luong, who had a large chunk missing from his leg, and nodded for her to help treat him. It was likely that Ghost was going to need to fashion another peg-leg at some point. The screaming had stopped. Now there were only whimpers as background noise. Chinny would tend to everyone else first. He'd fix his own wounds later.

Ghost Doc was looking like he'd *seen* a ghost. He seemed more distant than ever. His face was pale, his mind wandering. It was no good, no good at all. Something wasn't right with Ghost. His manner had changed, bit by bit, over a rather short time. In the beginning he was all fire and fury whenever he lost a patient or a friend, swearing revenge, fighting to go back into the bush to teach Charlie a lesson. Now he tended to stare out into the horizon, perhaps contemplating something… or nothing. When a man roared his pain out into the world, he *appeared* to be losing it. In truth, it was when he did nothing that one needed to be concerned.

"Ghost Doc." He did not respond. "Ghost?" Still no answer. Chinny hadn't realized how long it'd been since he'd used the boy's real name. It felt strange to do so, but perhaps necessary in his current state. "Jeffery?" He put his hand on the boy's shoulder. "Jeff?"

Ghost said nothing, and yet his eyes said everything.

Chinny pressed his hand firmly on Ghost Doc's shoulder. "Bury it, son."

The emotion left Ghost's face. "I'm… I'm fine… I'm fine."

"That's it." Chinny patted him on the shoulder and walked away.

He had Kim tend to him. She did so with a gentle and caring nature. He'd swing around in a bit and check on Ghost.

He walked about to each and every Yard, one by one. He asked them how they were. He brought each some water. He hated it, but he smiled and played the part. Some of them he spotted watching him out of the corner of their eye, waiting to see if they'd be tended to next. A big daddy type, he was. He appointed several separate squads to patrol the perimeter and stand guard. Whatever came for them last night probably wasn't coming back. However, creating a sense of safety was of the utmost importance at such a time. He'd have to take the little baby arm away from Kapaow when they started their burial ceremonies, but for now, it could wait.

Whump, whump, whump

The whirring of helicopter blades was often heard throughout the day, yet these grew louder, closer. He motioned to several Yards. Of course, Sinner dragged himself out of bed, and the rest able to arm themselves stood watch. The problem with Vietnam was the echoes sounded different. Chinny was still adapting in some minor respects. He listened closely and wondered.

Was it food?

CHAPTER 8
CHINNY

Whump, whump, whump
What are ya? Food, or some twat with papers to push on us again?
Chinny's stomach burned and tightened. The last thing he wanted was to deal with anybody's shite today.
Whump, whump, whump
"Crghk... sssss... Zero... ssss... crkrkrk... this is... over. Ssshhhhhsssss... pre... ssshhhh... resupply... ssssss... over."
Resupply? I'll be damned.
They had feared their last resupply request had been forgotten or deprioritized. He let out a sigh of relief. At the very least, they'd have enough medical supplies to make it through the tragedy. There had been ups and downs to their unique mission. Ups being less involvement from supervisors, downs being cut off from the regular supplies and always needing to be the beggar.
"Yeah... ss... again... crgkgkgkgkgk..."
The radios were buggy again. Ghost figured it had something to do with their location. Sometimes their signals were strong, other times rather faint. Of course, it was always when they needed them to be clear that they were crackled. The chopper floated for a moment, cargo dangling from its belly. After a few more garbled comms, the crate dropped. In that instant, the entire village was alive again, rushing the supply drop. Chinny waved to the chopper, and the men inside waved back. Chinny was knocked on his arse by a group of ankle biters.
"Hello! Stop shoving, now. It hasn't been that long, has it?" It had. "We'll get this opened right up, and we're *all* going to share, yeah?" Chinny said firmly as he pried open the crate. He looked inside and felt, among other things, unbridled anger. "Bloody rubbish."
"What is it, boss?" Sinner asked.
"Shouldn't you be resting?" Chinny jabbed back.
"What the fuck is this shit?" Sinner turned around and yelled. "Who the fuck ordered ammo? We got ammo, goddamn it! We need meds."
"Ammo's good—" Ghost started.

43

"Yeah, yeah," Sinner interrupted dismissively. "You gonna make medicine out of bullets? Huh?" Sinner snarled.

"Easy. We'll put in another order. Least they didn't send lady's undergarments, yeah?" Chinny said, hoping to lighten the mood.

While everyone slumped away from the crate, Chinny remained, staring at the bits and pieces of people that once had names. He shouldn't have tried to make a joke, not at a time like this. It was hard for Chinny. He'd already been through all this a dozen times before. It didn't feel the same to him. He was ready to move forward, to detach. He took a breath. *Just gotta wait for everyone else to catch up.* While everyone continued to gather the dead, he headed for his tools. They needed to rebuild something before the day was over.

He grabbed the papers from his bullet-ridden hooch. His hands were still bloody, he realized, when he noticed red fingerprints on their makeshift blueprints. He tried to wipe them away, but only managed to smear them. He put the plans down and got the wood ready for measures and cuts. He turned slightly to remove the sight of the carnage from his peripheral.

He looked at the plans. They were a bit complicated and there were some cuts that needed to be angled cuts, which he hated. Most of the morning was already gone and he'd have to work faster to make up for lost time. He checked his watch, and for a moment, simply observed the tremors in his hand.

He noticed something on the ground that had not yet been collected. He felt lightheaded and fell to his knees. The sensation of pins and needles formed all over his body like an orchestral crescendo before someone plummeted to their doom. It was a piece of a body, a tiny body. A piece of a child's skull, the eye was still attached… he couldn't… he couldn't do it anymore… *no… no… no…* he felt dizzy.

"No, no, no, no." His words were crackled like the static-ridden comms.

"BOSS? BOSS!" Ghost's hand landed onto his shoulder and squeezed so hard he felt like his shoulder might dislocate.

"What?" Chinny pretended to have no idea what the problem was.

"Are you all right?"

Ghost seemed very concerned. Again, Chinny played the fool. Pretend long enough and it would be whatever one made it out to be. Chinny pretended to be fine.

"Yes… yes…" He forced a smile. "Ha, of course I'm all right. Hell, I was… I was worried about *you*."

"Um, yeah brother. Yeah. I'm okay now. You're okay?" Ghost didn't sound convinced at all.

"Yeah. I'm okay."

Ghost pulled a bandage out and wrapped one of his wounds. Then he slowly walked away.

Oh, wait. The skull.

"Oh, Ghost, just a tick… over here, something strange about this body…" He pointed towards the piece of skull with the blue eye, but it was gone. *Where'd it go?* "Ummm, odd. Never mind then… Sung must have picked it up. Hey, Ghost?"

"Yeah, boss?"

"Who here has blue eyes?"

"Ummm… seriously?"

"No. Sarcastically, Because I always make quips about fuckin' eye color next to a pile of dead fuckin' bodies," Chinny said more crossly than he had intended.

"Fine. You, me and Sinner. Why?"

"No, an infant."

"What? Did you take your malaria pill?"

"Yes."

"You sure you're okay, boss? It's okay if you need me to check you out."

"Yes, yes. I'm fine. It's nothing. I suppose I'm still a bit shook up."

"Yeah, you and me both, heh… I'll get you some water."

"Appreciate it."

He listened to Ghost murmur to himself. Chinny looked down at the papers with their designs Ghost had sketched on them, covered in blood. He looked at his tools and sighed. He'd let someone else do it. He was *not* skilled at carpentry.

He wasn't too bad with a knife, though—a couple of dead men could attest to that. He wasn't good at drawing blueprints, but a rifle felt nice in his hands. He could chuck a grenade farther than most—accurately, in fact. Under stress, he could still put 'em all in a fist at ten meters with a pistol. Didn't even need to look down the sights to do it. He was classified as an expert marksman. Try as he might, he was still pretty damn good at surviving. If one made it easy, it was suicide, and he couldn't have that.

War was all he was, all he could be. For two seconds he thought about joining that party last night. He thought about having a brew with Kapaow. Maybe dancing with a lady was on his mind, too. Now he was staring at a pile of dead. War was all he was and this was the consequence if he tried to fight it.

"CHIN! Shit, CHINNY! Brotha, get over here man, *now*," Bleak yelled.

"What do ya have then?" Chinny asked, concerned.

Bleak was hysterical. "They're *gone*, man, just like last time! Fuckin' gone!"

"Hold ya'self there, mate. Did you say gone?"

"Yes! Gone. Every last one of 'em, man! There's too much fuckin' blood… caked into the mud, on the trees, fuckin' everywhere, man. Too much fuckin' blood for them to be gone, Chin! Too much fuckin' blood!"

"Hold yourself you damn fool!" Chinny raised his hand and Bleak recoiled from his anger. The look in Bleak's eyes… Chinny backed down. "Just… relax a bit. They always try to carry their dead out. You know that."

"Get the trackers in there, man, there's marks that look like muthafuckas limpin' outta there and shit. No way those guys were only wounded. With that much blood, they all had to be dead."

"Impossible. If that were so, their bodies would still be there. I'm not questioning anyone's marksmanship, but let's be real: I heard you using full auto on that awful rifle. It's not so crazy to think we missed more than we'd like to admit. Take it easy now. Have a swig and take a breath, Bleak."

"Send the trackers in! Shit, man! Shit… I want out of this fuckin' place. I can feel shit crawlin' on my skin, man. I want it off."

"Stay *calm*." Chinny spoke as firmly as he could without crossing the line. "I'm not sending the trackers in because I already know what happened, right? And so do you. They take their dead. We do the same. I sent *you* in there for intelligence. Ya got any?"

"Tell him, Sin, tell him what you saw last night." Bleak gestured to Sinner, who looked uncomfortably at the ground. "You gonna do me like that, Sin? You know what we saw, that muthafucka wouldn't go down… okay, okay." Bleak nodded frantically. "I see how it is, little pansy ass muthafucka."

"All I saw was a coked up Chink that didn't want to go down. I don't know *what* the fuck you're talkin' 'bout, clay face," Sinner shot back.

"That's *enough*," Chinny snarled through his teeth.

"Look in my eyes, Chin." Bleak's eyes were wide, but unwavering. He looked like a man who knew exactly what he'd seen, and yet what he claimed to know made no sense. "I'm not saying we need to go, cuz I ain't one for running away, but we need backup, Chin. We need help. You need to ask for help."

"Then get on the bloody radio!" Chinny yelled. "Tell them we've got missing bodies so we need a small army to come protect us. I'm not saying we're not fucked. I'm just saying your people don't give a bloody shite about it!" His statement brought silence to the entire village. "Call in the *facts*, nothing more, Bleak. Nothing more. You call in the facts and you let the higher ups decide what to do. Yeah?"

"Fuck that shit, blood. We need to handle this."

"Everyone takes their dead, Bleak. We do the same thing. Ghost, do us a favor and have a look at him, yeah?"

Ghost checked Bleak's pulse. Bleak seemed unaware that he was being touched. "No, we always try to *come back* for our dead. A fight like this, we'd been ordered to burn the pavement on up outta here. Wouldn'ta been no time to get the bodies. They took *everything* with them. Even the blown up flame thrower. Where'd the fuckin' bodies go, Chin?" Bleak demanded. "Where'd the bodies go?"

The question agitated Chinny.

CHAPTER 9
CHINNY

"Son…" What was the best way to talk to a man bordering on hysteria? "I'm only going to say this once… *calm down.*" Chinny felt angry at Bleak's loss of composure. They were suffering enough without Bleak being his usual paranoid self.

"Hell no. Don't give me that shit. You tell me what the fuck happened to the bodies!"

"Bleak, shut it."

"Fuck you!"

"Carl!" Chinny's hand began to shake.

"Fuck you, Chin!" Bleak spat on the ground in front of him.

Chinny looked down at his shaking hands. He ought to take out his pistol and point it right between Bleak's eyes. That'd show him. Teach him not to disrespect him in front of the men. Bleak was supposed to be in charge of this whole thing and Chinny just the advisor, a trainer of sorts. Instead, Chinny had to take charge and teach Bleak how to lead, too.

Bleak continued to scream and carry on about missing bodies. Chinny continued to demand his silence. Chinny's hand pressed against his holster.

Why not? Fuck it. This bloody arsehole thinks he's so tough? Show him what real fear is.

Bleak, Ghost and Sinner, they were all too young to know. Trapped in a hell-hole, death for every meal of the day and yet still starving while being caged like an animal, too weak to fight back, too scared to end it.

Too right. Put a bullet in Bleak's head … that'd show 'em all.

Bleak's lip quivered. Chinny remembered staring at his own reflection years ago in chest-high waters from inside his cage. His own lip had quivered, for days. He was scared then, too. Bleak was just afraid. His hand stopped shaking. That's all it was—fear. The key to fear was to do the right thing in spite of it. Keep pushing forward even when one wanted to double over and yuck up their breakfast. He wanted to shoot Bleak, but it was fear, that's all. He'd walk away while his hand still touched his holster.

From the corner of his eye, someone approached rather quickly. Chinny snapped his head around, but there was no one there. He could have sworn he saw someone. *Strange.*

"There's nothing else on the matter, yeah? Come on then. Get hydrated and we'll fix this place up a bit, Nice coat of paint, some drapes... good as new..." His words trailed off at his attempt at wit.

"That's some bullshit right there."

"Duly noted. Doc, make sure we're all hydrated, yeah? Pop some salts everyone. Today's gonna be a hot one."

Chinny took his bloody hand off his holster and breathed deeply. Fear, if it took hold, could make a man do anything. Too much love could make him do stupid things too. Too much anything could kill.

Deep breaths, Chin. It's gonna be all right.

Chinny just needed to stop feeling. Then he'd be in control. Then he'd be strong. As he turned to walk away, he bumped into Kapaow. The Yard was staring out into the forest. He wasn't catatonic. No. Worse yet, he was afraid like Chinny.

"Kapaow? Ling Pao?" He tapped him on his arm. "I'm uh, uh—I'm—I'm sorry. Me sorry. Sad for Go Doc, sad for Mamma Ling."

It looked like Kapaow was going to hug him. Chinny didn't know what to do. Was he supposed to hold his arms up? Should they shake hands? His were too bloody for that. Kapaow stepped forward. Chinny felt his stomach fall through the floor and stepped back out of reflex. Then Kapaow walked away. He went to Ghost Doc, both of them looking at the stain that was once Kapaow's wife and newest baby boy. Next time. He'd give a hug next time.

Yeah. Next time.

Chinny was a horrible leader. Lax in his duties, the proper guard that should have been up at all times was allowed to join the party. For only a moment he was weak, and that was the moment they were attacked. The *one* time. A terrible leader indeed.

The seven dead were now sorted into rows and their body parts matched as best as could be, considering the carnage. The women were washing and preparing them for their ceremonies. A blue twinkle caught his attention. It originated from a tiny purple face on the ground, its one remaining eye still open, watching him. Something shimmered. He knelt down and looked closer into the brown iris. So close it looked like the gills of a mushroom. Something blue.

"Dooahhdeee meeee oooahhh," Sung shooed him away from the bodies. He looked back again. Baby Go Doc's eyes were indeed brown.

Odd.

He looked at the two men from opposite sides of the world kneeling side by side, staring at a spot on the floor, their brass bracelets matching. Only good men should be rewarded. Ghost Doc was a good man and deserved to be a part of the Yard family.

"Ghost?" Chinny tried to get his attention again, hoping to get his mind off of things.

"Huh?"

"We've got structures to rebuild. We need your help. The plans are all mucked up. We need ya. Kapaow, you too. We need ya, mate."

Kapaow followed Ghost, who put his arm on Chinny's shoulder and spoke softly, "We need you, too."

It caught Chinny off guard. His emotions mixed and confused him. Where was the world when he needed it decades ago, where was it when he needed it hours ago? There was just so much anger. He needed to know what the bloody hell had happened last night, why they were attacked, and how *did* they get the bodies out so fast?

Where to start? Where to look? Bleak had called in what happened, minus the insane parts of course, and they were told to sit tight. Chinny wasn't sure what that meant. Sit tight as in, "Wait for help," or sit tight as in, "Wait so we can see what happens to you next?" Why had there been vague responses instead of firm commands?

Chinny felt someone brush by. He looked, but there was no one there. The tension was exhausting. His senses came on alert once again when he turned to face the jungle. He listened, he watched, he sniffed the air to see if he could detect anything out of place. Chinny knew something was wrong. More wrong than simply being in Vietnam, more wrong than an attack on their village. Wrong in a way he'd never encountered before.

Chinny scanned the tree line again. He took a deep breath. For a moment, he examined a series of tiny interconnected structures in a tree above him. Ants had crawled over the trees and around their crops, dragging things together into what looked like little bird nests. He looked at one closer. It made him cringe the way the nests seemed to move, when in fact they were simply infested with hundreds of thousands of smaller ants crawling around inside.

He flicked the edge of one such nest and an instant panic came over them. Larger ants came to the site of the disturbance and stood guard. Chinny stared at one that seemed to be the most aggressive. It stood at the edge of the nest, tense and rigid. It *knew* something was wrong, but its antennae couldn't tell it exactly what. Yet, still it knew. He turned his attention away from the nest and back to the tree line.

What are you planning, Charlie?

CHAPTER 10
GHOST DOC

"What's this? The fifth time this year?" Bleak rambled.

"Why do you *always* have to bring this stuff up all the time? It's bad enough I'm out on patrol instead of back at base doing something important. Now I have to listen to you and your bleak outlook on everything, *Bleak*," Ghost said as quietly as he could without sounding any less annoyed.

"Yeah. Whatever, man. When the ghost soldiers get you, you gon' be all like—*Bleak! Save me, Bleak! You were right all along, Bleak!* Heard that, Phong?" Bleak whispered his mockery as he smiled. Phong smiled as well.

It was Ghost's turn to join patrol. He hated it every time it came around. Luckily, there were so many skilled fighters in the village that his turn didn't come up often, allowing him time to focus on the real work: helping people. The loss the village suffered took only a few minutes to inflict, but would take several months to repair. Despite attempts to make contact, an evac never came for them. Not that it mattered. They made due—surprisingly well, in fact.

Ghost again fell into the trap of trying to make sense of the killing. The very existence of life was an anomaly. Nothing in the entire universe worked in favor of it, and everything was trying to end it. Yet, it was created every day. Diamonds and gold were on other planets, but not life. Ghost couldn't understand how people disrespected it so easily.

Ghost's more scientific side argued that overpopulation could result in disease and famine. The truth was, more people had to die than what natural causes could provide alone. In some respect, any death could be considered natural cause, since it was human nature to kill. Ghost's more emotional side couldn't argue the point, yet it continued to feel it was wrong all the same.

It wasn't even that he minded death. He and Death had an understanding. He harvested plenty of souls for him. It was the depravity of the VC and NVA that confused him. Killing was one thing, but what they did was worse than killing.

"I'm sayin', Ghost."

"Be quiet. You're gonna get us killed ... or I'm going to kill you. Whichever comes first. *Ya dig?*" Ghost's threats didn't sound as threatening when he whisper-yelled them.

"I'm in charge, *jerk.*"

"Yeah, says the guy telling everybody we're—"

"Yup, see, here we go."

"Shhhh! Let me finish. Says the guy telling everybody we're fighting a bunch of ghosts."

"Whatever, man. Can't none uh ya come up with somethin' better, so I don't see why my story's gotta be so crazy."

"Because we *do* find dead bodies, and we *do* find weapons, *and* intelligence. It's like fishing, ya know? Sometimes you get a bite, sometimes you don't."

"We found like eight bodies in that tunnel that one time, remember?"

"Yeah, and I'm sure they were coming back for those too."

"Chin said we killed about eighty of them muthafuckas last time, so you're telling me they moved seventy-four bodies before we got down in there? *While* we were chasin' 'em?"

"Ummmm ... eighty minus eight is seventy-two ... just sayin'."

"What? Aaaww, fuck you, man. I'm here trying to figure out what's going to happen to us and you're off checkin' my math. Fine. Could the VC carry out a *boatload—*"

"Seventy-two."

"A *boatload* of people like it was nothin', *while* being on the run? No. So where the hell'd the bodies go, Ghost? Huh? Where?"

"And it wasn't *eighty.* Cheese-and-rice, we're not *that* good. It was more like thirty of 'em... I guess maybe eighty *percent* casualties. What's that? Like, twenty-four kills? I could see *that.*"

"Fine. So eight people."

"*Six* people. What is *with* you?"

"Whatever man. Six people... no It was eight. I remember that much." Bleak always made this weird snappy, clicky noise with his tongue whenever he didn't like what someone was saying to him. "There was eight there. Now you got me all twisted up."

Ghost loved to mess with Bleak when it came to numbers.

"So *eight* people carried out twenty-four? Can you carry three dudes at once?"

Ghost didn't have an answer for that one. The two looked at each other sternly. How could they argue when neither of them knew what was going on? During the attack, Ghost could have sworn he tagged at least seven. He'd heard them scream. So what was the answer? What about the night the village was attacked? How many were carried away by how many? He never saw any more than eight VC at a time, but they just kept coming. There had to have been more. Were there only eight the entire time, eight ghost-soldiers? Did they just walk away?

Don't be crazy, Ghost. That's what Bleak's for.

"Maybe they got some kind of armor we don't know about yet," Ghost offered.

"Oh, right. An entire army outfitted with top-of-the-line armor and ain't nobody found it yet. Like that happens. Remember that gun they were testing out, the one with the little thing to the side?"

"Yeah," Ghost said with deep exhaustion.

"Found that, didn't we? That was some top secret shit. Feel me?"

"We don't know if it was top secret."

"Kapaow said it was top secret from the intel, so guess what? Top secret."

"If you don't quiet down, I swear to God I'm going to dose you with morphine." He wouldn't actually dose Bleak, but Bleak didn't seem so sure.

"You shouldn't take the Lord's name in vain like that."

"I didn't take it in vain," Ghost argued.

"Yes you did. You're not s'possed ta swear at God."

"I was swearing *to* him, like promising."

"Nope. Can't do it."

"Okay, fine. I'm sorry… I was caught up in the—"

"It's all good, Ghost."

"Stop talking." Ghost was actually getting a headache from all the whisper-banter.

To pass the time, he checked the immediate area for any number of things that might kill him. Something like thirty different snake species in the area were poisonous. The ones with round heads, round eyes and double rows of plates going down their back were generally non-poisonous, but not always. The triangle-headed snakes with elliptical eyes tended to be poisonous. In the end, it was best to just avoid all snakes. For the most part, snakes avoided people. So did scorpions and poison tree frogs. Disease-ridden mosquitoes, however, did not. If he had to guess, more casualties were from disease brought on by mosquitoes than from gunfire. That could be an over exaggeration, but it sure felt that way.

Ghost tapped his watch and everyone took out a malaria pill and swallowed it with a swig of water from their canteen. Their canteens were bladder types made by the Yards. The standard issue would make sloshing sounds when half full, something else that could get them killed in Vietnam.

This patrol had proven quite boring. A more exciting patrol was a "Faux Team" or "bait patrol." They'd take some guys such as Binh, Hieu, Phong and Vinh patrolling down a trail, and they'd be dressed up like VC. If any actual VC, or even NVA for that matter, showed up, the idea was to ambush and retrieve intel. If the force was really huge, a forward observer would let them know and they'd all hide and let it pass on by. They'd radio ahead to Chinny and let him know what was coming. The trickiest thing about bait patrols was staying far enough away from the bait-team that they didn't spook any potential prey, but close enough that they could take care of business if necessary.

Today wasn't a bait patrol, though. Today was basic recon. This consisted of sitting in the bush, painted green, trying not to get bit by scorpions, snakes, or mosquitoes. Trying not to rub up against any toxic vegetation was also high on the list, right next to avoiding booby traps. Though being a boob wasn't required to get caught by one. They were pretty darn hard to spot.

The Yards didn't seem too concerned about any of it. They were still trying to egg on Bleak and his crazy conversations. Hieu was wearing a drab green bandana. It was very John Wayne, except for him giggling like an idiot with missing teeth.

Wild boars. They had to keep an eye out for wild boars, too. If a guy crawled into the wrong area and made a boar feel cornered, he was pretty much certain to get his face eaten off. Sit in the jungle long enough and death was pretty much a guarantee, no matter how much camo paint was smeared on.

Boredom was almost as dangerous as venomous snakes, tree frogs, disease-ridden mosquitoes, wild boars, poisonous vegetation and booby traps, because Charlie never came when anyone was ready. It was always when someone was defecating or when they were celebrating a new life coming into the village that Charlie showed up.

Aside from the things trying to kill them, there were things that could get them killed. Even if a team did everything right, some Curious George hoping to steal someone's hat could give away their position and get them killed. Crickets falling silent, birds that stopped chirping, a sprig of grass or a tree branch that wiggled as they passed by–they all had the power to end lives.

Dehydration, that was another one. Even surrounded by rain almost all the darn time, which was also hazardous to their health, dehy—

Cghrk

The static "click" that came over the comm meant to return to base as soon as possible. He'd be happy if it weren't for the fact that it meant something was wrong. As they were all scanning the area before getting up, Ghost noticed something bright purple in the distance and stopped. He squinted as he glared up the trail just a bit. It was a flower.

Sometimes Ghost felt like the jungle was a single creature, a monster in the night waiting for him to make a mistake, and when he did he'd be gobbled up. Yet, here was this radiant purple flower with a bright yellow stamen. It was something so beautiful, growing in something so awful. Regardless of how bad the jungle could be, goodness still lived there. Goodness worth fighting for. His gaze drew the others' attention. Some took a moment to realize what the fuss was about. Then they all shared a faint smile. They had to enjoy the little things.

"Bukametan chow!"

Their heads snapped toward the sound. Ghost honestly thought he'd have learned the language faster. He still had no idea what anyone was saying.

They all froze. Bleak was dead silent. *Thank God.* From behind the green face paint, each of them met eyes with the next. All of their hearts were racing. Bleak held up a fist, signaling everyone to settle in. They weren't supposed to engage the enemy. He hoped that they were camouflaged well enough to avoid detection.

They waited while the noise grew closer. The first to come into view was a tiny little girl in a tattered, dirty tan dress. Its shabby appearance didn't stop her from looking any less adorable, with little bows in her hair. His heart thumped in his chest. Her hands were bound.

Next came a woman, most likely the mother, her face purple and swollen like a hotdog about to burst, her lips bleeding and split, her dress torn to shreds and dangling like used dishrags. Ghost struggled not to shiver. Then eight VC came around, two of them dragging a man, most likely the father, a Yard bracelet on his wrist. He was being kicked and beaten. Ghost knew how this was going to end.

Unless they did something.

CHAPTER 11
GHOST DOC

The Yards stirred, as did Ghost. He looked to Bleak for an order. Bleak jerked his fist tighter, reasserting the need to hold their position. They obeyed. Had they been running a Faux Team today, they could have taken the chumps out.

Not being able to tell the future could get you killed in Vietnam, too. The little girl wasn't crying, but she looked like she had been for so long she had run out of tears. The VC were yelling, and screaming, and laughing, and carrying on. As soon as these Melvins passed, they'd take them from behind and capture as many as they could while saving the family.

Bleak tightened his fist again. They were not going to engage. It wasn't the smart move, even though they wanted to. Ghost looked at Bleak as if he were insane. Bleak looked at Ghost as if he were stupid. Ghost started to move. He could drop at least three of them, guaranteed. Bleak jerked his fist and clenched his teeth, so Ghost backed down. The fist stayed up as a reminder to all.

One of the VC kicked the little girl, causing her to fall on her face. When she sat up, her mouth was bleeding and covered in mud. Her knees were bleeding, too. Another VC laughed and extracted his tiny little thing from his pants and pushed it in her face. More laughter.

Bleak snarled, his eyes locked onto the sight in front of him. His hand began to shake. His chest rose and fell more quickly. He turned to his men and made piercing eye contact with each, tracing his hands in two small circular motions until he clenched his fists. They'd silently take them as soon as they passed. Ghost felt the fear and kept it close to his stomach. *Use it enough to keep you sane. Ignore it enough to keep you fighting.* That's what Chinny always said.

Bleak held up one finger with determination. That meant leave one alive. He withdrew a tiny pistol given to him by Chinny. He then withdrew the matching suppressor and screwed it on. It wasn't a powerful pistol, but it was quiet. Bleak extracted his knife with his other hand. The rest of the men drew their knives. Ghost looked around and saw the signs of adrenaline on all of their faces. Tactically, they could wait, let Chinny set up an intercept, but what would happen to the family by then?

Ghost closed his eyes and breathed slowly. He had to turn some switches on, turn others off. He tried to feel the looming sensation in the air… *Death*. He breathed it in and let Death inside his lungs, let it become a part of him. In a moment, he'd do its bidding.

Then the group stopped, too far up the gosh-darn trail. Bleak's little pistol needed them to be closer for it to prove effective. The Viet Cong soldiers started whipping the mother's feet. The one with his *thing* out mashed the little girl's face into the reddish mud, so soupy she was nearly drowning. Bleak was shaking all over now. Still, he kept his fist up.

Make the call, man.

One of them took out a machete and Ghost froze, they all did. He nonchalantly hacked off the mother's right foot. The blade made a ringing sound for a split second, and then her screams pierced the air. He went to stand up and fire on them, but Bleak again shook his fist for everyone to stay down. How could they sit here and watch this happen? Another ringing sound and her screams grew even louder. The VC enjoyed the sounds of her misery. They weren't men. They were parasites, sucking the life out of the land. They needed to be sterilized.

Yet still they waited.

Ghost read somewhere that soccer became popular in England because the English had a blast kicking around the severed heads of invading Dutchmen.

The guy with his thing out situated himself on top of the little girl, giving her a chance to raise her head and gasp for air, mud pouring out of her mouth as she choked. With a toothless smile, he rammed himself forward, hard. The little girl screamed in agony. Ghost could feel the shrill cry piercing his teeth. It was like being stabbed, cold and bloody. A single tear trickled down Bleak's face, dissolving his camo paint as it trickled down. He *slammed* his fist down and stood up. Everyone's mouth dropped.

He walked with his shoulders broad, a bop in his step. This must have been what he looked like walking down the streets of Brooklyn, looking for trouble. Bleak was ready to die today. Phong stood up next and quietly jogged up to Bleak's side. A few VC were huddled around the father, beating him with their canes. Another cut the ears off the mother while she screamed and those remaining watched and laughed. The man on top of the little girl with bows in her hair had his eyes closed, a smile on his face as he rocked back and forth. One of his hands held her face down in the mud.

The rest of the team followed soon after, but Ghost was still in shock.

Are we really going to do this?

Ghost took a deep breath, deeper than he had in a long time.

Walk through the valley, Ghost. Walk on through. Shake it off.

Ghost got up and joined the rest of them. They were a wolf pack, hell hounds. Reapers. They were stupid. This wasn't going to end well, and they were too close to each other while being too far away to close the gap.

Another ring and the mother lost a hand. The sound made Ghost queasy. She passed out and they all started kicking her, her husband cursing their attackers in a deep, demonic voice. Then the poor man cried when he saw her wake back up. The machetes swung down onto her as she screamed again, her back splitting open. The sound of her husband screaming–it was as if they were cutting him too.

Ghost wanted Bleak to open up on them, but the little pistol just couldn't be trusted so far away. Surprisingly, Charlie was so engrossed in their activities none of them knew what was coming. Ghost half expected Bleak to press the end of the suppressor right on the rapist's head just so he'd know what happened to him before he died. Instead, he thumped the hammer-butt end of his Ka-Bar knife down on the man's skull, knocking him unconscious.

He flung the guy's body on the ground, flipped the little girl on her back and motioned Ghost to check her. Ghost paused for a moment while Bleak raised his pistol up and shot the nearest man in the base of his skull. It was an excellent shot, causing him to rag-doll forward and land on top of the mother. Ghost went to work on the little girl.

At first, Charlie didn't seem to know what happened. They all started laughing at their friend who had fallen. The gun, when fired, sounded a bit like a plastic bubble being popped by a wire brush, followed by the clack of the slide popping back. If the VC hadn't been laughing so loudly, the noise of the suppressed shot would have drawn immediate attention. It was their joy that truly silenced the pistol and did them in.

Compress, then breathe. Come on. Breathe.

The service taught him a technique for bringing people back to life. It was amazing how often it worked. Compress the chest and then breathe into the mouth. Would it work now?

Come on. Breathe.

The next guy in Bleak's line of sight caught it just under his nose before he could say anything. At that point the Yards were airborne. The VC whose backs faced Ghost attempted to turn, but the Yard blades impacted with their necks before they had a chance. Each Yard twisted his knife ninety degrees and raked it out of the front of their target's neck. The gurgling and violent tearing sounds of ripped leather and pea soup slopping on the ground finally caught the attention of the remaining men who were still beating the father.

Please… come on! Breathe, little girl! Please! Please…

Bleak fired the rest of his clip at the men. They were too far away, and while they were injured, they didn't drop so expertly as before. It did, however, buy the Yards enough time to close the gap. They slashed and stabbed and hacked through the men. They screamed as they fought, but none of it would be loud enough to draw attention from far away.

No… Death! No… How can you do this? NOOOO!

She was… tears started to form… but anger choked them back. Ghost got up, all of the right switches turned on. *You owe me this now, Death.* He glided toward the enemy, a specter with a blade. He stabbed one guy in the kidney first, then up under the armpit, turned him around by yanking his weapon away and pushed the knife into his sternum, withdrew the blade when the man pulled his own knife in an attempt to fight back. He cut the man so deeply near his elbow that his entire arm flopped down, heavy and useless. The weapon dropped from his hand as Ghost swung his knife around and sliced down from the base of the target's ear to just below his jaw. No tears, just rage. Vengeance was supposed to be wrong… but it felt right.

The motion threw the man off balance. Ghost grabbed his arm and pulled him back. His knife thrust deep, piercing the top of the trachea and continuing up toward the medulla oblongata. The blade was stopped by bone and instead of dying, the man went into convulsions. Ghost reached around the back of the target's head and forced the knife deeper. It felt like stabbing through a T-bone steak and scraping the tip of the knife down the bone until it screeched across the ceramic dinner plate.

His opponent continued to convulse. He should have gone limp. Had Ghost missed the brain stem? The man reached for Ghost and tried to claw at his eyes. How was he not dead yet? He struggled to pull the knife from his throat. He wanted to yell for help, but they needed to stay quiet or risk attracting attention.

Die already!
"GUYS! HELP!" Ghost screamed.
The man was strong, almost stronger than before.
Finish it, Ghost!
He pulled the knife out and stabbed him again and again in the neck until his head hung from a string of flesh. Exhausted, he turned to check on the others. They were all staring at him, their heads cocked to the side as if staring at a diseased person.

"Ya done yet?" Sinner asked.

Ghost got up, stumbling with his first step. The guy's hand was clinging to his leg... Ghost looked closer at the body... something felt as if the dead body had tugged on him ever so slightly. That was a little too intricate a move for a death twitch, wasn't it?

His hands shook. It was like a cockroach had crawled inside his mouth. He saw its eye move.

"AAAAAHHH!!!"

He hacked at the arm until it too was dangling from a string. Ghost stared at the body suspiciously, waiting for it to move again. He kicked the corpse in its head again to see if it flinched, but it didn't move.

"What the hell is up with you, blood?" Bleak asked.

"Nothing." Ghost breathed as best he could. "He... he just wouldn't... I don't know."

"Wouldn't what?" Bleak's eyes widened.

Ghost didn't want to get into another conversation with Bleak. Whatever had happened, it could likely be explained by... by... drugs... or... something. Something other than crazy. He took a deep breath and buried it. He could sort it out on his own later.

Just then, he heard more rustling. What now? Phong was on the ground. Someone had gotten back up. How juiced up were they? Had they all taken the same substance? The guy fought with Phong and managed to land the butt of an AK across his head. The guy was messed up. He moved strangely, like something was wrong with him. Perhaps Phong had messed him up pretty good and it was just the drugs keeping him on his feet.

The muzzle of the guy's AK was bearing down on Phong. Ghost brandished his knife and charged. There wasn't enough time to get to Phong's attacker. He was too far away and slipped trying to move faster through the mud. He pulled Suzanne, who slipped from his hands into the mud. There wasn't enough time to clean it off and fire. He tried to get the M16 off his back, but the sling snagged on his clothing.

Death? What are you doing?

Everything slowed down when he realized he wouldn't make it. He'd been practicing throwing knives with Kapaow, who was actually quite good at it. Had he gotten good enough to throw it now? Death was coming for Phong. He could feel it. Ghost hated to disagree with the most powerful force in the world, but he went ahead and flipped the knife over, grabbed it by the blade, and launched it toward Phong's attacker.

Please, Death. Let us kill evil and let good remain.

The knife flew end-over-end, hurtling toward the man's back. Good. It was flying right for his spine. He worried that if he asked too much of Death it would turn on him. So he let go. Either the knife would land or it wouldn't. Either he'd save Phong, or he'd live with the memory of watching him die.

Whatever you want, Death. Whatever you want.

Finally the knife reached its target… and landed handle-first in the guy's spine. All it afforded was a pause of confusion, and the man turned to shoot Ghost.

Nuts.

The guy's eyes were vacant, barely focused on Ghost. He *must* have gotten some kind of brain damage from his injuries. He looked like a giant bug more than a man, twitching as he moved. The AK's muzzle pointed at Ghost's chest seemed enormous. Just then, Ghost Doc saw little hands come around the attacker's neck, a length of rope between them. The hands jerked back and before the trigger could be pulled, the killer was airborne. The guy dropped his rifle and struggled with the rope around his neck.

It was the father of the little girl with bows in her hair. He strangled the guy with the same rope they'd bound his hands with. The father was very small, but extremely powerful, lifting the much larger VC onto his back and holding him there. The man was jerking and kicking violently, trying to throw himself to the side. Finally, it worked, and he tumbled off to the right, but the little guy was ready for it and jerked the rope in the opposite direction using the VC's body weight against him. He could still hear the guy choking, but the rest of his body gave up the fight, probably a broken neck. Minutes in a battle seemed like days. It took days to kill this guy, but he finally died.

Their eyes met. Ghost was looking down at him, the little warrior looking up, tears streaming down their faces. Ghost cut the father free. He took his hand and brought him over to the unconscious rapist on the ground, motioning for the man to hold him down. He reached into his med pack and pulled out some ammonium carbonate, then he grabbed a handful of mud. He cracked open the smelling salts and waved them in front of the rapist's nose. He jerked awake, opening his mouth wide, and gasped for air. Ghost immediately shoved in the mud. He held his hand over the creep's mouth so he couldn't spit it out.

"Bleak! Get over here. Hold him down."

Bleak was more than happy to help. Still holding the rapist's mouth closed, he looked up at the father and nodded. There was a brief pause, a look of doubt. Ghost motioned toward the baby girl lying in the mud, her hands folded across her chest. The little man looked at the murder scene over his shoulder.

A few moments passed before the father looked back. Then, without hesitation, he pinched the rapist's nose closed. Ghost had never seen someone die like this. He wasn't even sure where the idea came from. Had they taken action a minute sooner... they were so far away, though. Maybe they'd all have just died. He watched the rapist struggle. Why was it that people who felt superior always did the most pathetic and inferior things?

Ghost pressed down harder on the man's mouth. Only a minute had passed. The guy was still struggling. He broke an arm free and grabbed a stick and hit Ghost right in the jaw. Ghost punched him in the ear as hard as he could and covered his mouth again.

Just choking someone was more painless than simply cutting off their airflow. When someone was choked, blood was prevented from reaching their brain, causing the victim to pass out. Truly being suffocated took much longer. He was beginning to choke on the mud. It'd feel like drowning.

Death? Am I wrong? Send me a sign.

Just then, it started to rain. This wasn't exactly an epic occurrence, since it rained all the time. For it to happen right as he asked for help seemed pertinent. Now, the question was: which type of sign was it? The rapist broke an arm free again, but the heavy rain made the rock he reached for slippery and it fell from his hands. It was settled. Death wanted the rapist's soul.

Copy that, over and out.

Two minutes had passed. Ghost Doc looked deep into the rapist's eyes. Ghost forced him to look the father in the eyes. Little Guy stared down at the thing that had taken so much from him. Three minutes had passed.

Ghost could feel the diaphragm spasm. Ghost knew what this felt like. It was starting to burn inside as the rapist's body convulsed uncontrollably. They passed the four minute mark. When they reached the five minute mark, that was when the body started to get past the fact that it was going to die, and then there was a certain sense of peace where the body let go and started to shut down to afford a painless death.

That's when Ghost reached over and moved the father's thumb, letting air in through only one nostril. It was brief, just enough time to gasp, to come back to life and start feeling again. For the body to think it was getting air only to be instantly cut off again. It did nothing for the swine but bring the pain back. The diaphragm jerked and bucked back and forth. The pain must have been twice as much now, burning and drowning at the same time. They held his eyes open, too.

At eleven minutes and thirty two seconds Ghost Doc handed the father his knife. Very ceremoniously, the poor soul plunged the knife into the chest of the man that raped and drowned his daughter, and then… it was quiet. They all looked at each other. Then they looked over at the bodies of the man's wife and daughter. No one really felt any better.

"Ya know zebras are actually black with white stripes, Bleak?"

"Really?"

"Yeah. Shave a zebra, he's all black."

Ghost breathed deep and tried to calm down. What had he just done? Combat was combat, but was this considered murder? Had they become murderers? No. That scum was a murderer. They were something better. He felt a breath across the back of his neck and jerked to see who the heck was there… but he didn't see a thing. It made him feel very cold inside. Something was wrong.

Just then, three more VC arrogantly strolled up the trail like they owned it. The first one stopped when he saw the bodies and the next two bumped into the first, creating a triangle shaped cluster. Everyone froze. Everyone except for the heartbroken father. He charged.

It must have been strange, staring at dead bodies, looking up, and seeing a tiny little man leap into the air. Even more odd when his feet flew past either side of the lead guy's head and collided with the throats of the two men in the back. Downright insane when he grabbed the lead guy's neck with his thighs and flipped over.

The little guy was smart. One hundred and thirty pounds, give or take, wasn't much to fight with. Using his entire body weight, the little man crushed two esophagi and broke the neck of the leader. In one fluid motion he was on his feet, heel striking down on one of their noses.

He hopped over and kicked the guy to his right square in the testicles and raked his fingers across his eyes. He swung back around and punched the one to his left in his already-bloodied nose, then punched the right in the temple and punched the left on the nose again. He punched the crater where the nose used to be, again and again, and when his hand hurt too much, it was elbow strike after elbow strike.

He jumped high into the air, kicked his leg straight up so his foot went past his own head and swung his heel down into the same exact crater with the precision of a Swiss watch. He screamed, looking up into the heavens as if taunting God himself, damning God for allowing this to happen to his family. The pain in his voice was familiar to them all, far too familiar. Little Guy turned, eyes like a tiger, and grabbed the head of the last survivor. He gouged his thumbs down into the eye sockets. The eyeless man, with his throat caved in and his face beaten to a pulp, flailed his arms and grabbed at the father's wrists to no avail. He went limp. The little man turned. It was as if he were waiting for some new feeling to emerge. He gasped and choked, screaming out his tears. There was no making up for what he'd lost.

"KAAAAAHHH!"

The sound was deafening in contrast to the soft jungle chatter. All of them got up. It was like ice water had been forced down his throat, like needles were piercing all over his skin, like tiny claws were scraping their way down his body. Sinner backed up. Bleak backed up. They all backed up.

"What the fuck?"

"What the fuck?"

"What the heck?

Ghost forgot that anyone else in the world existed. All he saw was a man that should be dead, but was crawling toward him, reaching for him. He fired into his head and a piece of his skull broke away, but he didn't stop. Ghost fired again and again and again, some rounds hit so close to the surface that the shockwave caused the skin to split and tear away like overcooked sausage.

"Die! Die! Die!" Ghost screamed, drawing his knife when he ran out of ammo. He stabbed him in the neck as he clawed at Ghost's face. He tasted his blood in his mouth and it made him ill. "Die!" He stabbed. "DIE!" he screamed, and stabbed, and sliced, over and over and over, until finally the body went limp.

Ghost was shaking. He had never shaken so badly. His mind was falling apart attempting to find an answer.

They lost too much blood. There's no way. The brain trauma was too severe. There's no way. That big of a drop in blood pressure would have made them pass out.

Maybe they hadn't been dead, but unconscious temporarily? Perhaps some drug was capable of this kind of tenacity? Something he had never heard of?

Ghost held his hands together, one trying to stop the other from shaking. When that didn't work, he held his head, hoping it would make it easier to think. He rocked back and forth.

He looked around, and everyone had the same expression. The bodies were limp on the ground, but they all watched, waiting for them to move again. One of the dead men's arms fell flatter on the ground and they all flinched.

"You still think I'm crazy?" Bleak mumbled.

"Yeah," Ghost softly replied, "but that wasn't natural. I haven't figured it out yet, but I will. I promise."

"You better." Bleak whispered.

Cghrk

"Eh, fuck." Bleak seemed to snap out of his trance. He'd forgotten to double click back to Chinny, which meant Chinny was worried now. "Now boss man's gonna chew me out. You assholes probably ain't gonna say shit either when we get back, are ya?"

"Say what, Bleak? Huh?" Ghost challenged.

Bleak ignored Ghost, instead choosing to look at the father, now covered in blood. He sighed and turned away as he spoke into his handheld. "Yeah, boss, we encountered a light resistance upon prepping to RTB. What do you want us to do with the bodies and intel? We have one survivor, over."

"*Crghk*, Say a—*shhhhkah*—over."

"Come back, base." The radio crackled back with an empty sigh. "Base, come back."

"Roger—*ssshhhh*—for interrogation. *Shhh* the rest of 'em and hide the bodies best ya can, over."

"Come back, base. I can't hear you."

"Roll the *krggghhh* of 'em and hide the bodies best ya can, over."

"Copy that, but the tangos had civilians in tow, one surviving. Charlie's dead, over."

"Say *shhheee* over."

"Copy that, but the tangos had civilians in tow, one surviving. Charlie's dead, over." There was a three second pause, not long, but long enough to know that Bleak was in trouble.

"Copy that. Bring back any intel and survivors. *Shhhhh* another team out for the *sssshhh* bring the bodies back. We'll burn 'em. Hopefully *sssshhh* won't come asking questions. Out."

"Piece of crap radios," Bleak muttered.

Ghost Doc pulled out some antiseptic and cared for the wounds on the father's hands inflicted by the sharp edges of crushed bone. He was wrapping them with a piece of petroleum gauze and going over that with dry gauze when Bleak grumbled under his breath.

"We're bringing him back. Chinny will send another team for the dead."

"Good. Let's get out of here." Ghost's voice shook as he spoke.

"Yeah, well, the dead better *be* here when we get back."

Ghost turned back to give them one last look. His heart dropped from his ribcage and his body turned cold. What he saw was what they had all seen. Yet, just a split second ago, as he'd turned to pay his respects... he could have sworn he saw their heads turned up, as if the bodies were looking their way.

"Guys... I..." He didn't want to say anything. Somewhere deep in his gut, he could not let the team down. "I... I think something's wrong with me."

"What do you mean?" Bleak asked, sounding more concerned than angry.

"I..." He wanted to tell them what he saw, but didn't want to get laughed at. "I think I saw something that wasn't there."

"Ghost, look at me," Bleak said sternly. "Whatever you saw, you tell me, and I'll believe you."

Ghost parted his lips, but didn't speak. He started to feel tired, and achy like he was sick. His stomach turned and his mouth was dry. Had he been drinking water? Ghost tried to think back... he started to feel dizzy and lost his footing.

"Damn," Bleak said, catching Ghost before he fell. "Fuck it, we'll talk about it later. Let's get everybody back home on the double so I can hurry up and call in more reports and get chewed out about how much I'm fuckin' up everything I touch, but I should be grateful because not a lot of coloreds out there get the chance I do, boy. Fuckin' assholes."

For a moment, they all stared at the bodies.

I wonder if we're all getting chewed out for this mess.

CHAPTER 12
BLEAK

"I once shot a man right in his heart from ten feet away. Not only did he not die, the bloody bastard almost choked me to death before I finally took him down. I know it's scary, but it's not uncommon, yeah? Now, listen up. I'm not gonna ask, ya hear? I'm just gonna tell. You get sent out on recon-only, you *avoid* contact at all cost! *Recon* is more important than *revenge*," Chinny growled.

"Come on, Chinny. I was just tryin' a do the right thang, man," Bleak said, arguing his case.

"I don't wanna hear it, mate. We need ya. We can't afford to put any disciplinary action against ya, but you're not comin' next time we visit the theater."

"What? No John Wayne?"

"No John Wayne."

"Awwwww, damn. Come on, Brooklyn."

"Kapaow, find out where he lives and get a ten-man together and escort him home."

"Don't start ignorin' me now, Chin."

Chinny waved dismissively at Bleak. "What's done is done."

"He no want go," Kapaow said.

"What?" Chinny and Bleak asked at the same time.

"Him want to stay."

"Why?" Again they asked together.

"No one left where he from."

Chinny and Bleak shared some silence for a little bit.

"Well?" Chinny asked Bleak.

"Okay…" Bleak replied, unsteadily, "yeah… let him stay. We need the manpower. Kapaow, put him on a detail. Get a list of his skills. We'll put him to use."

"Find out what happened at his village and we'll hold a ceremony for his people later," Ghost added from a distance.

"All settled then, yeah? Great. Now you," Chinny pointed at Bleak… *shit.* "Water detail." Bleak moped away. "Bleak!"

"What?"

"Forgettin' somethin'?"

Shit. Now I have to call in and report this shit. Bleak hated reporting in. Comms never worked and the assholes on the other end never understood anything even when they did work. Anytime he ever tried to get genuine orders they would just tell him some generic nonsense so they could cover their own ass in case things went south.

Their main radio was dead, but in one spot—of course it was a hike to get to—he could get through with the smaller unit. After about twenty minutes of clarifying, he got told the Yard father they'd saved was a non-priority.

After the stupid conversation was over, Bleak got back on his stupid water detail. He flipped the bird at the general direction he knew their orders were coming from. It was some bullshit.

Fuck I'm supposed to do? Just let 'em rape a damn kid? Fuck that. Pale face muthafuckas always trying to weigh down on a brotha. That's right. They wanna see a black man fail. They wanna see a black man lose his damn mind. Stickin' someone out in the bush, in charge, and then get mad when he takes charge. Uh, that ain't how it works. Believe that. Now I gotta figure what to do with this crazy ass Montagnard muthafucka.

Chinny again approached Bleak as he returned with water and grabbed up on his arm, pulling him aside. Chinny looked around a bit, some old mean ass look on his face. Like he hadn't chewed him out enough, he had to come in for some seconds. Bleak looked at the sky and rolled his eyes. He didn't need this dumb ass shit.

"Look here, mate." Chinny was whispering now, looking around to make sure no one was listening. "You did good, son. Real good. We can't have any cowboys out there, so I gotta punish ya on the outside, ya hear? I can't *condone* it, ya understand? We can't have a policy of saving every single person that's in trouble or we put the village at risk. The punishment stands. Next time we head on in, you're staying back for work detail." Bleak made his pissed-off-clicky-noise with his tongue. Chinny grabbed his arm again. "Hey, listen: some things ya just can't reward. Right then. Run along now."

Bleak felt a little less heated over the whole situation. Chinny was all right. Them Australian cats were some badasses. Neither Chinny nor any of Chinny's friends ever called him "boy" or looked at him funny or anything like that. They were all right. He could dig it. Not wanting everybody and their mamma poppin' off gooks left and right. That'd be bad for business.

WALK THROUGH THE VALLEY | 73

The crackers back home set him up to fail, as usual. Chinny had more experience, even fought in a jungle before coming to Vietnam. Bleak got trained and sent to Viet-mutha-fuckin'-nam as his first assignment. Really, he didn't even know what made him Spec Ops. He was more like Spec Train, because all he had was special training. "Special Operations" was plural. He only had one operation so far and the shit wasn't even complete yet. He knew that shit showed too.

He could have gotten everybody toe tagged trying to get revenge for a little girl. There were tons of little girls getting that shit done to them. What made him think he had the right to step in and do something to stop it? Who was he to meddle in the lives of others? They shouldn't even be getting involved in these people's problems. Right?

Man... fuck that pussy ass pansy bullshit. What the fuck kinda fairy fuckin' nonsense is that? Of course, Bleak was justified in stepping in. He should have moved in sooner. As soon as he saw them coming he should have had everyone just go loud with the M16's and smoke them all. Then that crazy little Montagnard would have his family.

Should have gone sooner... Come to think of it... why didn't he? He wanted to do something, but instead of taking action he just watched. He'd gone and let his heebie-jeebies get the best of him. There weren't any ghosts out there, but he hesitated for a moment to wonder about it. After that, it took everything he had to gather up the courage just to stand up. Everybody got scared, but why'd he have to get scared then, at that specific moment? Why couldn't it have been some other day? Why couldn't it have been something that only put *his* life at risk? Why'd it have to be a mother and daughter?

"Hey, coon face."

"Yeah?"

"Damn... you all right?"

"What do you want, Sin?"

"Well... look, man..." Sinner looked out onto the horizon and bit his lip.

Bleak tried to read his face. He figured Sinner had to say something he didn't want to say. Whatever it was, it'd have to be something Bleak was real sensitive about, otherwise that honkey would just blurt it out.

"Fuck you, Sin. I know what we did up there. You sayin' the shit didn't happen?" he said quietly, though angrily.

"Hey, hey, hey! I didn't say it didn't happen. I'm just sayin' Chinny makes sense. Some people are just tough, man. Would *you* go down if you was shot? Or would you keep fighting and fighting until your body wouldn't let ya? Hell, I've heard stories of guys getting shot in the head and not even notice."

He was right. Bleak wouldn't die unless he had to. Still, with the type of wounds they'd inflicted, how *couldn't* those muthafuckas have died? He listened to Sinner sigh, long and slow, squinting at the sun on the horizon. He watched Sinner wipe the sweat from his brow and sigh again. He shifted his weight, back and forth, back and forth.

Come on, Sin. You gotta believe me.

"I tell ya what. Things get squared away here, we'll run through what happened. I'll get our notebook and we can add this type of shit to it. We'll try and come up with some... whatever you want to call it... failure to stop. We'll come up with failure to stop drills."

"Sin," Bleak said firmly. "We shot the *shit* out them muthafuckas."

Sinner had an exhausted half smile on his face, the kind used for crazy people and stupid kids. "Fuck's his name anyway?" Sinner changed the subject.

"I don't know. I say we call him Crazy Mont." Bleak was happy to get off the subject at that point.

"Why?"

"Because, dummy. He's a Montagnard," Bleak replied with attitude.

"I know *that*, you walkin' stick a shit. I mean *why* crazy?"

"Because that muthafucka is *crazy*."

"Ooohh... serious?"

"Blood... *that* muthafucka is *crazy*. Ya dig? That Crazy Mont's gonna come in handy."

"So what did you find, Sin?" Chinny came over and broke up their private conversation.

Sinner scratched his head slowly. Bleak could tell he was trying to think of the best way to say what he had to say. Since Sinner rarely gave a fuck about how his words sounded, it was obviously straining him.

"Whelp... whelp... my guess'd be..." Sinner hesitated as he looked at Bleak, then at Chinny, then back at Bleak again. "My guess'd be... Charlie come around and... got the bodies again. Place was empty." He paused and looked at Bleak. "Now *don't* start that—"

"Ohhh, shit, man. See. I *told* ya'll. I *fuckin'* told ya'll, but you didn't want to listen! Now it done happened *again!*" Bleak yelled.

Sinner tried to shush him. Fuck that bullshit. These muthafuckas wanted to sit there and make fun of his ass all the damn time. Some shit was going down. All around them, there was some shit going down. Bleak started to look around. Scanning the trees, he concentrated. Sinner was talking, but Bleak was so focused his words fell to the background. Something wasn't right. Bleak could feel it, different from the usual sense of danger. Something else.

It felt like eyes staring at the back of his head.

CHAPTER 13
KAPAOW

"Quit now? Are you crazy? There's *never* a reason to give up, Kim. Never!" Kapaow yelled. "What do you think this is? I mean, really. What do you think is happening?" He walked up to Kim and stared into her eyes to make his words sink in. "We don't fall in line, as a *people*. We were born free, and we *can't* live as slaves. You see the difference? We *can't* live as slaves. We're incapable. So they'll just get rid of us."

"Yeah. A lot of good that's done them." Kim rolled her eyes and laughed.

"You're right. We're strong. We've always been strong... and our numbers have always dwindled. Little by little, sliver by sliver, we're being shaven away from existence. That's not what's killing us, though, Kim. What's killing us is that no one else cares. That was our mistake, you see? I realize that now, what Grandfather was trying to make us understand.

"We avoided the rest of the world. Hoping to not be infected by their way of thinking. Hoping to not catch whatever it is they have that not only makes them willing to submit, but *eager* to do it. All that time, hundreds of years, *thousands,* we never once lifted a finger to empower anyone but ourselves. We were greedy and small-minded and here we are, the sand slipping between our fingers, soon to be nothing. We need help. We needed it long ago, but we need it now more than ever. So I need *your* help."

"I understand just telling them the truth won't work. That's not my problem with what you're asking. I just think they're too stupid to be of any use. Let us assume," Kim said skeptically, "that you somehow manage to get these men to open their minds and they are somehow able to resist the influence of the tree-fairies, we—"

"Look. Just help me guide the men towards the truth."

"Why, Kapaow? Why do you think they are special? If their own cultures have been infected, how could they ever help us? *Why* would they ever help us beyond the orders they receive?"

"They are outcasts where they are from. They are talented, brave, smart and valuable, but they do not fall in line, so they are pushed aside by their own societies. None of these men fit in where they are supposed to belong, and they never will. You see? They never will. I have seen rebels fall in line, but I have never seen these men fall in line, at least not completely. They follow orders as they see fit and allow for what's right to exist whenever they can. They offer a quiet defiance to their own command, but they are waiting. Waiting for something they believe in so fully it allows them to justify shining in the darkness. They want to stand in the face of what controls them and say 'no more.' They just can't see what truly controls them. *Yet.* So they wait. I will show them when the time is right."

Kim's face shifted slightly. A subtle look of surprise revealed itself. Even she was beginning to believe, whether she wanted to admit it or not. "As you wish. But getting back to my point..." Of course she would be defiant and continue her argument. He wouldn't have expected anything less. "Say they do resist *them.* Perhaps instead of going mad and slaughtering each other, they simply have a bit of a struggle with reality only to find their way. Fine. None of those accomplishments will matter once the dead are implemented. Once the dead walk, *everyone* loses their nerve. You know this, Ling Pao."

"*We* held it together, Kim, for *thousands* of years. Do you think we're the only ones capable?"

"We had people in our lives who valued openness, who valued connection, community, family, friendship and love–valued it so much they never let it be taken from us, at any cost. We had ancestors that would die to preserve us."

"They don't have that," Kapaow agreed. "But imagine if they did."

"The fact that we are surrounded by millions of empty, lifeless husks that do only as commanded by a perverse influence terrifies me more than the dead, Ling Pao." Kim revealed the truth of her doubt. She was afraid of facing the enemy head on.

"How many times do I have to tell you to call me Kapaow?"

"No. You blew up a fifteen-year-old boy and they applauded you for it and gave you a name to match the deed. I will *not.*"

"They gave me the name for blowing up *three* fifteen-year-old boys with a single shot in *record* time. That was after we caught them slaughtering babies from the High Hills village up the path and they opened fire on us, which you seem to have forgotten. Perhaps the fairies *do* have a hold on you already?"

"I have not forgotten!" she screamed, tears welling up in her eyes. "I certainly am not captive to *them!*" she growled, folding her arms in disapproval.

Kapaow looked at the soldiers. Kim punched him in the shoulder. "I thought we weren't calling them fairies?" she mocked.

"That was their first day, Kim. The first thing they saw when they got here. Little children, little babies. You did not see their eyes... Chinny's eyes, the look in his eyes... it surprised me, the endless pain he felt. *Endless,* though he did not want to show the emotion at all. I saw it. *That's* why it's Chinny out of all of them. His empathy. I hate to say it, but I am glad. If it had to happen, I am glad they saw it, because now they *know.* You heard them, Kim. Where they are from, no one knows we exist. They think it is about communism and not us, and when that lie does not serve their leaders, it will be something else that fuels the war, but never us. For all's sake," Kapaow scoffed, "they think the Chinese are the indigenous people and not the invaders! No one cares that we were here first and they have been trying to kill us all off and take our land for thousands of years. It has taken them thousands of years, *thousands* of years of us resisting them, Kim, but they are doing it. They *are* killing us off. In fact, they are almost *done.*

"One day we will all be gone, and the world will not stop. It will keep going without ever noticing. People will not remember us. We, and I am certain a few other cultures, have protected the people of this Earth from *them.* We deserve better than this! We deserve to fight back and win!" Kapaow allowed a moment of silence to compose himself and let his words absorb into Kim's mind. "The truth is: it does not matter if the Americans can or cannot succeed. They are the only chance we have left."

Kim hung her head low, unable to argue against Kapaow's logic. "So what will you try this time?" she asked, making no attempt to hide the mocking tone in her voice.

Kapaow had already tried and failed. His father had already tried and failed, and as the stories go, his entire lineage had tried and failed to bring others to their aid. Still, as far as Kapaow was concerned, he knew more about *them* than any other entity in the world. There were too many things lining up in their favor for it not to work. It *had* to work. It had to.

"I cannot *tell* them, Kim. The truth does not work in words. I have to *show* them, and even then belief isn't guaranteed. You have mocked me plenty for all the hardened men that came through here, were shown the dead, and were reduced to nothing more than crying children in the face of it. What I have learned is that we have to bring them to an instinctual, spiritual, and intellectual acceptance. These points need to converge at a precise moment, a delicate dance, but I believe it will be effective this time. We cannot make a mistake in guiding them to their own answers, otherwise they will never believe it and it will drive them away from us."

"Why do you think the soul matters so much in a battle of weapons and warriors?"

"The warrior wields the weapon and the soul wields the warrior, Kim. The heart is the route of everything, and if the heart is numb, it feels nothing about anything–has no opinion on any matter, is willing to stand by and watch. It will do anything, accept anything. We need to wake these warriors up, bring feeling back into their lives, help them see what they are *allowing* to be taken from this world."

"What makes us so special? So important?"

Kapaow grabbed her by the shoulders and shook her. "You matter. Everyone matters. You understand me?!" His eyes bored holes through her, his teeth gritted, tired of her doubts. "The small things have much bigger impact than you realize," he said more calmly. "Basic things like leadership, family, friendship, love: these are tools in the battle. The battle starts in the mind, and with these tools the mind is forged into something capable of resolve; of making the right choices. Each of them has something. Leadership, family, friendship… but none of them have love. Love is what helps us choose for ourselves. It forces us to become transparent, to be vulnerable, and by being vulnerable we cannot hold back, and we release our ultimate potential. Even more than that, with that sort of openness, the truth of the world becomes more obvious. Truth is nothing without the will to act, and love gives us the will to act."

"How do you think you know this?" Kim was almost in tears.

"Because we are still standing! More than that, we are still fighting! We are *not* victims! Our story is like no other. We did not bow, we did not die, we did not cower! Most of all, in spite of our suffering, we are the happiest people I have ever encountered! Not at this very moment, because you're being a royal pain in the ass, but usually!"

She smiled.

"No other culture can say this. To have suffered so much and still love, still feel, still smile, without living as victims, without wallowing in our battered past, without living with endless rage in our souls, without accepting nothingness, without falling in line and bending to *their* will! We are the last memory in a world that is steadily forgetting what it means to live!"

"Now you just sound arrogant."

"Our culture has given us the tools to resist their influence, but it isn't a perfect resistance. We need to learn from our ancestors' mistakes and share these tools, not squander them. That is not arrogance, that is fact."

"What if it's something else? What if it has nothing to do with our culture at all?"

"What else could it be? No. My heart tells me it will work. Somehow, it will work. I do not know exactly how, I do not know when, I do not know the impact it will have for us. All I know is it will bring good things to our people."

"Wonderful. So we just need to get these professional killers to understand the meaning of true love *before* they start to lose their minds and face off against an army of corpses… a flawless plan."

"Chinny is the key. I saw it in his eyes. He is a good man. Bleak is intuitive and his instincts are faster than lightning, but he gets lost in it all. Ghost keeps them focused but doesn't want to lead, and Sinner negates their doubt in favor of action, but none of them have the empathy that Chinny does. It is the ability to feel that allows us to rise above the fog. Chinny will see. We just need to wake him up. His scars have not made him incapable of total connection, only afraid of it. We need to help him face his fears."

"This is manipulation, *Kapaow*."

"It is *communication*, Kim. We are translating what he needs into terms he can grasp so he will know he needs it, nothing more. His team represents all pieces of a puzzle, pieces I will use to teach Chinny everything he needs to be. The others will play a role as well, perhaps greater roles than Chinny, but he is the spark. He is the thing that can hold them back or push them forward. It needs to be him."

"It needs to be him, but we cannot tell him it needs to be him."

"I know it will be difficult."

"It will be next to impossible, especially when you account for the fact that when you speak English you sound like an overgrown child. He will never take you seriously."

"What? I speak fine."

"Ha! Goo goo, ga ga, Kablaowey!"

"Hey!" He pulled her hair playfully. She flicked his nose with her finger. "What?" he asked as he rubbed his nose "I do. This will work, Kim, I promise."

"I hope it works, Kapaow. I really do."

"It will work."

Please let this work.

CHAPTER 14
BLEAK

As he stared into the distance, Bleak wondered if somewhere a sniper had his crosshairs on his nose. No... that feeling of eyes staring at the back of his head; it felt close. A cold chill ran down his spine, the hairs on his arms stood up on end. Sinner put his hand on Bleak's shoulder. Bleak shrugged it away without looking. Again, Sinner put his hand on Bleak's shoulder. Bleak turned to tell that fool where to shove it. His heart almost stopped.

Sin was standing ten feet away. There wasn't nobody near Bleak at all. Not near enough to put a hand on his shoulder, too far away to have grabbed his shoulder and run—trying to mess with him. He looked where a man *might* be, had he placed a hand on Bleak's shoulder a moment ago. He looked and looked... but there wasn't anybody there.

"I think he's losin' it, Boss. Gotta get Doc to check him out. Maybe he ain't take his malaria pills or some damn thing." Even though Chinny and Sin were whispering to each other, he could hear them.

Why had he waited? Why had Bleak waited to attack those chumps? Why did he wait while they hacked up that lady, while they murdered that little girl? He was scared, he had to admit, but wasn't he always scared out in the bush? It's not like fear ever stopped him from doing his job. Why, then? Why right at *that* moment had he been so scared he couldn't move?

Anger swelled inside him. It wasn't his fault. It was Chinny's for always tellin' him to get intel and not worry about the people. They were supposed to be winning hearts and minds. *Hearts and minds.* Those were Chinny's words, and yet anytime some dangerous shit came along they were supposed to wait. Why was Chinny always so calm? Why was he always acting like he knew what was going on, meanwhile nobody else had any clue? What did he know?

"Where'd all the bodies go, Chin? Huh? Where'd all the bodies go? Ain't no way Charlie came and went that fast, man. No fuckin' way."

Chinny grabbed him by the arm *again* and pulled him aside to whisper. It was gonna be the same damn conversation. He wasn't crazy. Nobody could explain any of it, but they were all real quick to explain him away.

"Bleak, listen, all right? Do you *honestly* think that—what? We're fighting ghosts? Do I need to start worryin' about ya?" Chinny stared at Bleak like a man ready to put down his rabid dog.

"I know what you wanted me to do, Chin. I know. See... you think I'm crazy... but I know what you wanted me to do. I know." Bleak nodded his head over and over.

"Well, if ya knew that you'd have done it, mate." Chinny let go and rested his hand on his sidearm.

"You goddamn right I didn't do it. I didn't do it, 'cause..." Bleak yelled the next part, "... I'M *NOT* CRAZY! Shoot, man. You talk about winning the hearts and minds, Chinny. You *talk* about it. You don't *do* shit though."

"You're gettin' too attached, mate. I'm warnin' ya now."

"Ya know what, Chin? Someday soon, I'm gon' be better than you. Everybody's gonna stop lookin' to you and start lookin' to me and when they do, we're gonna stand up to these assholes, not hide and watch them all the damn time."

"Have you been taking your malaria pills?" Chinny finally asked.

"Why does this have to be anything other than you being a pussy, Chin?" Bleak didn't mean to say that.

"Hold ya'self, mate. You're gettin' out of line." Chinny was starting to puff his chest out.

"Go fuck yourself, Chin. Ya stupid fuckin' fairy!"

"Bleak ..." Suddenly Kapaow was at his side, his hand on his shoulder, looking in his eyes like he understood what was going on inside him. "Breathe, my friend. Breathe."

I'm losin' it... shit... I'm losin' it. Bleak breathed.

Ah, fuck that. Chinny could take a long walk off a short pier as far as Bleak was concerned. Like he knew so much better. That motherfucker didn't know shit. How the fuck was keeping a safe distance supposed to help them connect with these people? Chinny didn't have no bracelet... Bleak didn't neither, but Ghost *did,* and he didn't have *no* distance from the Yards whatsoever.

Gotta calm down, Bleak. You're just afraid, that's all it is. Just calm down. You'll be all right. Gotta have faith, son.

"I'll let this go, but I think you're wrong, Chin."

"I wish I was, Bleak. I wish I was."

"And yes, I been takin' the damn pills. Ask Ghost. He know."

"You'd tell me if somethin' else was wrong, though, wouldn't ya?" Chinny asked as the two stared at each other for a good ten seconds.

"Yeah… course," Bleak lied.

"I won't judge ya."

"I got ya, man." Great. Now everybody thought he was crazy. He had to put them on something else. Distract them.

Bleak watched as Kapaow whispered in Chinny's ear, then Chinny spoke, almost like he forgot Bleak was even there. "Sin? You get any intel?" Everyone looked at Sinner.

"If you could call it that. Found a piece of a map. Ain't goin' be much use. Here. See? We got a few circles, an 'X.' Goddamn tic tac toe."

It was several circles spaced out in a nonsensical way. A man didn't mark a bunch of nonsense on a map, though. Had to be targets. Key points for something. What was the X for? The target? One circle stood out from the rest. Hue City. He knew that place, had been there once. Nice tail in that area. It was the circles that were targets. How? Hue was a good size city. The VC couldn't handle that kinda fight alone. Unless maybe they were looking for a suicide run. The VC was like that, crazy and stupid. Chinny always said they got… *peels? Zeel?* Some shit, whatever that meant. Bottom line, the VC couldn't do shit like attack a whole damn city and expect to get anywhere. They had to be getting help, and a lot of it.

"Get this. The X is right about the same distance, give or take, from these three circles. There's gotta be a cache or somethin' there. X marks the spot, right? The VC probably got orders from the NVA to go do something and they're moving their weapons around to get by our patrols. Ten to one that's a village or some shit hiding the weapons." He searched Chinny's eyes. *Come on, Blood. Agree with me.* Maybe he needed a little more. "It's gotta be a large scale coordinated attack. If we take a map, we could prolly guess where there's an X the same distance from these other circles. Two for the price'a one."

"Large scale attack by what? Ghosts? You're making wild assumptions without any facts," Chinny said, shooting him down. "No worries, mate. It ain't much to go on, but we can send it up the line. If it does well, we'll make sure the powers-that-be know to thank you." Chinny didn't seem convinced.

A rumble of choppers in the distance inbound on their position scrambled his thoughts. He hadn't heard of any NVA aircraft in the 'Nam... but he couldn't help but feel on edge whenever the sound got close to his position.

"We heard 'em comin' just a bit ago when I signaled you back. Got a scout out in the tree line, but the radios are buggy again," said Chinny.

"How long's it take to get over here in a fuckin' chopper?"

"They been flying in circles it sounds like. Whoever they are, they're not the usual," Chinny said with a sense of doom.

"You don't think?"

"What do *you* think?" Chinny asserted, while Bleak hesitated.

"Everybody up," he called out, to which people slowly obeyed.

Sin, Ghost Doc, Kapaow and Crazy Mont came up alongside him. He looked over at Crazy Mont, whose eyes were still bloodshot from crying. Bleak took his pistol out by the barrel and motioned toward him.

"You can use?" he asked.

Crazy smiled and nodded quickly. Bleak was a little worried though, didn't feel like getting shot in the ass. When he saw Crazy Mont keep his finger off the trigger, point the gun in a safe direction, and check the chamber for a round, he knew the guy could handle himself. He passed him his extra mags, too. Bleak looked back at the rest of the village staring at him like they didn't know what to do. Bleak turned around and lifted up his gun and raised his eyebrows like, "Stupid? Get ready." And everybody started running around getting armed. On guard, behind cover, they waited.

And waited.

And waited.

And waited. He clucked his tongue again.

A friendly chopper peeked up over the trees. Shark teeth were painted on its nose and redneck music blared from loudspeakers. For a minute, Bleak understood why Chinny hated Americans. Regardless, they could relax. It was nice to have a resupply. Maybe they'd get some "clean clothes" this damn time instead of some "water hose." *Fuckin' radios.* When it landed, the dry red dust of the earth swept up into their faces.

A bunch of good ol' boys emptied out as the engine died down. Bleak clicked his tongue. *Man, no resupply.* They looked everybody over and, of course, stared right at Bleak like someone might stare at snot on the ground. Bunch of chinks all over the damn place, they gotta look at the one nigger. Same way a bunch of pasty ass Billy Bo Bobs always looked at him. He wasn't scared of any of them. He'd knock them right in their fucking heads, each and every one.

Fuck em, lookin' all pissed off they got their boots dirty. Fuckin' twinkle toes.

"Oi! Did I say at ease? Everybody at the ready! Resupplies are prime targets for the enemy ya twats! Everyone relaxing like it's a bloody vacation. Eyes open!" Chinny spoke like Bleak didn't *just* get done tellin' everybody to get ready.

"There's the nigger. Where's the chicken choker? Says his name's *Cock*-ington? Heh heh. That you?"

Oh, shit! Bleak felt light in his stomach like he really, really wanted to laugh, but he tried not to. They just called Chinny a chicken choker—this was about to be a brawl.

Come on, Chin. Get 'em.

CHAPTER 15
CHINNY

It was yet another unfit nickname. Special Air Service Regiment members were sometimes referred to as "Chicken Stranglers." Not only was his nickname Chinny, but Chinny was indeed a chicken strangler. Chinny the chicken strangler. Cockington the Cock Strangler. *Explain that to your mum.* Chinny stared into the man's eyes, finding much weakness in them. He bypassed the comment.

"Brooklyn Cockington, Special Air Service Regiment. What can I do for you boys?"

"Nothin'. I just think your name's hilarious. Where's the man in charge around here? Who was it again?" he asked, gesturing to one of his lackeys.

"Green, sir," one arse kisser responded while peeking over his shoulder.

"Green?" the assistant whispered in his ear. "The nigger? Green?" he asked, motioning at Bleak. "Swear, every place I go it's some spook in charge. The whole damn world's gone crazy," the man grumbled under his breath.

Chinny continued to stare at the man, more and more like he intended to murder him. At first he just stared at his face. He was sort of fat. A fat-ish man. The likes of someone who perhaps was once in shape but with a change in lifestyle was starting to lose his desire to exercise. Then he stared at his eyes. Beady little things they were, with a sort of blankness to them. Not the kind of blank stare a man got from torturing himself over the things he'd seen. No. This fattish man's eyes were blank because he didn't seem to contemplate much of anything except his own self-worth. With every ounce of rage he had, Chinny looked into the man's soul. The fattish man looked away.

Suddenly, Bleak was nowhere to be found. *Little bastard.* Where the hell had he gone? Chinny was stuck talking to the bloody Yanks while Bleak was hiding somewhere avoiding confrontation. It was so unlike him, but every once in a while the boy surprised him with his actions. That's how he'd say it to Bleak: *I'm off yacking with the bloody Yanks while you're having a shy moment. Big man, always talking a big game until the brass shows up. Then it's your tail between your legs, is it?* Then he'd laugh at him. Chinny was counting on Bleak to take over his role. He was teaching him so he wasn't needed anymore and could leave.

"Uh… he's otherwise engaged at the moment. I can take the orders and relay them."

"Says you're just the advisor."

"I'm also his assistant," Chinny said without hiding the aggravation in his voice.

"Okay… well look here, man: do chicken chokers like to turn their radios off? Been trying to get in contact for days now."

"It's on the fritz. If you have a spare we'll take it."

"You're supposed to report in."

"Just as soon as we get a new radio. We've got some Prick Sixes and a pack radio. The main one's shot. Recently we've been getting a lot of interference. The big boy was the only thing that could transmit through it."

"Right. Well, anyhow, ya'll are ordered to report to the Mike Force unit over at the A Shau special forces base. We got word there might be an attack and we're callin' all cars."

"They might be ordered to do so, but I don't answer to this specific chain of command."

"Actually, I have here a signed document saying you do." The fattish man smiled.

Chinny caught himself before he started arguing with him. It was a chance, a chance to break free from the village. Still, to leave without properly transitioning out would make a still-fragile emplacement vulnerable to attack. The village was as tactically important as it was politically.

He was put here for Australia. Now, apparently, he was fighting for America. The civilians wouldn't be allowed to come, only the fighting men. Chinny needed to leave enough weapons, ammunition and fighters behind to keep the place safe until the men could return. The orders demanded everything they had. The elderly, women, and children in the village would have to defend themselves with only seized weapons and whatever ammunition they left them.

"You waitin' on a sign from God, boy? See that there? That means I'm the ranking officer in this here area so what I say goes. Ya get me? I'm in charge. I'm the man. Ya understand? Me. An' I'm sayin' get your shit ready. You'll be picked up at the rendezvous and shipped out. Understand?"

"Why wouldn't they pick us up here?"

"I'm in charge, not you."

"What does that even have to do with what I'm ask—"

"Clayton!"

"Yes, sir?"

"Radio's on the fritz. See if you can fix it." The fattish man looked to Chinny and spoke softly, nodding while pushing his lower lip up like a bulldog. "Did you guys try jiggling the antennae?"

Just going to glance over the fact that half a bloody village has to risk their lives through the jungle because the Yanks don't wanna spend the gas? Ya bloody twat.

"Of course."

"What about the wire where it goes into the box thing. Did you jiggle that?"

"No."

"Yeah, Claybald, tr—"

"It's Clayton, sir."

"S'what I said. Try jigglin' the wire a little." Chinny and the fattish man shifted their gazes to the ground, an uncomfortable pause followed.

"Sir?"

"Yeah? What is it?"

"I think I know what the problem is."

"It's that wire, isn't it? Yeah, just give it a jiggle then."

"No sir, it's—"

"It ain't the wire?"

"No sir, it's—"

"Well, spit it out. I ain't got all day."

"There's a good fifteen bullet holes in it, and I think the wire's been—melted off." The fattish man looked at Chinny with a touch of shock on his face.

"As I said ... shot."

"Oh... all right, well, *Cock*ington. Why did the commanding officer of this circus-act choose not to call in and request a replacement?"

Why didn't he call on the broken radio to order a replacement for it?

Chinny blinked.

"Why didn't you call in for a new radio?"

"We came under fire, thus the bullet holes in the radio, thus the lack of calling anything in thanks to the lack of radio. We've got wounded we're tending to. If we leave now…"

The fattish man picked his teeth. He leaned in close to Chinny, puffing his chest out. "We ain't training these people to sit around and do nothing," he whispered. "To be honest, I could care less about your chinks or your damn village, but there's dying to do, boy. We'd rather use up the locals first. You readin' me? Less expenditures that way."

Don't break his nose... don't.

"*Your* orders have been received. We'll get squared away and move out."

"Sir," the fattish man replied.

"I'm sorry?"

"You'll get squared away and move out, *sir*," the fattish man asserted.

Bloody hell. The twat was asking for it.

"Come again?"

"Say it and salute, soldier."

Fat Fuck. The fattish man had just been promoted to the Fat Fuck.

"Snipers are pretty fierce out here, *Sir.*" Chinny saluted. "We tend to not salute the important targets. Wouldn't want you catching a bullet clean through the teeth, now would we?" Chinny saluted again. "But as I said, *Sir.* orders received and we will carry them out, *Sir.*" He saluted again.

The man glared, so Chinny looked at him like if he glared for too long he might get shot in the face. He'd read Fat Fuck's eyes. He'd fight back administratively. He'd make himself feel better through paperwork and favors against Chinny. Thankfully, it'd be a while before such paperwork was received, if ever. As Fat Fuck walked away and the chopper's blades whipped the air before takeoff, Bleak approached and had the gall to ask Chinny what was up, son, blood, ya dig? Jive turkey... *bloody fuckin' hell.*

"What the *fuck* are you doin'?" He shoved Bleak, hard.

"What?"

"Don't 'what' me you little prick. Ya got me off talkin' with the fuckin' Yanks. That's *your* job."

"Fuck those guys, man, fuckin' fast tracking me into this shit. You know as well as I do I don't even fuckin' belong here, man."

"Nobody gets put in a position of leadership unless they earned it, mate."

"Yeah, right. They just wanted to put a black man in charge, watch him fail and then be like, '*See*, black people can't lead.' Fuck them. Trying to get me killed. Shit."

"You're a damn good marksman." Chinny was almost hurt, though not surprised, by Bleak's lack of belief in himself. "You're a good leader when you let yourself be, when you're not off being crazy or... bleak. You're so worried about *why* you're here, you're forgetting what ya need to be doing now that you *are* here. Forget about why. You can turn this around in your favor, mate. Like Ghost always says: ya gotta walk through this, not around it, yeah? You're here. Walk through the valley."

"More like *die* in the muthafuckin' valley."

"Shut it! I've had enough of your shite about this and that." Chinny spoke in a mocking tone. "Maybe it's ghosts, maybe it's aliens, maybe a bunch of loser twats in pajamas are going to coordinate a full scale military attack. Maybe we're all just gonna be one big happy fuckin' family in a jungle that smells like rotting cartilage with a bunch of toothless fucks! This is a fucking *job.*" Chinny started growling through his teeth. "A fucking *job*. You punch in, you punch out, *that's* the end of it. You *pretend* to give a shite, but you never really do. That way, when they swoop you up and drop you off in some other Godforsaken place, you're not stuck dreaming about the last hell hole! There is no home. Ya understand? This *isn't* our home."

Chinny turned to face the entire village staring at him.

CHAPTER 16
CHINNY

Chinny's face burned with embarrassment. Had the Yards understood his angry ramblings? Kapaow would know not to take it personally. So would Kim. The rest of them, well… the Yards' morale was somewhat durable.

He took a deep breath and tried to think of some form of apology. *Bloody fuckin' hell.* It wasn't his fault, and he wasn't going to apologize for it. What did they expect? It wasn't like it all wasn't true. He turned away from them and turned his attention back on Bleak.

Chinny was fuming. The kid just didn't listen to anything. A hundred times he told him politely, a hundred times Bleak defied him. A hundred more times he told him sternly, now he was screaming at the top of his lungs, and suddenly Bleak was hurt.

He just couldn't win. Now *he* was the bad guy for telling the truth. All he could do then was sigh and walk away, find someplace to calm down. He bumped past inquisitive villagers he didn't have the desire to explain himself to and searched for a place to catch his breath.

"Why didn't you call in for a new radio?" Chinny asked himself in the best redneck accent he could gather.

What a twat. His hooch was a sieve, right along with most of the others and the radio room as well. He lay back on his sleeping mat and surveyed the room that had been his quarters for a good while. His walls were bare. The floor was dirt, yet seemed clean somehow. His gear was in a hole he'd dug in the ground and luckily sustained no damage.

It all served to exemplify the fact that he had nothing holding him to the village. It was fine to leave. The job wasn't to save anyone. It wasn't to make a difference. It was to do as ordered. In this particular case, the order was to leave.

Pap… pap… pap… pap, pap, pap… pap, pap, pap… pap… pap… pap, pap, pap, pap, pap...

"Oh fuckin' hell. I'm right here, mate."

"I have teeth… see?" Kapaow smiled big and bright.

"Well..." Chinny squinted as he looked in Kapaow's mouth. "Ya got *some*." Kapaow had several molars missing. He had the parts one saw the most, anyway; a full set of front teeth.

"We kill VC?" Kapaow asked.

"That's what we're contemplating at the moment."

"What is contemate?"

"Con-tem-plate."

"Con... dem... puhlate."

"Pretty close. To think in a very serious way, I guess is what it means. We have to leave to support another base that might get attacked."

"Might? So... might not?"

"Might not, but probably will."

"Oooohhh... not so bad! I tell others we fight!" Kapaow said with a smile, eager to share the news. When he stood up, Chinny pulled him back down to the ground.

"Kapaow, wait. Just... wait." Chinny took another deep breath. How could he explain this? How could he say it in a way Kapaow would not only understand, but obey? "We don't need you. You stay here, protect village. I take some, only *some*, go to base and protect."

Kapaow stared into Chinny's eyes the way Chinny had stared into the fattish man's. Kapaow was measuring him, evaluating his nature and determining what was really happening. His facial expressions seemed to mimic what he saw in Chinny's heart. The last face Kapaow made was one of grave concern.

"You come back?"

"Sure," Chinny lied.

"No... no... I think no... You no go alone."

"I *won't* be alone. Bleak, Sinner, Ghost, some of the others–they're coming with me."

"No... *you* ... *you* no go alone. You need friend stay close. I come, Chinny. I come." Kapaow smiled, shaking his head, his eyes closed as he waved his hand about.

"I don't want you to come."

"Yes, me go. I go. I go you."

"No." How was he supposed to get through to him?

"Yes."

"Kapaow... *no*."

"*Yes*."

"Fuck! I don't need you! You understand me?" Chinny shoved him.

"Chinny, I go!" Kapaow got angry too.

"I don't give a fuck about ya. Don't you get it? I'm just here until I'm not here. I mean, bloody hell, mate. You should be with your people." It was like talking to Bleak all over again. He just didn't have the time or the energy for it.

"You scared. Chinny, my friend." He touched Chinny on his shoulder, closed his eyes while raising his eyebrows and pushing his upper lip down as if to say no offense. "But he scared."

"Oh, come on, then." Chinny shrugged off Kapaow's words.

"Yes, scared." Kapaow snapped his head to the side and squinted.

"What? You see something?" Chinny got ready to draw his pistol.

"No… no." Kapaow shrugged off whatever it was and went back to his thought. "Afraid, Chinny. Demon." He touched a finger to Chinny's forehead and Chinny almost vomited at the thought. "Demon, follow you. You need friend." Kapaow snapped his head to the side.

"What is it?"

Kapaow paused longer this time, squinting, staring. "Nothing." Kapaow looked back, then jerked again.

Chinny became silent, the air became silent, the wind stopped moving and the truth of how ungodly hot it was became apparent. The humid moisture filled his lungs more than the air. It became hard to breathe.

Kapaow shook his head, shook off whatever idea he had about what was out there. He turned back to Chinny, opened his mouth to finish his thought—Chinny was close enough to see Kapaow's pupils dilate. This time Kapaow spun around and faster than a bolt of lightning drew his pistol and fired into the air.

KLOWWWWWwwwwwwww!

The shot echoed and made Chinny's ears ring.

"Shite! Fuckin' bloody hell, mate? What the fuck are ya doin'? What the hell's a matter with ya?" Chinny screamed.

Chinny came over to grab the pistol from him. The commotion of the villagers coming to see what happened swelled in the background. Kapaow grabbed at Chinny's shirt to stop him and pointed at the reddish-colored sand that made up most of the landscape. On the patch of ground Kapaow pointed to, something glistened in the red sand.

Chinny got down on his hands and knees for an even closer look. It was wet. It was red. It was fresh. It couldn't be what it looked like. He wasn't supposed to touch it. Ghost would get angry if he did. It wasn't sanitary. He needed to be sure, though.

He dipped his forefinger into it and rubbed it against his thumb. The smear confirmed it to Chinny. He stood back up with as much disbelief on his face as Kapaow. Together, they scanned the tree line. He checked his finger again. It was blood. Someone had bled there *very* recently, too recently to make sense. He checked himself and then Kapaow. It wasn't from either of them.

Whose blood was it?

CHAPTER 17
KAPAOW

What have I done?
What have I done?
What have I done?
What have I done?
What am I going to do?
What am I going to do?
What am I going to do?
How could they have known?
How could they have known?
I was careful.

Keep focused, Kapaow. Breathe. Breathe. Just breathe. Pretend like you do not know what you have done. Play dumb. Just play dumb. How are they so close? They weren't anywhere near this close yesterday. They doubled, maybe tripled their movements. My timetable was wrong. Did I shoot one? What did I do? Why did I do it? What was wrong with me?

Chinny. Oh no. Look at him. This is too much, too fast for him. I have to distract him, somehow. What do I do? How do I do it? I don't know if I can fix this. Kim. Find Kim. Let her in on the plan now. Everything is ruined anyway. All the containment, the generations of biding our time, making a formula to awaken the outsiders and in an instant it is all put to ruin. This was not my legacy. This was not my gift to our people. This wasn't supposed to happen like this.

Just let it go. Let it go, let it go. It does not matter anymore. What are you going to do now, Kapaow? That is all that matters. What do I do? What do I do? What do I do? What can I do? Think, think, think.

It's too late... isn't it?

All I can do now is go forward. I betrayed you, Chinny, my friend. I betrayed you without ever knowing it, but I betrayed you nonetheless. I am sorry.

There's no going back now.

CHAPTER 18
CHINNY

"What did you see?" Chinny demanded, albeit quietly.

"No know."

"Well you saw *something*," he whisper-yelled.

"… no know…" Kapaow's voice shook.

They stood shoulder to shoulder as the villagers crowded around them. He didn't know what they were saying. Considering the behavior immediately followed a gunshot, one could wager a guess. Their feet stomped across the red sand and mashed the tiny spot of blood. Chinny was so lost in what had happened he didn't even lift a finger to stop them.

Was it some kind of sleight of hand? A magic trick? A practical joke? No. Kapaow wouldn't discharge a firearm to make a joke. No way. Kapaow looked too terrified to be joking, and he was never much of an actor. Which left only insanity as his final option.

The crowd grew closer, pressing against Chinny's chest. The already-hot air became even more so, and every breath yielded less and less oxygen in his lungs. The humidity increased and his body felt heavy. They started to push and shove, and he breathed faster and faster, slowly falling behind into a state of suffocation.

Kapaow grabbed him and yelled something as he dragged him from the crowd which stood in a mass of curiosity. Having no answers for them was aggravating. They turned their backs to the patiently waiting crowd. Kapaow opened his mouth for a brief moment, and then shook his head no, disagreeing with himself. A moment later, Chinny did the same.

They knew something was out there. Their instincts were screaming, but they couldn't determine exactly what was waiting for them. Chinny struggled with every sensibility, desperately searching for logic in the scenario. He suddenly felt very tired, worn out, and uninterested. A voice echoed in the back of his mind, begging him to delve further into the matter. However, he found himself less and less concerned. Eventually, the little voice was drowned out by the villagers' voices.

They couldn't stand there staring at the jungle for the rest of the day, after all. Orders had changed, and life was about to go on. A sinking feeling crept into Chinny's stomach. It was time to get on with it. The truth was: there were simply more important things to be dealt with and not enough time for anything else.

"Kim! Where's Kim? Kim!" Chinny called out. "Kim! Kim! Where are ya? There you are. Can ya come here a tick? That's it."

Kim was a shy one, contrary to her behavior under fire. She shuffled her feet and stared at the ground, somehow magically gliding through the dense crowd without any hesitation. Kim didn't know anywhere near as many languages as Kapaow, but her ability to translate English was probably the best in the entire country. He needed clarity now. No loss in translation.

The customs of their village would mean that he'd need Kim to translate his message to Kapaow, who would then explain it to Cheng, the village leader. The villagers would want to hear it from a man, and the man in charge would also want to hear it from a man. When she got close, he grabbed her by the arm and guided her behind a hooch to speak in private. It didn't go well.

"Look. We have to go. You understand? We have to go. Simple."

Kim looked at Kapaow. The two shared the oddest of looks, and Chinny wondered what was going on between the two of them.

"Why?" Kim asked.

"Because we have to," Chinny replied instantly.

"You don't *have* to. Just stay." Her English was getting better.

"I don't expect you to agree. Just understand that we *have* to go."

"I'll tell them, Chinny, but you don't *have* to do anything. You *choose* to."

What the hell's that supposed to mean? Of course he had to go.

"I need you to explain to Kapaow that he's to stay, to protect all of you."

"Ling Pao will do as he wishes. If he chooses to go, he will go."

"It's not that simple."

"Yes it is. I need *you* to understand, Chinny," she said sternly.

"You're still young, Kim. You don't realize how complicated the world is. We're being ordered. Don't you understand? That means we have to go."

She giggled softly and uncontrollably, a tear rolling down her cheek. More tears followed, and she covered her mouth and shuffled away. It wasn't a laugh of joy, or ridicule. Just one of those laughs. He snatched her arm before she got too far. He needed to know that she would relay the message properly.

She swatted at Chinny and scratched his forearm. What the bloody hell was her problem? Bleak, Ghost, and Sinner came up behind her, staring at him like he'd lost his mind. He just wanted to talk to her. He stared at the tree line again, still feeling that sense of unease... what had sparked it? He tried to think back. It was only a moment ago. Something happened with Kapaow not five minutes ago. What was it?

"AAAAAAHHHHHHH!!!!!!" Off in the distance, perhaps hundreds of meters away, echoing off the mountains, they stopped bickering for a moment and simply listened to some poor bloke screaming.

The bugs stopped. The wind stopped, Everything was listening. It was strange to hear such a thing without any sort of gunfire or explosions accompanying it. The unfortunate soul might have stepped in a primitive trap, perhaps a punji or a more elaborate contraption.

"Help!" they listened to the soul cry.

It was too far away. Too many reflections garbled the bloke's origin point. He was on his own. Chinny listened while the man cried for it to stop. It was a strange sort of agony. Most men continued to cry for help, yet this man cried *stop, please stop,* and then... he cried someone's name. Chinny couldn't make out the name, but the hapless victim cried it out and begged the perpetrator to stop. What the bloody hell was going on out there?

"Weeoohhdwa aww," Kapaow rattled off some comment to Kim. Chinny had no idea what it meant, but Kim froze in her tracks, and the two just stared at each other. Chinny stared at them and swore his own heart stopped beating for a moment at the sight.

"Bleak, make a call. Maybe there's some work for us, yeah?" There was no time for strange ponderings. They needed to deal with tasks at hand.

"We ain't got no radio, Chin. Not one that works good enough," Bleak replied softly.

For a moment they all just listened. A moment of silence for whomever it was. There just wasn't enough time for all of this. Chinny waved his men away. They slowly marched off, confused, perhaps even afraid, but still marching. Everyone wanted to be in charge until it was time to make the hard choices. He watched Kapaow laboriously disperse the crowd.

Kim approached Kapaow after the last of the villagers left, then spoke to him in their native tongue. From time to time, Kapaow would glare at Chinny, depending on what she was saying. He then turned and explained it all to Cheng, even though he'd been standing there and heard everything Kim said. It was obvious none of them would take the news lightly.

Maybe Chinny should have brought a make-believe tea set in his kit when he arrived in the 'Nam. Then they could sip make-believe tea and chew on make-believe crumpets while pretending to be some big happy family. Of course, he wanted to leave this shite. What'd they expect?

No sense in feeling surprise, mate. Ya saw this comin' a klick away.

Chinny took his time stuffing his things into the largest pack he had. Of all his weapons and equipment, extra socks were the most important piece of gear. Second after that was foot powder. After that, ammunition and such. He hadn't named the rifle he was given in the 'Nam, an odd thing for a soldier. It was simply an M16. His did not fare well in the jungle. It didn't jam as often as Sinner claimed, but one would suppose it jammed too often. Still, it was an accurate rifle and the rounds did as promised. The VC called it "The Black Death." His pistol was just that, a Browning Hi-Power 9mm pistol that saw little use. Still, the extra weight was sort of like a baby's blanket–a mere comfort that helped to squelch anxiety.

He *had* named a rifle, once, long ago. An L1A1, issued to him in Malaya. Everybody called it the SLR, but his was named Victoria, after his lady. She was a beaut, both the woman and the rifle. It had a more powerful round, more reliable than an M16 and more accurate than an AK. The woman was blonde and curvy. She had blue eyes, too. *No… they were brown, weren't they? Right. Because her and I were surprised when …*

Thump

He could hear the sound in his jaw when something smashed him in the back of the head. He turned to see Kim, who had thrown something at him. Her voice stabbed into him.

"You go, we die."

If I stay, you'll die.

CHAPTER 19
CHINNY

He remembered the look of the gun, its nicks and scratches, the sound of the action sliding back and forth. He tried to remember her cheeks, her chin, her lips, her voice, her love. It was all black holes in the jungle, missing pieces from millions of years ago.

No worries. Not like you'll ever see her or anyone else again after this job.

It was freeing, really.

He pulled out his knife, the last personal thing he owned. He had chosen to leave the raw hammer marks in the blade even though the bloke at the shop said to polish them out. Every swing of the hammer was a piece of him. His soul was in that knife, and it was outnumbered by the souls of its victims two-to-one.

"Supah Mang?" Cadeo's soft voice emerged at his doorway.

"Umm... not today, mate. It's the knees again."

"Please?"

"No. Not today."

"No more days... please?"

"No, I really can't right now. Later," Chinny lied.

"No more laters... please?"

"Fine. Ya want to play the *stupid* fuckin' game? *Let's go.*" He grabbed Cadeo by the arm and dragged him over to their piece of shite bench and lifted him up by his one arm. "Get up there. Come on."

"Ouch." Cadeo rubbed his arm, his brow furrowed in concern.

"I got ya now. Jump." Chinny could hear the aggravation in his own voice.

"Too far."

Chinny stood a meter and half away. "Nah, it's fine. Come on, promise."

"You catch?"

"Yeah... I'll catch ya."

Cadeo wiggled. He licked his lips, something kids seemed to do when they concentrated. He focused on Chinny's hands. Chinny knew what he had to do. To get these people to understand that they weren't friends. This was just a job and the job took them somewhere else now.

Cadeo jumped, smiling, though his body tensed up. Chinny swooped in and caught him. He spun Cadeo around so fast his knees really did start to hurt. He let the boy go before he was perfectly steady and Cadeo tripped up a little bit, but didn't fall. He paused where he stood, staring at Chinny.

"It's okay, mate. Let's go again. Farther this time, I'll catch you… I *promise*."

Cadeo jumped, smiling. He stretched his arms out straighter than ever, his body flat as a board. He *was* Superman. The boy was so happy, so free, his eyes closed. Chinny dropped his hands. The boy landed hard on the ground, hard enough to bounce. He sat up, confused and looked up at Chinny, looking for some sort of an apology as if it had to have been a mistake.

"Up again. Let's go. This time I'll catch you. Come on." Chinny yanked the boy off the ground.

"You… catch?" Cadeo was rubbing his arm again.

"Yeah. Let's go. Promise. I don't have all day." Chinny snapped his fingers.

Something changed in the boy's eyes. A certain kind of disbelief Chinny hadn't seen in a long time. Chinny *had* to catch him, because how *couldn't* he? The boy wiggled atop the bench, looked at Chinny, wiggled again. He didn't ask if Chinny would catch him. He just closed his eyes and jumped again. This time, however, he was not relaxed. Chinny dropped his hands. The boy landed hard.

"Again! Come on. Let's go."

"No. You no catch!" Cadeo started to cry.

"Yes I will…" *What are ya doing, mate?* "I promise."

Cadeo didn't hesitate. He leapt even harder, forcing his eyes closed. Bruises were forming on his legs. He bit something in his mouth and a little blood trickled out. He cried and cried and Chinny just stared at him. Part of Chinny wanted to stop, but his body kept going. He scanned the tree line for a moment while Cadeo cried. Then he headed back to his hooch to finish packing.

"Why?" Cadeo screamed. "Why you leave?"

"I have to." Chinny said nonchalantly over his shoulder without giving the boy another glance.

After his bags were full, the rest of the time was spent honing the blade of his knife, inspecting its every tattered imperfection. He wasn't a very good blade smith, either.

On the ground next to his bed there was a beaded bracelet. Zhang, a skinny teenage boy with a rotten smile, had made it for him some time ago. He'd never worn it, never thought about it, yet he kept it near his bed. He went to add it to his bag. Maybe he'd tie it to his knife later as a lanyard. There were many different green stones on it. He'd wondered why Zhang only chose green when most of the other Yards had multicolored stones on their beaded jewelry. He went to drop it in the bag.

"No," he said to no one in particular.

He threw it across the room, and it smacked the wall so hard it wedged itself between two slats of wood. A man couldn't hold onto things, lest he enjoy seeing them taken away. He stared at the bracelet, his eyes heavy in his head, wishing it was a brass one. Chinny felt ill. He hadn't slept in a while. Maybe he could catch a couple of hours before anyone noticed.

He wet his mouth with a fresh swig of water before easing onto his comfortable sleeping mat, also a gift from the Yards. His knees creaked and cracked and popped. His lungs sighed. He laid back and breathed slowly, waiting to drift off. He hadn't felt this relaxed in years. It was so much easier to leave. He let his mind wander wherever it liked.

* * *

Chinny sat Indian style in an open field charred by napalm, his wrists draped over his knees. Wisps of embers floated through the air like hell's snow. He was meditating, but it was as if he were floating, watching himself. He observed from an outside perspective, yet still felt everything his body felt. Each hellish snowflake burned his skin, *tsss-tsss-tsss*, but he didn't dare move. He breathed in the smoke from far off burning bodies and blew from his nose. He could taste the dead.

In the distance he heard cries, perhaps a mother screaming for help. He wanted to get up and go to her. A deep, booming voice came to him from every direction. The booming voice said, "Sit." Chinny remained seated, and he felt a pat on his head. The cries became louder, and the voice said, "Stay." Her cries became louder and the voice said, "Look away." So Chinny looked away and closed his eyes. "Good dog."

He couldn't just sit and stay. He had to do something. His eyes were still closed, afraid of what they might see. His heart pounded from the fear, but if he stayed, what would happen to her? If he went, what would happen to him?

His feet burned with every step across the scorched earth. He felt the ground stir, the panic forcing his eyes open. There were giant rocks growing out of the dirt and they cracked and shattered like ice cubes in a glass of water. They hissed as he passed by. He'd heard the sound before, from friend and from foe, up close and personal; the air escaping from the lungs of a man as he slowly faded away. So many times Chinny had heard that sound. This was louder, more violent, almost angry, but it was otherwise the same sound.

"*hhhhhhhhhhh…*"

Her cries were growing louder. The sky was hazy and bright, but as he grew nearer to the cries of distress, dark clouds formed. Swirling about, he saw it all turn black. For a moment, the only light came from the red and orange glow of the burning ground. Thunder rolled in and the wind blew embers in his face and eyes. He was now close enough to see the woman. She was rocking back and forth, her blonde hair smoldering. His pace quickened.

He screamed to her, *"Get up! You have to get up! Please!"* It sounded like he was yelling from behind a wall. Everything was muffled. His steps seemed to drag, like running through waist-high water. She rocked back and forth, her arms tucked in, holding something that had to be her baby. Her hair burst into flames and he bawled, *"NO! PLEASE! PLEASE GET UP! RUN! YOU HAVE TO RUN!"*

The earth began to shake and lightning formed in the skies, each bolt veining the blackness with hazy red streaks. It was him. He was the cause of it. The closer he got, the more it was turning to ash. He tried to stop running, but the hand that once patted his head was now pushing him closer. He tried to fight it, but it was too strong, too inevitable.

He screamed to her, *"Get away from me! Stay away from me!"* He tried to warn her that it was his fault, that she'd only be safe if she ran, but she wouldn't move. She just rocked back and forth, wheezing coarsely through her crackling throat, her clothes engulfed in raging flames. She screamed with even more agony.

Flicks of bright red and yellow seared past his eyes. It was rain, but smelled of fuel falling from the skies. It was as if some silent battle with planes and helicopters raged on somewhere in the black sky, the fuel set ablaze, and the rain burned. He felt each and every drop cooking through his face. She tilted her head back and swayed side to side, screaming in one long, deep, desperate, crackled note. He grew closer to her, welts and blisters forming on his skin. He hated asking for help.

Please, God... God, please. Send something to save her.

Instantly, the sky opened up, patches of red sky showing through. There were thousands—*millions*—of planes and choppers ripping through the clouds. They dipped and dived between the black patches, the holes in the sky. Giant planes whooshed overhead, running low to the ground with their bay doors opened, dropping cool liquid over the landscape. It put out the fire on his skin and in her hair. He cheered, shook his hands above his head, and felt the wetness hit his face. He tasted copper in his mouth and his eyes burned. The liquid was slimy. What was happening?

The skin on his arms was melting. He looked into the distance and saw there were trees unburned by the fire a few klicks away. Their leaves were melting away from the liquid. When his eyes returned to his flesh, it was dripping off like fat searing from a spit-roasted pig. He ran. He had to save her, even if he was supposed to sit. Stay. Good boy. He held his hands out to try and catch the pieces of himself as they fell off and burned into the ground. His jaw went weak and hinged down. He couldn't call to her anymore. All he could hear was his open-mouthed, breathy moan of agony as he ran faster and faster.

He fell to his knees beside her and attempted to ask if she was all right, but his tongue was gone. He tried to turn her body but she resisted him. He was hideous and frightful, but he needed to know she was okay. He forced her to turn and looked her in the eyes.

The back of her head was scorched and blistered, but charred sprigs of hair remained in front. The hair clung to her face like a mask, only her eyes shown clearly. She kind of looked like Mamma Ling and yet she looked like so many others. He peered down. There was no baby. She was just looking at the empty space between her cradled arms. What was left of his stomach turned over on itself. Slowly, painfully, he brushed her hair to the side with a bony finger.

"Open your eyes!" he screamed, though his voice still sounded muffled.

She tried to pull her eyes open, but the lids had cooked together. He grabbed her face and screamed for her to open her eyes, again and again. He raked his fingers across and tore them open. Her jaw fell to the ground and sizzled on the coals of the earth. Blood dripped from her face like saliva from a dog, sizzling and boiling before it hit the ground. He held her face forcefully to gaze in her eyes. He stumbled back, threw himself away, his muscles dissolving as he thrashed his arms one in front of the other, hoping to drag himself to safety. She had blue eyes.

She grabbed him, digging her fingers through his calves like they were soft wax. Again and again her hoarse and desperate breaths made his heart race inside him. He tried to scream, tried to get away, but he had nothing left. He could barely drag himself over the coals, and was pulled back to her. She turned him over and held him down, staring deeply into his eyes. He tried to look away, but all his muscles were gone. All he could see were her eyes.

Her voice grew louder, louder than even the booming voice that'd told him to sit, stay, good dog. Louder, her voice grew, until it replaced the booming voice in the sky, and echoed through the clouds with each clap of thunder. *Why ... you (you, you)... leave (leave leave)?* The voice in the air breathed hoarsely like a dying animal. It sent out a growl so loud and deep it shook the ground around him like an earthquake.

WWWWHHYYYY ARRRE YOU LEEEAAAVVVVINNNG?

Suddenly, it was sunny and quiet, and he was lying in the grass, his head in Victoria's lap. Victoria was looking into the distance, and when she noticed he was awake, she smiled at him. The sun was so bright he could not clearly see her face through the glare.

"Why are you leaving?" She looked puzzled. She reached for his face.

* * *

Chinny jerked and flailed awake in the dark. There was a face staring at him–two glints in the night, eyes reflecting moonlight. He swung his fist out of reflex and reached for his pistol, which wasn't there.

The figure dodged the attack and countered by pressing his knee against his chest. When the blur of Chinny's tired eyes faded and his enemy came into focus, he saw it wasn't an enemy at all. It was Kapaow.

"What you see?" Kapaow asked, strangely without a smile on his face.

"What?"

"In you sleep. What you see?'

"Get the fuck off me, Kapaow." Chinny wrestled himself free. "I'm *fine.*" Kapaow just stared at him. It was an unsettling sight.

WALK THROUGH THE VALLEY | 111

He was outside of his hooch. His hands were covered in red earth, dirt caked under his fingernails. He'd been digging in his sleep again. His heart was beating so fast and so hard he thought he might die. He quickly got up and walked over to Ghost Doc's hooch and snuck inside to wake him. After having a pistol pointed at him for a very brief moment, he asked Ghost outside. The medic checked his vitals and then looked at his watch.

"I don't know, boss. Other than being startled, I think you're fine. What was the dream?"

"Dream?" Chinny was embarrassed Ghost knew it was a bad dream. "I don't remember, I had it a moment ago, but it's slipping away. I guess we all have nightmares at some point."

"Yeah. I keep dreaming about Go Doc. Kid had my name, sort of... ya know?"

"Just bury it."

"What?"

The words came out of Chinny's mouth before he even realized he'd thought them. The only thing left was to bury it. Tuck it away in some horrible place built for housing the worst. Bury it and move on. It was the only way. One could always let it out when it was time to kill.

"There's no making it better, Ghost. Ya try to make it better and you'll just make yourself insane. Bury it and keep moving. You'll be okay." Chinny walked back to his hooch. "Get some rest, Ghost. Tomorrow's gonna be a busy day."

"Hey, Chin?"

"Yeah?"

"Any idea what happened with Cadeo? He's all banged up, but he won't say what happened."

Gunfire erupted in the distance and people screamed. Ghost and Chinny turned toward the sound. He knew they were both attempting to calculate the direction and possibly a rough estimate on the distance. The gunfire continued, but the screams seemed to grow louder.

"Die!" Gunfire. "Die!" Gunfire. "*Die!*" Someone screamed long and hard, but no gunfire followed... instead the bloke screamed a completely different sort of scream, one of suffering.

"Sounds closer than last time," Ghost said.

"Could be."

Chinny went back in his hooch. He hadn't realized how badly Cadeo had been hurt. He felt sick in his stomach from the guilt. He buried it with everything else. He sighed. One little question wouldn't hurt anything. He got up a few moments later and leaned back outside.

"Ghost? How is he?"

"Cadeo? He's all right. Hanging out with Sinner on night watch."

"Not safe, mate. Switch Sinner out with one of the CIDG and tell him to get some rest. We're gonna be up for a few days, I gather. We're all gonna need the rest. These blokes need to take care of themselves now." He hadn't meant to sound so cold, but hadn't exactly meant to sound warm, either. Ghost stared at him confused. "CIDG, Civilian Irregular Defense Group."

"I *know* what it means." Ghost snapped. "Since *when* are they CIDG and not just *Yards*? Besides–shouldn't Bleak be switching people?"

"You're right. Tell Bleak to do it."

Chinny went inside, sat down on his mat, and tried to forget his current situation. Instead, he tried to think back to his dream. He remembered the fire, the ground of embers. What else was there? He had a strange inkling toward something, but it was so vague it couldn't be important. Whatever it was, he remembered the color.

It was blue.

CHAPTER 20
KAPAOW

"I told you he'd lose it," Kim pouted.

"He's not losing it, and I'm not losing it either, Kim. You just don't understand what we struggle with every day. *They're always scratching at our minds, one scratch at a time. Each scratch isn't enough to cause any real discomfort, but ten thousand scratches later you're in a pool of your own blood. They're scratching, Kim."

"We should run."

"No. They wouldn't be giving us so much attention unless we were doing something right. We need to adapt, that's all. If I had to guess, I'd say they've been scratching at Chinny his whole life. He's strong. He can handle the torture. Trust me, These are the guys."

"What if you're the guy, Kapaow?"

"How would I be the guy? If I was the guy, we'd be safe, not worse off than ever before."

"Well, look at how much you've lost."

"No. You can't look at it that way. Look at what we've gained. If I can do my part correctly, Chinny will change, the rest will follow, and they won't stop until we're all safe. It will work. America came to us first. They won't betray us, Kim. They believe in us, just as I believe in Chinny. This will work."

"We should run."

Kapaow took Kim by the hand and dragged her over to a toolbox Chinny often used. From it, he took out a ratchet, and placed it on a nut that had been used to fasten a new metal railing to an old wooden house. He put the ratchet on an angle that would suit his lesson perfectly.

He motioned to Kim. "Push up while I push down." Of course, she was confused, but she pushed. Kapaow fought with all his might, but eventually she heard the ratchet click and saw that it had traveled up and stayed in its new location in spite of Kapaow's efforts. Kapaow continued to push down. "You see? You can rest, but I have to keep pushing, because I do not know what you will do next, when you will do it, or with what tenacity. So while you rest, I grow tired. Now push."

She did, and eventually Kapaow was completely overcome and could no longer stop the ratchet from moving. She was tired, but not as exhausted as Kapaow, who smiled with pride over his lesson, as it did clearly explain what they were up against.

"I love you, Kim, but you do not understand the scope of things. In that little exercise, you were *them,* and I was the rest of the world. You are weaker than me, but it did not matter, because the system you utilized was designed to handle such a truth. They rest, and they follow and they watch and listen. They influence, but eventually they make a move. We are never ready, and once they are done, they can rest again. Eventually, we will have lost it all."

"So how do we win, then?"

"I don't know, but I'm going to try and break the ratchet."

CHAPTER 21

CHINNY

"See all this? I warned ya." Chinny threw an I-told-you-so at Bleak.

"Yeah, yeah. I feel ya. But you're not hearing me."

"Zip it. We'll discuss it later. Now instead of shoving off, we're dealing with all this. Ya happy now?" Chinny was genuinely annoyed.

Sinner pushed Cadeo to the ground when he tried to hold on to him. Cadeo looked up into Chinny's eyes, assuming he'd object. Chinny dragged on and turned away from the little boy. He was kind of surprised by how much this was killing them all. Such strange behavior. People came and went all the time. How was this any different?

Chinny tried to explain the logic of leaving, how it made sense. The explanation didn't change the fact he was taking roughly sixty of the villagers with him. No. They all knew the truth no matter how much Chinny lied. The village was doomed.

"Go on. *Git!* Ain't got no place for ya where I'm going. Ya hear? Get your little gook ass up on outta here 'fore I unzip your face, *zipper head.* Go on. Get outta here." Sinner pushed the boy again.

Sinner at least understood the way of things, unlike Bleak and Ghost. Cadeo was a kid, and kids got attached easily. They also moved on quickly. Someday he'd forget it ever happened. Sinner pushed the boy down into the ground again. Finally, Cadeo stopped trying to chase Sinner. He sat in the dirt and cried.

Chinny continued on, only to be halted by the warm tickle of tiny fingers intertwining with his own. It was Cua, a tiny little boy with big green eyes and a sprig of hair that would never sit down no matter how much of his mother's spit was applied to it. Cua squeezed his hand and looked into Chinny's eyes, not with sadness or anger, or even confusion. Chinny wasn't sure what he saw in Cua's eyes... he wasn't sure what Cua was seeing in his.

Priorities, mate. Priorities. That's all it was. Sure–staying would have been nice, but a man had priorities. Priorities dictated they leave the village and back up their fellow soldiers. He didn't need family. He needed a promotion. He didn't need the loud cries of a child in the middle of the night. Chinny cleared his throat. He needed a raise.

They headed down the trail, their backs saying goodbye for them as the entire village waved and cried. Mostly women cried for Sinner. Spread out a good distance from each other, the sixty some men formed a dragon slithering its way down the mountainside to await pick up. Sinner took point with his shotgun. Bleak covered the rear while Chinny and Ghost mixed themselves in the middle. Chinny was relieved when he saw the look of cold focus on each of his men's faces. Soon, the pain they'd felt would be gone. The village slowly vanished behind the hillcrest as they traveled to the rendezvous point.

"NO! YOU DON'T LEAVE! HATE YOU! HATE YOU! HATE YOU!"

Silence.

Chinny turned to see a tiny figure at the top of the crest that bordered the edge of their former village. His arms were pressed at his sides, and he was screaming so loudly he was certain to damage his vocal cords. Chinny bumped into the man in front of him as he looked over his shoulder. His entire line had slowly come to a halt. A faint concussive force filled the background, followed by muffled cracks as some sort of firefight broke out in some unseen part of the jungle.

Splunk, splunk, splunk...

Wet, jogging footsteps emerged from the hollow silence, growing louder with each step. Perhaps one of the Yards was having second thoughts. This could be a serious issue. Others might follow. While the sloshing of feet slowly approached him, he tried to formulate what he'd say. He threw his hand out to stop the fellow in his tracks and talk some reason into him.

"Mate, we gotta—" It was Sinner! *What the bloody hell?* Sinner jogged right by, didn't stop for a second, all the way back up the hill. He dropped to his knees and hugged the small figure, who turned out to be Cadeo.

It made no sense. Since when was Sinner any kind of mush about anything? What had made Sinner so suddenly attached to the boy? More black holes, more blurred memories, and more graves strewn about his mind. Then, something broke free. The boy always had followed Sinner around quite a bit, hadn't he? But the man always seemed so annoyed by it.

Sinner was constantly tripping on Cadeo, who loved to hop about, leaping into Sinner's footprints. The kid changed the way he walked to match Sinner's gait and would echo what the man said, learning the worst form of English possible. Sinner had always been quick to tell Cadeo to "git" whenever he caught the boy imitating him too much. What, then? What was it? Chinny strained to remember.

Chinny felt a sharp pain stab through the softest parts of his brain and grind through his optic nerves. Suddenly, he felt very tired, very disinterested in all of it. Then, another strange memory–random pointless: that of a coat rack tipping over and landing in a puddle on the floor. He couldn't even access his memories properly anymore. Again pain stabbed through his eyes all the way to the back of his skull. His throat was so dry it felt prickly, like he'd been gargling needles. He swigged a bit from his canteen to, but the pain lingered.

He wiped his mouth, scoffing at how tiny the boy was, too scrawny to even lift an AK-47, much less shoot the bloody thing. What use was he? As Chinny thought more, he remembered that Sinner *was* the one who took the time to teach the weapon's manipulation to the lad while Chinny told Cadeo to hide during a battle. Sinner worked with the boy until he knew everything about that AK: how to hold it, shoot it, take it apart and clean it. He even forced Cadeo to name the rifle. How much did that really matter? They were all small things.

Come to think of it, when the boy watched while his best friend Ling Ting–Kapaow's first son–was set ablaze, Cadeo blamed himself. It was Sin who took the time to explain that he probably saved a bunch more by fighting. At the time, the two didn't hug. Sinner said what he said, pushed the kid's head to the side, and walked away.

Kapaow appeared at his side. "We forgive Chinny. Chinny must forgive Chinny."

Sneaky bastard.

"Do I look like I want forgiveness for anything?" Chinny asserted. What the bloody hell even gave him that idea? "We still don't need ya, mate. Go back up the hill."

"Dinki Dao, hummooah talama ti fo ho menzalaca tak ooomooaahh, Bac oohnomenataow."

"I'm being crazy… something, something, something… something, something, get myself shot, something, something. I don't know, mate. What?"

"Yes, what. I speak this many." Kapaow counted out seventeen on his hands, one finger at a time. "You speak." He held up one finger.

"You speak seventeen languages poorly. If a translator was what I needed, I'd bring Kim."

"Hey! Kim speak only few. Me speak many, beddy, beddy good. Beddy John Wayne I so good."

"Yeah … you think so."

Kapaow was valuable as a translator. Hell, even if he wasn't, Chinny hadn't seen the Blooper cycled as fast and fired as efficiently as when it was in Kapaow's hands. A really good grenadier was hard to come by. A really good grenadier that was also a good translator was a hunk of gold in a land of shite.

"I go. No more talk. I go." Kapaow waved his hand at Chinny dismissively.

Chinny shook his head no. Kapaow nodded his yes. Chinny shook his head no with more vigor, to which Kapaow nodded yes more ferociously. And back and forth they went. Chinny threw his hands up, snapped his fingers and shook his head no, this time with anger in his eyes. Without waiting for a response from Kapaow, Chinny started back up the hill.

Sinner was a teddy bear; albeit a foul-mouthed, ignorant, filthy one. No two ways about it. Chinny had moved so many times in his life, leaving didn't mean anything anymore, but these men weren't him.

That was it, then. Something had to be done. When he reached the top, everyone there turned in unison to glare at Chinny, who was steadily becoming the bad guy. He couldn't feel remorse for such things. A leader did what he had to.

He settled in next to Sinner, surveying the crowd on the hill. Something needed to be said. Something needed to be done. The men had to leave feeling right about what they were doing, or their hearts wouldn't be in it. Without their hearts in it, without their minds focused on the task at hand, they wouldn't be in the fight. He needed to say something inspirational.

It would seem failure was imminent.

CHAPTER 22

CHINNY

Chinny wasn't one for failure.

"We have to go. To fight the VC."

He needed to rally them to his cause–to win their hearts and minds.

"We have to go," he continued, "to stop them from taking the lands around us. If they circle us, we'll die." The crowd made no reaction to his statement. "I promise you all that we will return." Still no reaction.

Bloody hell. Do they even know what the fuck I'm saying?

"Oh, *fuckin'* hell. Where's Kim? Kim?" There was no response.

Chinny's heart wasn't in leaving, yet somehow it wasn't in staying either. He couldn't commit to one path and so, as he could see, his words held little meaning or power.

"Che chi ma sooooahh," Kapaow said, appearing at his side.

Chinny's body was present, trying to say something inspirational. His mind, however, was absent, trying to figure out what they would do to make up for lost time. His heart was off in a completely different direction, wishing for those calm, slow days so long ago when he'd toss the ball and AJ would bring it back. If Kapaow could not make his point to the crowd for him, they'd never let go of their ankles.

He needed to dispel the concern that they'd never return. He needed to lie in a way that even if they knew he was lying, they would prefer to believe him. He took his rifle and handed it to Cheng. As the leader of their village, it'd be understood he was making a vow to return. He handed over all of the ammo. He looked to Kapaow and said, "I'm coming back for those. Take good care of 'em."

Kapaow translated, and Cheng cracked a half smile and a nod. He shook hands with the leader. The man hadn't been a man for too long, yet already his face was scarred with worry, the way all true leaders' faces looked. Cheng wouldn't let go of his hand. Chinny looked up. Cheng yelled something.

The back of the crowd parted, and little by little, the opening moved closer to the front. Great. They'd want him to say goodbye to an elderly woman. Chinny sighed. After a bit of delay, she was finally to the front. Cheng said something and then gave Chinny's hand over to the elderly woman. The bracelet was cold and smooth as it slid over his skin. It was ornately designed, with detail he didn't think possible when looking at the tools they used to make it. A little brass bracelet made from spent bullet casings which littered the ground no matter where one traveled. He... he felt... he felt so...

Bury it, mate. It'll just break your concentration and get you killed later.

He looked for Bleak. Seeing the bracelet would prove that Chinny's choices to date were in fact the most appropriate. Since Bleak wasn't getting a bracelet, the lesson wouldn't even require words. This newfound respect Chinny would enjoy from Bleak would give him a chance to complete things and ensure Bleak could handle his unit without hesitation once and for all.

He hugged the elderly woman, whose name he sadly could not remember, and he kicked himself for that. Xiau or something, if memory served. The old sheila whispered something to Cheng, who then said something to Kapaow to translate.

"When you bed-dee all piece, you digem mop," Kapaow said, but Chinny struggled to understand. There was an awkward pause then Kapaow repeated it. "When you BED-DEE ... all PIECE ... you digem MOP... yes?"

Chinny's face twisted in confusion.

"Oh, buddy hewl. Kim!" She came when *Kapaow* called.

"When you've buried all the pieces," she translated, "dig them up."

What the bloody hell did that mean?

"Not *just* you, Chinny, but especially you," she added.

"We'll do our best." He smiled an awkward smile and looked to Sinner, who was pretending to box with Cadeo. "*Now*, Mister Sinner. If there's nothing else, we'll be on our way." Chinny was half ready to vomit as feelings and things sloshed about in his gut.

"You got it, boss." Sinner went to leave, and then quickly turned back around and handed Cadeo a pocket watch. It was an item Chinny hadn't seen before. "Keep it safe," he told Cadeo, "I'm coming back for that."

Sinner winked at the kid and then nodded to Chinny. They walked away into the setting sun. It was a long hike to make it to the rendezvous on time, and they'd likely be on the move most of the night. Perhaps some luck would fall on them and they'd get there without losing anyone.

Bleak was waiting halfway down the hill with his M14 rifle resting across his shoulders, his wrists dangling over the stock like the yokes they used to carry water to the village. Chinny waved at him, and Bleak responded by holding his rifle toward the sky in a high ready position. It was an awfully hot day for the boy to be wearing a long-sleeve shirt. Chinny kept quiet. No sense in mother-henning every little thing the boy did.

"Fuck you lookin' at, spook?" Sinner said.

"Oh, that's some dirty words for such a sweet boy. You give that little man a hug? Huh? Is that what you did?" Bleak smiled.

"You better hope there ain't no planks of wood on this here trail, Bleak. I'll string you right up on a makeshift cross and light that sucker on fire."

"You goin' give me a hug and kiss goodbye before you light the match? Ha ha." Bleak laughed.

"No... shut up, Bleak."

The men moved out, more willingly this time. Chinny had mixed feelings about the bracelet on his wrist. He'd lied to the village. Had they lied to him? Even if they hadn't lied, did the bracelet lose its meaning, knowing what Chinny knew? Who knew? Maybe Chinny really would return to the village, someday. Even in his own mind, Chinny didn't sound convinced.

"Hey, bud dee," Kapaow whispered.

"Now are ya saying bud dee as in, *buddy*," Chinny asked, "or bud dee as in, *bury*? Or bud dee like, *bloody*?"

"Oh buddy hewl, Chinny." He smiled. "Toc," he said somberly, pointing toward the visitor. "They got attack, like us before. Came to thank us for teach them to fight. It hep beddy much," Kapaow whispered.

"Why are you whispering?"

"No want scare Bleak," Kapaow whispered even lower, forcing Chinny to lean closer. "He come for answer. I send him home."

"Answers to what?"

"Bodies gone, only small pieces left. He ask where they go."

Chinny felt a moment of panic pierce the air; felt his hand quiver in the slightest way. He thought back to the drop of blood in the sand. Why had they not investigated that further? Suddenly, he felt lightheaded, and he rested a hand on Kapaow's shoulder to steady himself. What did it matter? Orders were orders. He needed to keep his mind right and focus.

"Look, mate—"

"I know, Chinny. I know," Kapaow assured him. They walked together in silence for a moment before parting ways for the last time.

A glimmer, followed by a thump in the distance, caused Chinny to flinch. For a moment, he felt like perhaps a sniper finally *had* caught him in his scope. No. It was a small explosion in the distance. Something had caught fire. He could see it in the tree line. Chinny pulled out a pair of binoculars from his kit and got a closer look. It looked like the fire was moving. It strung out, then did something strange and sort of circled inward a bit.

He searched his pack for a larger pair of binoculars. The larger lenses gathered more light, and the more powerful magnification gave him a better view. The light from the fire helped some, and hurt some, as it made more shapes and shadows. He couldn't be entirely certain of what he saw, but it appeared to be a group of men huddled up. It was close. The closest odd incident to date.

"AAAAHH! AHHHHH! AH! AH! *AH!*" someone screamed.

He saw something get thrown into the air. It was as if the men were... *digging?* No... *fighting?* Perhaps, but as the man screamed louder with each drastic movement of the crowd, Chinny realized he'd seen such behavior once before. He couldn't be certain, but part of him couldn't help but wonder if he was watching someone being ripped apart. Whatever it was, the person was alive while it happened. Of that he was certain.

"Bleak, try and call it in."

After a few unsuccessful tries with their smaller radios, Chinny decided to let it go for the moment. They'd let someone know when they got to the base.

"Goodbye," Chinny said to Kapaow. He packed up his gear and left.

He felt hollow as they hiked several klicks to the rendezvous point. They waited a full two hours longer than was planned, plenty of time to fester over past regrets. The old sheila's words haunted him more and more. While Chinny, his men and the sixty or so CIDG waited, concealed in the jungle for a night pick up, the words echoed in his mind. *When you've buried all the pieces, dig them up.* What the hell did it mean?

He listened to the sound of Hueys inbound. Who cared? Apparently *he* cared, because he couldn't stop thinking about it. He climbed into the nearest chopper and pointed his rifle into the darkness. He turned to check who was with him while Bleak got a headcount over the comms. Chinny's blood began to boil.

He was staring at someone who wasn't supposed to be there.

CHAPTER 23
SINNER

There was a difference between a man who possessed something worth measuring and man who did not. A man worth measuring knew there was no point in measuring, for he had more than enough to be happy and needn't compare himself to anyone else. Meanwhile, the other understood the same fact, but also understood he needn't compare, as he would no doubt lose such a contest. That reality bred a certain bitterness in that type of man's heart.

Such a man measured in other ways–hoping to appear larger, perhaps large enough to one day hide how small he really was. Sinner figured that concept explained everything that was wrong with any organization, but especially the armed services.

It wasn't even ten seconds after showing up in a big fucking triangle that they were getting chewed out. Not saluting, not saying *sir*, not being dressed to code. Bunch of pig shit. Sinner didn't like the look on Chinny's face. Somehow, he could just tell that the roo-muncher had orders for them to head out on patrol. They just fucking got in and were already being sent out on patrol.

Couldn't been all bad, though. There was some new kind of M16 in Chinny's hand; smaller, lighter. Sinner figured he'd been out in the bush too damn long to know what the latest thing in zipper zapping was. Why didn't he know anything about this gun? What was the barrel length? How did that stack up against the cartridge? What was the muzzle flash like? The twist rate of the barrel? The thing about the bean counters was they'd hack anything up and then order everyone to call it pretty. Just because it passed their tests didn't mean it was good enough.

Sinner held out his hand and Chinny gave him the new rifle. He inspected the ejection port and checked to make sure the weapon was clear. He shouldered it and checked the controls. He looked at the short barrel and laughed. All this damn time they spent designing the gun, and the first war it fights they go fuck with it and make a bunch of hasty changes.

It was a good size for dragging through the brush, but used a cartridge meant for a twenty-inch barrel. He wondered what the loss in velocity would do to the tumbling effect of the bullet–the main thing keeping the round effective in combat.

Not to mention, they had already gotten used to using the regular-sized M16, as annoying as that was, especially since they'd been trained on the M14 and were then handed the Tyco rather abruptly.

He couldn't risk anyone trying out some newfangled idea their first time in unfamiliar territory. Sinner slung the carbine over his shoulder and handed Chinny his own M16. The Lady Antoinette would be Sinner's main gun anyway, but if they got into a pickle, he'd switch over to the shorty-rifle instead of reloading and see what it could do. Chinny gave him a thankful nod. They all geared up.

Sinner looked over his stuff. A while back, one of the Yards had stitched up some old leather that was lying around. A big "El Paso"-looking bandoleer held about sixty shotgun shells. A shell holder on The Lady's stock placed another five at his disposal. With its extended seven-round tube, he had something like seventy-two shells with him. It didn't sound like much in a war. The key was to view the shotgun as a really powerful short-range rifle instead of a magic wand delivering walls of lead at the enemy. Sinner always aimed for the important parts, always hit them, and always had shells left over when the smoke cleared.

Next, he started on his camouflage. Applying the paint to his face was tricky on account of him being covered in sweat. He toweled himself down a few times before he was finally able to apply it. He wasn't an artist. He just painted his whole face green, a couple of wiggly lines here, then darker green there, to break it up. Then he was done. Camo was interesting in that it didn't really matter what colors were used. As far as the human eye had to say, any broken pattern was harder to see than a regular one. Paint someone in bright pink tiger stripes and it would still make the enemy stop and squint, wondering what the hell they were looking at. At least for a moment. Matching the colors gave a man more moments.

Chinny always wanted him to teach some classes on proper camo, though Sinner couldn't understand why. Any damn fool with common sense could figure it out. Fact of the matter was: the training manual didn't cover it so great. A man can't just paint his face and think he's good to go. He's gotta break up the outline of his body with foliage and the like. He liked to put floppy twine and stuff around his feet so it draped down a little and covered the black on his boots. He also liked to camouflage his smell. He kept a mix of different animal poop and goat piss in a little flask and dabbed it on a couple of cloths to tie around his boots. A real seasoned dog could track his masked scent, but most dogs didn't live long enough to be seasoned.

He put a mosquito net around his head. Mostly everybody just got rid of them, but he liked them. It broke up the outline of his noggin, and helped in case the face paint started to run. Mainly, he just liked it because it kept the skeeters off his neck.

He strapped the bladder-style canteen to his leg along with his medicine pouch. Sinner noted the way the Yards loved putting fringe on everything they made. He threw a small Buddha figurine on a necklace. This was more to make Kapaow and the other Yards happy. Stupid som'bitches honestly thought that wearing the little three-dollar trinket warded off bullets coming from the NVA because they were Buddhists. He got tired of listening to them bitch about him not wearing it, so he wore it. Now… he kind of felt naked without it. He felt naked without his machete as well, so that went on next.

"What the fuck are you, son? Some kinda Injun?" said some idiot.

"He no fucking Injun. He cowboy, pahtnah," said Kapaow, who wasn't even supposed to be with them.

"The fuck that gook fuck just say to me?" asked the stupid idiot fuck face.

"What's a matter, asshole? Don't ya speak English?" asked Sinner.

"English? That whatchu call it, boy?"

"I speak-a dah damn good English punky Joe!" Kapaow said over Sinner's shoulder.

"Ha ha ha ha haha … ha *HAAA!*" the idiot mocked Kapaow.

WAP!

Sinner decked him.

"Aahhhh! *Fffuck!* Boy, I'll have your hide for that stunt!"

Right. Just as soon as you stop the bleeding, fuck face.

A couple of guys came to back up the idiot asshole. Kapaow and Crazy Mont flung themselves into the air, spinning like tops. When they landed, each had a leg extended, their heels an inch from their throats. Sinner walked over to the idiot.

"Yeah, and I'll have your scalp," Sinner smirked as he pulled out his Ka-bar and winked at him. He walked over to Chinny. "We ready to do this or what?" They all looked at him strange for some reason. "What? I forget something?"

"Ummm… not at all, Sinner. You look fine. Yes, we're ready." Chinny had an odd smirk on his face as well.

"Come-uh high flive!" Kapaow smiled ear to ear.

"Would you stop it with that fairy flim flam?" Sinner's attitude turned Kapaow's smile to a frown. "Oh, fuckin' zipper heads, man." Sinner gave Kapaow the high-five. Kapaow smiled.

They headed out. Having Crazy Mont watching his back was like having little Cadeo yipping around his ankles again. Not to mention the man was small enough to be picked up with one hand and used as a human shield if things got sticky. Not that a body stopped bullets, but it was bound to help at least a bit. Sinner took a deep breath.

Fuck, it's hot.

He tried to keep his mind from wandering. It usually happened at the beginning of a hike. He hated hiking. A wandering mind was on Ghost's long list of things that could kill a man in Vietnam. Sinner didn't bother to tell him the worst one. In fact, Sinner was a bit surprised Ghost hadn't discovered it yet.

He was staring at it right now.

CHAPTER 24
SINNER

The deadliest thing in Vietnam, as far as Sinner was concerned, was the crest of a hill with dense foliage on either side. There wasn't any way around the crest without backtracking quite a ways. Unfortunately, the work they were doing was deemed "time sensitive," which meant there wasn't any time for doubling back.

If he rushed over that hill to try and catch whatever was on the other side by surprise, the presence of an enemy would be just as much a surprise to Sinner as the gook waiting for him. *Dead.* If he tried to peek over, heck, a slow target was easier to hit. *Dead.* There wasn't any good way.

He looked back at Bleak, who nudged his shoulders like, *What are we waiting for?*

Sinner threw his hand up as if to say, *Just relax. I need a second.*

Bleak moved his hand in a circle like beating an egg, as if to imply, *Okay, fine, but hurry the fuck up cuz we don't have all day.* Then, Bleak widened his eyes as if to add, *Cracka.*

Sinner raised his eyebrows and pursed his lips like, *Hey! Watch it, man. You're not the one up here, all first-to-die and shit.*

And Bleak went and rolled his eyes and flopped his hand down like, *Whatever man.*

Finally, Chinny stepped in and threw his hand to the side, as if to say, *Cut it out, you two.* He looked at Sinner darkly and tapped his wrist. *Time's a wastin' brother.* He looked concerned.

Sinner curved his hand as if to say they should go around.

Chinny looked around. They were in a small valley, which would force them to go *all* the way back and take a new path. Chinny shook his head no, and Sinner took a deep breath.

Fine. Guess the redneck's gonna be the first to go. Why can't the nigger go? Shouldn't the darkies die first?

He turned back around for a second to look at Chinny as if to—nope. He just got pointed right back up the damn hill.

Fine... damn it.

His knees started to feel a little weak. The sweat on his hands had him holding Antoinette like a damn cherry virgin.

Take a deep breath, Sin.

He closed his eyes for a second and saw red, the light shining through his eyelids. He inhaled as deeply as he could and exhaled slowly.

Everything's gon' be okay, partner.

What would The Duke do? He'd mosey up to that hill and shoot the shit out of every gook fucker over the top with one hand tied behind his back, a cigarette in his teeth, using eighty-seven bullets from the same six-shot revolver without reloading. How the fuck was that going to help him here?

Calm down, Sinner. No sense talkin' bad about John Wayne.

He took a step forward, looking down the barrel of The Lady, watching that bead sight, finger off the trigger but ready to fire. He took another step forward, and he could see the tips of ferns on the other side. He crouched down as low as he possibly could. He looked at the ground before heading up to the crest. Twigs up the middle, dry leaves off to the left. He'd have to lean more toward the right side. The ground was softer there, perhaps able to mask the sound of his movement. He was crawling now, slowly. He took a deep breath in... and let it out. Slow and controlled, *breathing is everything, breathe.* He really didn't want to die.

God, if I can ask for this: save me and my men. But this time, instead of takin' Bleak, can you take the bastard that sent us in without any preparation?

He looked down at his Yard bracelet. This whole coming-over-the-crest nonsense must have been God punishing him for leaving the village. He supposed he earned that one. He took another step, but not because he had to. He could just walk away, go back home to the Yards and all the crispy—whatever that stuff was called that was so tasty—he could eat.

Just turn around, Sin. It ain't worth it. Just turn around and go home.

His mouth went dry. He tried to lick his lips, but his tongue was like sandpaper. His heart was beating so fast it was hard to tell one beat from the next. Something came up on him from the side. He snapped his head around... swore he saw a man staring right at him. Sinner's chest was heaving as he breathed like a scared rabbit.

He *swore* he saw a man... felt him staring. It was a sign, wasn't it? Gooks over that crest. Yeah, they were surrounded. He could feel it. He should run. If they tried to stop him, hell, he could just take The Lady and...

And what, ya dumb fuckin' redneck?

Something sure wasn't right. Sinner felt hazy, like something was off with him. He figured he should let the guys know he was off and let somebody else take point. Then he wondered what would happen the next time, and the time after that. If he showed weakness, even for a second, would he lose his spot in the team? Would someone else take over as point man? What would he do without his role? Shit, what would the team do without him, in all his bad ass glory, to take point?

A few slow breaths later and he was getting control of himself again. The thought of running kept repeating in his mind.

Yeah, but then what would Chin and the rest of them knuckleheads do? Probably get shot and die.

Sinner was afraid of dying. He was man enough to admit. Still, being the cause of *their* deaths scared him more. He needed to stay, to keep them alive, even if it meant dying. Fear was all it was. It was go time.

Scklunch.

Something clamped down on his ankle! His heart swelled as his lungs shrank. He must have died already. He didn't even hear the shot. Death was grabbing him by the leg, dragging him down to the Underworld to suff–

Oh, no, wait. It's that little Crazy Mont.

He nudged his chin forward, raised his eyes, and gritted his teeth like, *WHAT, MUTHAFUCKA? YOU SCARED THE SHIT OUTTA ME!*

Crazy Mont put his finger to his lips, even though Sinner hadn't actually made any noise, and then pointed up at the top of the crest.

When he traced the Crazy Mont's finger, he saw a tiny little shrub.

So? What? Nice foliage this time of year? What the fuck is your—ooooohhhh.

Sinner turned back to the Crazy Mont and nodded, then looked over to Chin and held his thumb up with his lips mashed together so as to say, *You cool with that, boss?* Chin gave the thumbs up. Sin and the Crazy Mont switched places.

Crazy crept up the hill. Standing, he was as tall as Sin on his knees. The little guy tucked himself right behind that tiny bush and was able to see without being seen. Insults aside, Crazy looked like he knew what he was doing. After a moment or two,

Crazy crept on back down the hill and scooted over to Kapaow. They spoke for a few moments before Kapaow translated in a whisper.

"Maybe company strength. Slow move, them keep looking back, probably more coming. Very far away, for now."

"Right then, gents. Let's head back, yeah? Report the scenario."

Patrols were mostly plagued by boredom, but today, they were plagued by scaring the living shit outta Sinner just shy of crapping his pants. He could not *wait* to get back into the base, get cleaned up, eat some American chow, sleep in a cot up off the ground and hear some Goddamn music that didn't involve chinks not being able to carry a tune.

Sinner turned for a moment to look back at the hillcrest. Hopefully he didn't have to go back there and mess with that ever again. They took their time returning. The patrol was a short one, at only four hours. Before he got halfway through the base, he was already out of most of his gear, dragging it behind him like a dog on a leash.

Some asshole came out all pissed off and loud as hell. "Who the fuck sent them in?"

"I did, sir," said some skinny little bastard.

"Damn it, Larsen! I said *night* patrol. Get 'em ready, they're going back out."

"I'm sorry, *sir*. Did I hear you correctly?" Chinny sounded pissed.

"Yes you did, you chicken chokin' son of a bitch. You heard me when I said *night* patrol. Don't play any games with me. You're double shiftin' today for that little fuck up. Get ready to head back out, kiwi."

There's no way we're going back out again already… is there?

CHAPTER 25
SINNER

Sinner listened, but he couldn't believe what he was hearing.

"And your patrol was too damn short anyway."

"With all due respect, we have time sensitive information, sir," Chinny said.

"Yeah. I don't want to hear it from you. Come here, *boy*. Report," the man said to Bleak.

Sinner's fists clenched up something fierce. *I outta knock that bastard right in his nose.*

"Sir, we got what we was lookin' fo', so what's the deal?"

"Oh, you gots what you was lookin' fo's, did ya?" the asshole mocked Bleak. "Get outta here, boy. Let me talk to someone who can at least speak straight. Listen here, Cockington: birds in the sky already radioed in about the platoon or two. We're not concerned with that."

"Then *why* send us in *at all?*" Chinny asked more forcefully.

"Why send us in at all..." the asshole puffed his chest out.

Great. Here we go with the dick measuring again.

"Why send us in..." Chinny sighed, "...*sir.*"

"Let's be clear: I don't expect much from you boys. I don't expect much from your little Indian project, either," the asshole said, referring to their time with the Montagnards. "So excuse me if I don't weep a river over your afternoon workout. Now, we need to know what the enemy is carrying and such. So guess who's gonna find out? Ya can get cleaned up, get some chow. Wait thirty minutes before diving in the deep end, but after that, you're going back in."

Chinny stood there with eyes of fire. Then he turned sharply on his heel and headed to where Sinner and everybody had dropped their gear.

"Well, boys, looks like we're heading back out." Chinny spoke like a broken man.

"Chinny, friendlies or not, I say we just fuck them cats up and do things our way. Ya dig?"

"Cut it out, Bleak. That's not going to help the situation," Ghost said. "Chin, what's going on with these guys? How'd you get on their bad side so fast?"

"It's... complicated."

"Whoa, whoa, whoa. Hold the lid on that shitter. What you mean *complicated?* You *know* these little turd knockers?"

"Yes, Sinner. I do. One of them, anyway. He's in charge of the Mike Force company that's here."

"So what's the problem, Chin? Come on, brotha. Spill it," Bleak pried.

"No, no. Quite all right. Nothing worth stirring up a big mess over."

Chinny "Bowl-a-Nails-for-Breakfast" Cockington was getting bashful? Chinny was ready to leave a whole damn family of gooks like he just met them seven minutes ago, but that asshole was working Chinny up into a tizzy? This was too good to pass up.

"Oh, hell no, Chin. Whatever it is, you gotta do the cat-thing and cough it on up. Come on, boss man. Let's hear it." Sinner's teeth were showing in the biggest smile he ever did have since setting foot inside this big fucking triangle-shaped base.

"It's... it's nothing, really."

"Come on, Chin. It's cool. We cool. Just tell us, blood," Bleak urged.

"Uhhh, well... he's... eh... he's got something of mine."

"Okay. And that would be?" Ghost was itching to know too.

"It would be...uh... my dog."

Sinner was waiting for some juicy tidbit to bust a gut over, but they all quieted down.

"Well, shit, boss. Let's go get him back," said Sinner.

"*Her.* It's a her. AJ's her name."

Just then, that asshole sack of shit stains came walking out, all the nerve of a tight-assed three-star general except none of the tin—with Chinny's dog on a fucking leash. That asshole had the nerve to crack a smile as he walked by.

"And salute next time you pass a superior officer, and address me as sir, goddamn it. Come on, AJ. Let's go." The asshole jerked the dog's leash so hard you could see her wince. "Come on, damn it." He choked her harder.

"AJ!" Chinny said firmly. The dog stopped and came to attention. "AJ... go!" he said sharply. The dog whimpered. "Go!" The dog looked away, took a step, then came back to sit. "GO!" Chinny yelled. Her head hanging low, her footsteps soft, she obeyed, occasionally looking back over her shoulder.

"How the fuck does *that* asshole have *your* dog?" Sinner spat, breaking the uncomfortable silence.

"I left her with my friend Andrew. He was going off to do something with more tracking. Bomb sniffing—that sort. I *wanted* her to go with him. She's the best. Ya understand? I wanted her to keep him safe. According to that arsehole, Andrew's dead, but AJ was assigned to the unit, not the man, so..."

"God*damn*, Chin." Bleak sounded stunned. Who could blame him?

"No worries. Doesn't matter. Wasn't really my dog when you think about it. Don't get attached, Bleak. It's what I keep tellin' ya. Anyway," Chinny said, changing the subject. "When should I kick all your arses for sneaking those two on board?" He pointed at Kapaow and Crazy Mont.

"They're here 'cuz they want to be, boss. Look around ya. We can use all the help we can get," Sinner replied.

Chinny smiled vacantly. "I look up as soon as I get on the Huey and I'm staring at Kapaow and all I can think is, 'How the fuck did he follow us the whole way without me spotting him?' I nearly shat myself."

Chinny had a tired look in his eyes for what was becoming a long list of obvious reasons. The man found out in the same minute that the Yards were now under that asshole's command, his friend had died, and someone had stolen his dog. Sin made a lot of jokes a lot of the time, but there was nothing funny about parting a man and his dog.

God, forget everything I done asked so far. You make that asshole cry like a little bitch and shit hisself and I swear I'll haul off and smash myself right in the testicles as penance. My word is bond on that.

"Uh, come on, boss. Let's get you some chow, get ya a seat around here somewhere, get ya near some good old rock and roll," Sinner suggested. "Rolling Stones I think was on last."

They all went off and wrangled different things. Sinner went after the food, Bleak went straight to finding some music, and Ghost nabbed the water. They met back where they'd left Chinny and sat down wherever they could. Kapaow had been talking to Chinny, but it seemed to just agitate the man even more.

The food was anything but sweet and far worse than disgusting. Sinner was wishing he had some more of that green stuff, or the sticky rice, or those sweet little balls of whatever the hell. The Yards could cook.

The radio sucked. Some gook bitch just kept talking about how much she loved the American GI.

Yeah, 'till she slits your throat while her brothers rape and kill your children and take their ears for souvenirs.

Stupid Spec Ops pussies were glued to that radio bitch. The whole place sucked. Everybody was tight knit and not interested in letting some FNGs horn in on their party. It didn't matter if they were here to help. Everybody was so different from Sinner and his team. He and the team were always getting the raw deal, pissing off important people without ever trying and suffering for it. What the hell made them so different?

"Oi. You all right, mate?" Chinny's voice made Sinner jump.

"Yeah, boss. You good? I'm good," Sinner lied.

"Stuck in your head a bit there, yeah?"

"Shoot…" Sinner tried to think of another lie.

"I hear ya, mate. We've all got something, yeah?"

"Heard that," Ghost added. Bleak nodded in agreement.

"Huh?" Kapaow wasn't listening, too busy enjoying some kind of pot roast in a can instead of the usual ham and fucking lima beans.

"Just bury it. It's the best thing you can do. *All of you*," Chinny said.

"Just bury it," Sin repeated to himself.

No one else repeated it, though. They all just looked at the ground. There wasn't but so much room in a man's gullet for him to bury things. Sinner had to imagine they were all about full-up. Sinner tried to bury it, but forcing things down seemed to jostle other things back to the surface. That had its own dangers.

An ache crept up in his belly. It was the kind of ache left behind when a person that should be present was not. Sinner'd been stabbed, shot, and burned, but he barely felt any of it.

This pain–boy, it was like pain for the first time, every time. Lurking in the darkness, clawing its way to the surface, was a very old memory of a special, beautiful girl, dragged away to her death. He pretended to smile at Chinny's advice, yet struggled to make use of it.

Bury it.

CHAPTER 26
BLEAK

Bleak was tired and cranky. Too damn tired and too damn cranky to be out in some damn jungle. Things hadn't turned out the way he'd imagined they would at the base. Everything was laid back. *Too* cool. People weren't alert even though the base was on alert, and they *knew* the damn attack was coming! How stupid was that?

BOOM ch-chick

Sinner's shotgun startled Bleak.

BOOM ch-chick BOOM ch-ch

What the hell was going on?

BOOM ch-ch BOOM ch-ch BOOM ch-ch BOOM

"CONTACT!" Sinner barked.

Sinner was running as fast as his honkey ass could carry him. Bleak turned to run, but hesitated. No. Wait. He should stay, cover the guys. Bleak corrected his need to burn pavement and forced himself to stay and do his job. Kapaow started unloading on the enemy just as Sinner passed him. When he went dry, he ran past Ghost, then Chinny, and so on. Bleak flicked the selector on his M14 to semi-auto and peered into the darkness.

Bleak turned his head to tell whichever one of them assholes was still at his side that they needed to go... but there was nobody there. The light from the flashes of gunfire must have been casting shadows all over the place. It looked like shit was moving right next to him. He closed his left eye. When things went dark, he could open it back up and hopefully his night vision wouldn't be ruined. Then he'd be able to see better. It was a trick Chinny used.

ZzzzzzsssssssSSSSSTHWAPTHWAPTHWAP!

The sound of fastballs covered in bumble bees whizzing past his head at a hundred miles an hour freaked him out. Shit was impacting all around him. He squinted, trying to focus on what was out there.

Gotta block it out, Bleak. Block out the noise. Focus, Chinny'd say. *Funnel the aggression.* A dark, blobby-looking figure came over the hill. He exhaled slowly, leaned into the rifle, and pressed straight back on the trigger as evenly as he could. He capped the first black blob and watched the sucka hit the dirt right next to that little bush Crazy Mont had hid behind just a few hours ago. More blobs were coming, each popping off a few blind shots before trying to get below the crest. There was no easy way to come over a non-negotiable crest. With each even and controlled press of the trigger, he saw the blobs plop to the ground. Here and there he could see a cloud of dark, bloody mist spurt into the air.

The guys continued to retreat as Bleak went empty. He yanked hard on the flap, holding the next mag in its pouch. The buttons were snapped so fucking tight the shit always lifted the whole damn kit up just to get a magazine out. Fast as he could he rocked that magazine into place and sent the bolt home.

He had these bitches. It was about to be a party up in here. More figures came up, forming a big blob of black. It spread out and grew big and tall, just like in that movie *The Blob*. The shit was eating up the jungle trying to get at them.

Slow and smooth, Bleak. Slow and smooth.

He relaxed in his crouching position. Chinny passed him and slapped him on the shoulder.

"Heavy contact! Blow out, mate!"

Bleak pressed and pressed his trigger while Chinny took off running. Each shot shrank that blob little by little. When Bleak went to stand, a big clump of dirt flew into his face and something hit his knee so hard he fell to the ground. No time to check it. He laid out prone and took aim again.

CRACK CRACK CRACK. He tried not to blink with each shot–to keep his eyes on the prize. *CRACK CRACK CRACK.* He tried to make sure every single shot hit something important. Not just the blob, but the little pieces of the blob. Not just the little pieces, but the center of the pieces. *Aim for the nose, not the head.* That was Sin's saying. He fired again and again and again. When he was dry, the hill was quiet. Bleak nudged himself up a bit and checked his leg. No bullet holes, and it didn't feel broken. He wiggled it. It hurt like a muthafucka, but it could carry him out. He reached in and pulled another magazine out.

Something yanked on his shirt and was choking him before he even knew what happened! Where the fuck did they come from? He hopped up, landed on his feet, and tried to spin around.

"You dumb ass nigger! We're blowin' out. Goddamn it."

zzZZZZzzzZZZSSssffffffffthwpop, tapap papap sshhhhheeerrrrrwwwww

Chunks of bark, mud and lead flew in every damn direction. Bleak yanked Sinner into the mud and went back to shooting. Sinner started capping single shots as they lay side by side. That short M16 was loud as hell and threw fireballs out like a fucking flame thrower. It was giving away their exact position while blinding them at the same time. Bleak ran dry again and went to reload, looking ahead at the edge of the crest for movement. It was quiet again. Then another skinny blob moved up the hill, right where that one fucker fell near the bush.

Not like before, though. This one was wounded or something. It hobbled up the hill, like something was pulling it by its arms, up to the top. That cat was messed up. Sin squeezed off a round at the blob, then another round... it hobbled back.

The blob got hit, so the fucker should go down. Sin shot him *again*. Bleak's sights were bouncing all over the damn place. Every thump of his heart was making it harder to make the shot. He fired, but must have missed. The guy jerked like he was startled, confused, maybe shell shocked. This time, Bleak went real slow with it, braced himself so his bones did the work of supporting the rifle instead of his muscles.

"All right, Sin. Go. I'll cover you!"

"You go."

"Go, man. I got you. I'm right behind you. *Damn*. Go!"

Sin took off running. Bleak squeezed off a round. He *definitely* capped that bastard. Black mist sprayed out and everything. That was it for Charlie. The blob stumbled back and paused, probably watching his life flashing before his eyes. Charlie's arms rose up and he jerked himself forward again.

Why won't you people just die!

Bleak shot again. More mist. Then his sights started to shake wildly. *He* was shaking. He stopped. It was doom, damnation, panic, fear–it all swept over Bleak like a swarm of locusts. No way... it couldn't be... couldn't be.

Bleak's heart raced faster than it ever had raced before. Sin gently touched his shoulder.

"Sin, I said *GO,* muthafucka!"

Bleak's eyes widened. It was there, then it was gone. He saw it. He knew he saw it. There was no flash, no kind of illusion. Cold poured into Bleak's heart. Those eyes. Was he losing his mind? Someone was there one second, gone the next. He had to be losing his mind.

Run, Bleak. Run.

Bleak stayed.

Hide.
Bleak didn't budge.
Shoot.
Bleak stared.
Bury it.
Bleak tried and failed. He desperately wanted to look back up the trail, but his instincts fought him, keeping his eyes on whatever was *but wasn't* there. Lightning crashed. He felt breath on his neck. He spun and fired wildly, but no one was there. The crest stole back his attention as things continued to move.

The darkness climbed over the hill like a creaking wooden roller coaster about to make its death-dive a hundred feet, barely holding itself together. He looked down at that little bush, the blob where all the dead had fallen—it stirred. He shook his head. His lip quivered. He gasped. The clouds parted slightly and the moonlight made things more visible. It wasn't until the lightning crashed again that he truly began to panic. For in that instant, fully lit, he could see the details of the bodies. Every single one lying on the crest began to move, began to stand back up.

Run, damn it! Run!

CHAPTER 27
BLEAK

Bleak ran.

He ran how he always ran home late at night, worrying about some giant ants coming to eat him or some big ass tarantula or Frankenstein or aliens or some shit coming to get him. He ran, only this time it wasn't a game. His eyes blurred, his stomach froze, his lungs burned, his eyes welled. He wasn't any stronger now than when he was a kid, still running, still afraid.

He ran so fast he caught up to and then passed Sinner. Bleak kept running. There wasn't any time to explain. A week wouldn't be enough time to explain, but he knew. He didn't know how he knew, he just knew. He caught up with the rest of the team who waited, rifles aiming into the night. He yelled that Sinner was okay, since he should have been there before Bleak, and then broke protocol and kept going. He ran through the darkness, only a small part of him wondering if he was sure he was heading the right way.

As a kid, he swore he could feel the monsters' fingertips stroking down the back of his neck when he ran from them late at night. He'd swear he could feel them breathing on him. In the darkness, he could feel them all around, surrounding him, on top of him.

His legs started to ache. The team was chasing after him. They came into the perimeter. They were supposed to say some shit when approaching. Instead, he jumped as high as he could and hurdled the fucking gate post. Fuck this shit. He wasn't going out like a punk.

A hundred or more Civilian Irregular Defense Group members, the Yards included, stared at him, their jaws dropped. Meanwhile, the honkeys didn't even pay him any mind. He marched right up to the cat at the armory bunker. What could Bleak say to this cat to make him walk away? He looked him up and down. His eyes had dark circles under them, and he could hear his stomach grumble. He looked bored.

"Damn, brotha, You heard that new shit on the radio?"

"You all right, man? You seem outta breath. What new shit?"

"I'm cool. I was out on patrol, but my team didn't know about the hot meals just came in, so I ran to go tell them. You know I had to get some food of my own first though, right?" Bleak laughed in between huffs. "That's why I was running. Didn't want them to miss out, ya dig? I'm about to get cleaned up. I tell ya, man," he wheezed, "best damn jam I ever heard. No better way to finish off a nice hot meal. Ain't that right? Which did you have: the chicken or the steak?"

"The *what?*" The best lies were the ones people wanted to believe.

"The duck?" Bleak pretended to be confused. "You ate some duck there? Shoot, I'mma go back and get me some of that. Never had no duck before. Awww, damn…" Bleak laid on stupid real nice for the guy.

"What?"

"Oh, damn. You right. I forgot. Can't get no seconds."

"I didn't get any food."

"You didn't? Awww, fuck no. Tell ya what, bruh. I'll watch your post. You go get some food. Bring me back some duck and we square."

"I didn't say duck. I said, Wha—yeah, that sounds great, buddy." The little fuck walked away with a grin on his face. Jerks always loved getting over on somebody. Bleak smiled back.

Good luck explaining this shit to that asshole that stole Chinny's dog. Fuck the both of you.

Bleak eased himself into the bunker nice and casual, like he belonged there. He dropped his M14, picked up one of the M16s with a grenade launcher, switched out his kit so he could carry as many grenade rounds as humanly possible, plus two. Hand grenades, extra ammo. He could hear some raspy wheezing in the distance, clomping footsteps, sounded like a dying horse.

He grabbed a bag and emptied it out. A bunch of survival shit fell to the ground. He started packing it with Claymores. He'd get Kapaow to help him with that step. He strapped a machete onto his back. The clomping got closer.

"Bleak. Damn, boy." Sinner huffed and puffed, but couldn't blow a house down with a rocket launcher he was so tired. "I always knew you coon bastards was fast, but…" He huffed again. "What are they havin'? A chicken fry or somethin' tonight?"

"Sin, I'm glad you're here, bro. You know how to use this flame thrower?"

"Bleak? What's a matter? You wanna burn that jungle up or something? Don't all you little monkeys dream about going back to the jungle some day?"

"No, man. Not for the jungle. You remember back in there? That one you shot didn't go down, Ya remember?"

"He went down. What are you talkin' 'bout?"

"You hit 'em, right? Ya had to have. Right?"

"Fuck, Bleak. The only place you deserve to argue my ability is in spear chuckin'. I hit a bunch of 'em. They all went down. What are you getting' all worked up about?"

"Maybe it's the rifle. I heard one of them talkin' 'bout how they shot up this one cat and the guy ran away. All they found was a shirt with five little bullet holes in it. How's that possible, Sin? Five bullets not to kill a guy?"

"Bleak… s'wrong witchu?"

"Here, take this." He handed Sinner the bag of claymores and started packing another bag. "We should probably set 'em up with trip wires. All around the perimeter, so they can't sneak up on us. You see this vest? It's nice. It's got a lot of pockets for the Blooper grenades. Kapaow could hold a whole bunch more than he usually has with this. Extra pistols … just in case." He picked up another bag as he started to look around the room. How would he carry all this shit? He saw a few cut down shotguns with pistol grips instead of a stock and packed them into the second bag. "How's The Lady doin', Sin? Ya need more ammo? Yeah, I'll grab you some more ammo. They ain't got any pistols, but there's some forty-five ammo. Ya need some of that?" He grabbed handfuls of shotgun shells and stuffed them into his pockets, since he'd run out of bags. "Can you find some more bags? *Why* are M60s in *here*? Huh, Sin? Why they got the M60s in the fuckin' broom closet instead of set up out there ready to rock out? They should be out *there*. What the fuck is wrong with these honkies, man?"

"Bleak… Jesus… calm down. Bleak… what'd you see after I blew outta there?"

What *had* he seen? They was just gonna crack jokes on him again. No point in sayin' a damn thing. If Bleak was ready for it, he could get everyone else ready faster once they saw for themselves. He stopped for a moment, looking around at everything. It was a lot of shit, but it was also kind of a whole lot of nothing. What else would they need?

Think, Bleak Think. Rockets!

He grabbed three of the LAW rockets and filled another pack with rifle rockets and more grenades. "Hey, Sin? Can you get Kapaow over here, too? Ask him to grab all these... these here explosives, and, and... to start setting 'em up all around this muthafucka. Take that det-cord and, and he needs to just wrap it all the way around the inside of the base. When they breach, maybe we can cut up a bunch of 'em before they get in too far. Wait... no... that open ground over there... yeah... no... that's no good. We gotta get the C4 and shit out into that open ground, as far back as we can make it happen, Sin. We gotta stop 'em as far back as we can. If they try to mortar us, maybe we'll have shit booby trapped further out. How far does a mortar team stay back, usually? They taught us, but I can't remember right now."

Sinner was staring at him. "I'm gon' get the boss man on over here, Bleak. Everything's goin' be all right, bud. You just... just keep getting' prepared and I'll... I'll be right back." Sinner looked concerned, Bleak could tell. "Hey, Bleak?"

"What?"

"Be careful in here, all right? Don't hurt yourself or nothin'."

How would he get all the stuff out without getting himself in trouble? How heavy was everything?

Don't matter. Just get moving.

"Ya okay, mate?" Chinny appeared at the entrance to the bunker.

"Hey, boss. You know how to work a flame thrower?"

"Uh, yeah. Bleak... you all right?"

Why the fuck did they keep askin' him that? "Yeah! Boss, I'm good! What the fuck, man? Charlie's comin'. Ya dig? You see them cats out there, crackin' jokes and shit? They ain't ready for this. We gon' be ready. Ya heard? Mark my mutha fuckin' words: these clowns is goin' down. Where's Kapaow, man? We need to get the perimeter rigged, Charlie's gonna be comin' in a big way."

"What'd you see out there, Bleak?" Chinny asked, just as concerned as Sinner.

He couldn't tell them. They'd just laugh at him and think he was crazy. He had to lie so they'd listen. What was something believable that meant the same thing?

"They just kept comin' up over that hill, boss. No matter how many me and Sin shot, they just kept comin'. You know who keeps comin' like that? Someone who's got plenty of spares. Someone dead set on this place. Somebody that ain't gonna quit. Them crackas, they ain't like us, boss. They think they bad shit.

The people they supposed to be trainin' think they bad shit, too. You see how quick Sin knocked that one nigga right in his face? They ain't ready, boss. *We* gotta be ready, 'cause they not."

Chin's shoulders kicked back. It was a good lie. One he'd be on board for. Chinny was always bitchin' about the way the "Yanks" operated. He'd *want* to believe some shit like that. Once Chin was on board, he'd go back and let everybody know that Bleak was okay. Bleak was just shook up and felt like they were in this alone. He'd agree with Bleak, tell them to go rig the perimeter. Sometimes Bleak didn't want to be right, especially now. Right now he was guessing on one thing and wishing it wasn't true.

They really were surrounded.

CHAPTER 28
CHINNY

"Chin. Come on, blood. Don't do me like this. It's bad enough they got me in holding. Now it's gonna be for nothing. Just do what I said, man. Don't ask *permission*."

"We can't risk rocking the boat here."

"They ain't gonna do it if you ask. I know that guy's type. He ain't goin' play ball."

Chinny approached the arsehole, trying to drown out Bleak's whisper-yelled objections.

He spoke briefly with the arsehole. Even though most of the man's questions were answered in the first thirty seconds of Chinny's presentation, he had to repeat himself a little more with each question the man asked. After talking in circles for what felt like at least forty-five minutes, the man was still a big blubbering pile of clueless. Why were officers always so damned incompetent? Not all, to be fair, but most. Chinny sighed to himself.

"Yew wan' dew what?" The arsehole's face was very piglike in the predawn darkness.

"You heard right, *sir.* The men saw a force much greater than initial intel indicates. We want to install countermeasures both outside and within the confines of this base in case the walls are overrun. I'd like my man out of holding, too."

"HA HA HA!" That arsehole was choking trying to hold back his own laughter. "Fat chance on that. You ain't puttin' no Claymores in the base, neither, Kangaroo boy, *or* det-cord *or* C4. Don't you girls worry your pretty little lace panties. We ain't the ones been livin' in a damn gook patch up in the jungle while the *real men* been fightin'. Things ain't wut they used ta be, kid." With that, the gross little imp walked away. "Hot steak dinner? HA HA HA, boy. You really think if there was any I'd have left some for *you*? Oh, that's rich. Ha ha ha," he said to a rather confused individual.

Bleak wasn't being completely honest with him. That much was certain. Whatever he saw, he was spooked. He heard him talking to Sinner just before they hauled him off. He asked such

145

an odd question of the man: what would they do if bullets couldn't stop them?

Shoot at Bleak, and Bleak was fine. Give him something he couldn't understand and Bleak was a mess. Regardless of his penchant for the fanciful, Sinner corroborated Bleak's real-world findings. There was a lot more Charlie than they were ready for. Still, something bothered Chinny.

The lad was shook up. True. They all were. However, it was different this time. He couldn't quite place it. For that brief moment while Bleak was alone in that jungle, something happened. Something Bleak couldn't understand. He wasn't talking now. That meant he witnessed something a fella might get himself laughed at for recounting.

Whatever it was, it was too important and too real to risk having it picked apart and explained away. Bleak believed what he saw with his whole being. To trust a shaken boy with little combat experience, even after all they'd been through… Chinny wasn't sure.

Without warning, a dreadful feeling swept through Chinny, as if materialized from thin air. The kind of dread he felt as a boy standing in front of the class during show and tell. He took several deep breaths, but the feeling remained. Chinny flexed his fingers and rubbed the soreness out of them as best he could. Rain was coming. Chinny sighed, still aware of that feeling in his belly, like he was the center of attention. Was Charlie out in the bush watching him right now? Someone was. Of that he was certain.

The awful feeling in his gut amplified as the nearby chatter ceased, emphasizing the fact that he was indeed the center of attention. At least forty men stared at him, silently, patiently, like some unwelcomed outsider. His stomach burned and a big part of him just wanted to look away. To avert his eyes to the intimidation and avoid the conflict. They were right to stare at him like a fool. He was a man that wasn't as much a man as a very old boy incapable of protecting his men, his village. How many times had he failed? Through the black holes, he remembered many failures. Then, out of the blue, he remembered the sound of running water. What was going on with him? Why all the strange memories lately? He needed to bury it. Forget it, close it up, and lock it all away. He had more important things to deal with in the here and now.

Chinny looked down at his shaking hands. They knew, didn't they? The men who stared knew. That's why they were staring. What was Chinny doing here? Why wasn't he back at the village?

Hell, why was even at the village in the first place? He should have never joined the force. He should have just stayed home with Victoria. Chinny tried to remember what life was like before the service. It was like trying to remember a dream; the harder he tried, the further it drifted away.

He was supposed to be on the same side as these men who stared, yet their smug faces made him see otherwise. Chinny was terrified. His stomach twisted around in enough directions to make balloon animals out of his intestines. He buried that, too.

Put it all in that grave inside, pile the dirt up high.

That's exactly what he did. He buried it in the place where he'd forgotten his past and hoped the fear would be forgotten as well. The black holes gobbled it all up. When he'd buried enough, there'd be nothing left to bury. Then he could rest. That's all he wanted now–to rest.

Kapaow came up to his side, and they scanned the tree line. Then they scanned the base, all the men still watching them. After sharing a concerned glance, Kapaow shook his head. Something didn't feel right to him, either. He couldn't quite put his finger on it, but it was there. Chinny buried it down, just like he always did whenever something was too much for him to grasp.

"No sleepy time," Kapaow stated, and Chinny nodded in agreement.

Finally, the base was beginning to stir in preparation for combat. Shrug it all off. In the end, fear was all it was. Nothing new. Doubt was fear being sneaky. A man never got used to fear; he just got better at dealing with it. He controlled his breathing. He focused his mind on the task at hand. Chinny had found his resolve. He would heed Bleak's warning and prepare as best as he could under the circumstances. He patted Kapaow on the shoulder and they got started.

"Right men. Let's huddle up, yeah?" He was reminded of his school days playing footy. The men circled around him as he took a knee. Of course, back then his knees didn't creak and crack the whole way down. "Bleak thinks he got his eye on a much larger force than anticipated. Sin confirms for the most part. As has been since we arrived here, things are a bit lax in all respects. I proposition that we come up with a secondary plan for how to deal with Charlie if he becomes too much for the Yanks and their Civilian Irregular Defense Group. Once we have a solid plan, we'll filter it back through the base and let *our* people know the fix of it. It won't be perfect. Miscommunication's going to be expected, so we'll designate our own fields of fire and everyone will know what's expected of them."

"Roger, boss," Ghost replied.

"Right then. Let's get us some paper, pencils. Anybody got a map of this place worked out?"

"I'll dig somethin' up, boss man," Sinner said eagerly.

A few moments later they had everything. Chinny clicked on his flashlight and paused for a brief moment to formulate his thoughts.

"Right. So we're basically in a big fuckin'… triangle, yeah? Right. Now, we're set up about here. Judging from the look of things as we were coming in, we're weakest here, here, and here. So we'll make sure the men know to keep an eye on these areas especially. The machine guns are spaced out with overlapping fields of fire, so we don't need any more on the perimeter."

"What about Bleak?" Sinner asked, concerned.

"You get him out, by force if necessary, as soon as the shite starts. Take Crazy with you. We'll fall back to this position… here. Give Phong a few men. He's ready. Tell them to fall back to… here." Chinny pointed to a good spot with lots of cover. "Ghost, you go with Kapaow and raid the armory immediately after the first signs of attack. We'll stow caches all about, close to weak areas for fallback positions. Now, let's get some ideas goin' about how to handle far off threats and mortar teams. Bleak's not here, so find Pan. He's a pretty good marksman. See if we can sneak him off base to do a little recon with a few others. Any ideas on getting the men out unnoticed?" It was quiet. Sinner wasn't even paying attention, staring up into the sky. "Sin? You awake, or are we disturbing your slumber?"

"I think I hear somethin', boss."

Chinny stuck his ear to the sky. The faint, yet constant ringing in his ears made detecting things over heavy background noise more difficult. Sinner looked at Kapaow. It was a hum, but more high pitched than th–*shite!* Chinny knocked Kapaow to the ground.

"INCOMING!"

CHAPTER 29

CHINNY

THOOM!

The earth exploded, spewing chunks of rock and dirt into the air. None of them were wearing their helmets. It was right about then he wished he'd been stricter about safety gear. They couldn't stop bullets, but they could protect from falling debris.

"COVER!" Sinner screamed.

The best they could hope for now was to cover their heads and pray luck was on their side. A rock hit him in the back so hard he felt like he got punched in the kidney by a two-hundred-pound boxer. Rocks were pelting the ground by his face. All the men were wincing in pain as bits of this and that rained from the sky. The Crazy Mont opened fire.

"Kapaow! Tell him to stop firing. He's not gonna hit anything and he's just drawing attention our way."

"Weeleyohwaahh!" Kapaow shouted, swinging his hands in a downward motion.

"What about a Blooper that way?" Ghost yelled.

They didn't know exactly where the fire was coming from. He pointed in the general direction he thought they might be. Some explosives, an air strike, anything in the general direction would help.

"No boss. Too far!" Kapaow shook his head.

THOOM! THOOM! THOOM!

All throughout the base men were running for cover and diving into bunkers. The bunkers were shabby in construction, but could protect them to some small degree. Some men were firing wildly into the distance.

PAPT! PAPT! PAPT! P-tunk, praow! THOOM!

A concussive blast slammed through Chinny's chest as more explosions and even gunfire began to flood into the base. Maybe they could use LAW rockets instead. They had more range than the Blooper, although they weren't terribly accurate at distance. It was worth a try.

"All right. No worries. Sin, Crazy, get Bleak. Ghost, Kapaow, weapons. All the LAW rockets you can find, yeah? Let's do this!" Chinny screamed.

Screeeeeee!

Chinny tried to grab someone to drag them down again, but they had already started to disperse toward their duties. Chinny could almost see the mortar in the sky coming right for them. He looked at his men as if things had slowed to a crawl. He glimpsed the twinkle of gold as their brass bracelets picked up the moon and assorted flashes of light here and there.

Sinner was running instead of ducking. Apparently he hadn't heard that one coming. He was knocked to the ground by someone. Chinny felt a tinge of relief. It was Bleak! Bleak pushed Sinner to the ground as a mortar impacted just behind a wall of sandbags. Another cloud of debris showered their position.

"You okay, boss man?" Bleak was screaming at the top of his lungs, but Chinny could barely hear.

"Think so! Cheers!" He moved up and patted Bleak on the shoulder as they scurried over to the wall of sandbags. A glint of yellow light hit him in the eye. He looked toward the source. It was Bleak's wrist. He was wearing a Yard bracelet. When did he get one of those?

"Hey! When'd you get yours?"

"The day before we left!"

Violence all around, the two men smiled. When Bleak looked away, Chinny winced.

"I see! I see!" Kapaow raised his LAW Rocket and took aim. Pressing down on the switch, it was always a surprise at how much recoil the things had.

KRCGHKSSSSSSHHHHhHHhhhheewwwww ... poom

They looked out to see where the rocket went. It seemed like a miss. Kapaow picked up the next LAW rocket, a single-use weapon, and fired. Hopefully the shot found its way to the enemy. They took cover before the rocket made its full journey, so they were uncertain of the result.

"Kapaow! Check your fuckin' backsplash before you melt somebody's face off!" Chinny ordered.

"What?" Kapaow screamed back.

The bombing stopped. A quick survey of the base showed no real injuries. The ringing in Chinny's ears kept going. Men were already screaming at the comm station for a full evacuation. The fight hadn't even begun. It became clear that from a morale standpoint on the base, the battle was already lost. This wasn't looking too good for their survival. A full evacuation was impossible. Who would get picked? He doubted it'd be first-come, first-served.

More like rich first, then the poor, as always.

Air support came, to some degree, but not the kind he was hoping for. Regardless, air support was air support, a bit of luck in their favor again. Chinny looked to the skies and saw the lumbering, somewhat slow-moving aircraft known as "Puff the Magic Dragon," an old sort of plane that the Yanks slapped a few miniguns onto. Thousands of rounds of suppressive fire rained down on the enemy as it flew over the encampments of mortar teams.

"WWWEEEEEOOOOHH! Puff on that, Charlie!" Sinner was shouting. Crazy Mont grabbed him and pulled him back down before he likely got his head blown off.

Thunk Thunk Thunk Thunk Thunk

Off in the distance—*fuck*. It was anti-aircraft guns chugging away. The Dragon didn't stand a chance, and sure enough, smoke and debris whisked off the wing and the plane came crashing down. The men fell silent.

"Come on, lads. Can't expect Charlie to make it easy for us!"

THOOOMKAH!

Bleak had run off, searching for whatever could be used, and returned with a recoilless rifle. His adrenaline must have been pumping, because they were heavy, but he carried it like a broomstick. Kapaow was in charge of launching the shells down range. Essentially, it was very much like a cannon, shooting large shells that a person normally wouldn't dream of firing from a shoulder-mounted platform. Some of the gasses from the propellant were shifted to oppose the recoil of the shot, so much so that as Kapaow launched the shells down range, Bleak's task of reloading was quite manageable. Typically, they were deployed against tanks and other armor, but in their current situation, it would do.

There was a clamor of screams in the distance to the right. Chinny's head snapped around to see a horde of NVA charging the east wall. The sounds of ripping and tearing and splashing liquid echoed through the entire camp. The mortar team had stopped its barrage to allow the first wave of attack, which gave the Yanks enough time to maneuver. As the enemy breached the perimeter, they were met with a swarm of lead so large the fallen bodies ruined their chance at sure footing. Chinny cracked a smile, watching them trip over the dead in their charge forward. A few of the Yards from another village took hits. The Yanks had positioned them at the front line.

So that's how it's gonna be, yeah? Put the locals up front, let them soak up the lead before the evac gets here? Bloody fuckin' hell.

Chinny got up and signaled the men over to his position. They huddled up just behind a wall of sandbags. Had they had time to set up the explosives, the charge could have been halted in an instant and they wouldn't have to try and compensate for the Yanks' "bullet sponge" tactic. Could have, should have, would have, but didn't.

"All right. Ghost, Sin, Kapaow, break left. Work your way up and support the fella on the M60. Keep that gun in the fight, yeah? We're gonna need a wedge of covering fire. Not too much overlap. Keep our people from taking the brunt of it."

"I can't believe those honkeys!" Bleak yelled.

"I can!" Chinny replied. "Bleak, Crazy, on me!" The Crazy Mont nodded quickly, loading a fresh magazine into his AK-47 and racking the action.

"We're breaking right. Flank 'em on the side. Watch your fields of fire, foregrounds, and backgrounds before you shoot. Check your muzzle when you're on the move! Don't forget the basics! Let's go!" He crooked his finger to motion Crazy to come along. Bleak was weighed down with extra guns and ammunition and was much slower than usual.

"Drop that shite, Bleak. Speed is key, yeah?"

"Get this muthafucka!" Bleak fired from the M16 in a panicked fury. An NVA soldier had come into view and Bleak bore down on him with an entire magazine.

"BLEAK! BLEAK! What the fuck are you doin', mate? Calm the fuck down! Calm the fuck down!"

"Ya gotta shoot 'em!" Bleak replied, "A lot!"

What the fuck had happened to Bleak? He'd lost his mind. "What are ya waitin' on? Fuckin' move!"

Bleak emptied another magazine into the body on the ground. The boy *had* lost his mind. This whole mess was coming apart on them. The men were overworked. The chain of command had failed them. Now he had to try to pick up the pieces and rally the men. A group of five NVA were firing rounds into a Yard on his knees, his hands out, begging for mercy. His fingers detached from his hands and became shrapnel into his own face as his jaw was ripped off ragged and dangling. The blood poured out of his wounds like gushing water. Chinny raised his rifle too late and fired on the executioners.

He almost went deaf when Bleak again came full on, emptying another magazine at the enemy. The rounds jerked the NVA about, side to side, as bits and chunks could be seen flying out the backs of their bodies. One bloke, a bit stronger than the others, tried to return fire. The final few rounds from Bleak's magazine dumped into that one's head and shattered the skull like a ceramic dish covered in meat and hair. Shards of bone flew to the ground as the last of the five collapsed.

Chinny patted Bleak on the back and they bounded up the far right wall, covering each other and firing until they intersected the attacking NVA soldiers. While the regular base staff were retreating, Chinny and his men pushed forward. A faint little voice in the back of his mind wondered if they shouldn't do the same.

No. Fight into the ambush, mate.

Yet, was there not strength in numbers? Shouldn't they rally with the Yanks?

Fuck that shite. We'll show 'em how it's done.

Bleak emptied another magazine at one enemy. He was frantically smiling and nodding in approval of his actions as he reached into his pack, filled to the brim with freshly-loaded mags. He fired a round from the grenade launcher–inside the base.

"Bleak, what the fuck are ya doing?!" Chinny screamed. "Not in the fucking base! Bloody hell!"

Bleak continued to launch grenade rounds and fire entire magazines at the enemy. The gunfire got so loud, Chinny felt himself going deaf. Then it slowed, the background noise of combat chatter beginning to calm down. Fewer and fewer screams were heard. They were overpowering the enemy! Chinny moved up again and took cover behind the base armory, a circle of sandbags, the floor of the room a few feet below ground. He crouched down as low as he could and pulled the magazine from his rifle to reload.

Just then, like always, Charlie came knocking when Chinny was most vulnerable. A kid wearing a uniform that barely fit him opened fire. Chinny bolted off to the left and behind the sandbag wall. Bleak shot the fellow pursuing him from feet to neck with an entire magazine. Crazy Mont ran up to protect them both while they reloaded. Chinny got the magazine out of his pouch when an angry-looking teenager jogged past the structure and took aim at him.

Chinny dropped his rifle and scurried up the sandbags, climbing onto the roof right as Crazy Mont fired a cool and calm three-shot burst into the boy's chest. It didn't matter that the shaky-handed kid had pointed a gun at his face; it was still painful to hear his screams. Chinny got his wits back and pulled his pistol. Because of his stupidity, he was now going to have to fight his way back to the rifle he'd dropped. Kapaow was letting loose with his Blooper. That bastard could shoot and reload it faster than anyone Chinny'd ever seen. A blur came up into Chinny's peripheral vision. His pistol snapped forward–pure instinct.

PAP! PAP!

The nine millimeter rounds thumped into the target's clavicle and the top of his head. It was instant death. Bleak and Crazy Mont had pushed forward. He leapt to the ground and retrieved his rifle, slammed home a fresh magazine, and racked the action. He fired two shots into each of three men that ran by–the sound of melons hitting the windshield of a car. It was rice and tomato sauce as the bullets exited. He rounded the corner cautiously. His knees gave out at the scene before him.

It was Phong, a bullet hole in his clavicle, another in the top of his head. Everything around him became muffled as nausea and dizziness took over. Chinny's hands began to shake. His body convulsed. How could this have happened? He fell to his knees. The battle didn't matter to Chinny anymore. Bullets and bombs and bayonets, and yet still he remained. How many children had died because of his stupidity?

"This is what it's come to, is it? Want something done right, gotta do it yourself, yeah?" Chinny screamed to the sky. Was anyone listening? Was anything up there *ever* listening?

Chinny pressed the cold muzzle of his Browning Hi-Power against his temple. His eyes scanned the battle. One of Chinny's Yards was getting his skull crushed in by the butt of an NVA soldier's rifle. A circular pattern of holes formed on the attacker's chest, perhaps Sinner with his Lady Antoinette. He heard a man screaming for help. An NVA was walking straight into a Green Beret's gunfire. The soldier *was* Special Forces, but he looked like a small child, barely eighteen. The lad fired a few shots into the enemy, screamed for help, then fired again. Still the NVA drew near.

He heard something else, something distant and faint. It was a painful sound, hard to distinguish from the rest of the noise.

Slowly it'd fade, then it'd come back even louder. Whatever it was, Chinny couldn't help but feel it was important.

Waaaa

He was beginning to feel woozy, disoriented, lost.

Waaaa waaa

No. He was losing it. His heart pumped harder and harder to the point where it was painful. *A baby?* He *could* hear a baby crying off in the distance. *Hold yourself together, mate.* What the hell was a baby doing out there? *There's no baby. You know there's no baby. It doesn't make sense. It's impossible.* In training, they blindfolded him and rotated a group of dogs that would bark all through the night. Eventually, the barking started to sound like babies crying. Was that what this was? Or was he losing his mind?

He put a hand on Phong's shoulder. The boy had been a better warrior than he'd ever be. Chinny deserved to die, slowly and painfully, for the things he'd done, but not before he saved the baby. No more children would die because of him. *No. There can't be a baby. What are you doing?* He struggled to his feet, lurched over, and vomited, his abdomen constricting like a python and the citrusy acid burning his nasal passage. Something was going horribly wrong, and not just with him.

He scanned the area, moving as quickly as caution would allow. He snapped his body hard to the right and took aim at a glint of something in his peripheral, this time pausing to be sure of the target. It was an enemy, but he was already riddled with holes. His chin was red and dripping from coughing up his own blood. His face was pointed directly at Chinny, but his eyes moved about spastically. The man's shoulder jerked like someone was pushing him, and he struggled forward, as if walking had become a complicated motion. Chinny fired two rounds in quick succession; more of a mercy kill at that point.

The bloody mess lurched forward, his eyes circling around and around, the circles constricting in size until, finally, they made contact with Chinny's. Breaking and cracking as he moved, the poor bastard was an anomaly of human resilience. He had to respect an enemy with such tenacity. Chinny tried to ignore the crying in the background.

He noticed Sinner off in the distance putting shot after shot from his Lady Antoinette into an enemy soldier who continued to struggle to approach him. Off to the side, some of the NVA were walking in the same puppeteer fashion. The way they moved, it was like their bones were snapping inside them, all while somehow managing to slowly fire their weapons. One tried to throw a potato masher-style grenade, but it landed only a few feet in front of him. A moment later, it exploded. What was left of the man was writhing in agony, pulling himself forward with his arms a few times before falling limp.

Chinny felt eyes on his back. He spun quickly and bore down on whatever his instincts took aim at. It was Phong! He was standing there, shaken, but alive. He'd heard stories about people surviving gunshot wounds to the head, especially from a nine millimeter. He'd never actually seen one face to face. It was a message from God. Keep up the good fight, Chin.

"Phong! You're gonna be ace in just a bit, right, mate? I'm gonna go find Ghost Doc and bring him over to ya. Here, just hold up inside there. Keep your head down! I'll be back in less than a tick." He went to guide Phong into the little bunker, but Phong didn't move. "Phong, come on! There's no time!" Phong's eyes twitched and overshot their mark as he tried to make eye contact. Chinny tried to move him. Thumps and cracks transmitted through the boy's skin and into Chinny's arm. He almost vomited from the sensation. "Phong?" The boy's head fell to the side, his face pointed right at him, yet his eyes struggled to see him.

Phong grabbed onto Chinny's shoulders and brought his face close. He smelled of corroded copper. Chinny tried to push him away, but the more he pushed, the harder Phong pulled. He was drawn dreadfully close despite his every last ounce of strength. He felt Phong's teeth scrape across his face. Chinny screamed out, pushing as best he could without injuring Phong further. He screamed for help from anyone, from anything, but nothing came. No one would save him. He was alone.

Wwwwaaaaaaaaa...

The crying returned, calling to him as he felt Phong's tongue, cold and wet, on his neck. He shivered and screamed, pushing desperately to get away. He felt the teeth clamp down on his flesh as the crying grew louder and louder. What if it was a baby? How could he know for sure he was losing his grip if he didn't go and check? Chinny stopped being scared and started to get angry. Phong was gone, something wrong with his brain. What was done was done, and if Chinny died, who would save the baby?

He struggled to reach for his knife, which he managed to unsheathe, and pressed the blade firmly against the inside of Phong's elbow. Chinny hacked and ripped and dug into the flesh. He coughed and choked as he raked the knife back and forth, crunching about, searching for cartilage. He apologized. Phong was not in his right mind. Suddenly, the knife broke free. It was awful. He'd taken the boy's arm. Chinny collapsed as he cut himself free, yet he still felt pressure on his arm so powerful he worried it might break.

He turned to stab Phong, but he was a meter away, his arm missing at the elbow. Chinny looked down to see the forearm and hand attached to his bicep, still squeezing. He tried to remove it, but it was too strong.

Waaaaaaaaa!

The crying was louder. He cut the arm at the wrist as deeply as he could. The tendons could no longer flex the fingers and he managed to pry it free. The blood rushed through Chinny's arm and it was all pins and needles, purple and blue, but the feeling was coming back. He tried to pick up his rifle with the tingling hand. It wasn't going to happen, at least not quickly enough. He stood behind cover with his pistol in his left hand pointed at Phong, hoping he'd stop attacking. As he aimed, he tried to track the location of the crying. *It's nowhere. Come on Chinny. Don't give into it!*

Suddenly, his mind drifted, and a memory came forward, blotting out the battle. It was of a door with pale light shining through its cracks. A baby was crying from the other side. *No!* Chinny swatted the memory away, clawed at it and buried it deep at the bottom of his inner grave. *Hold yourself together. Fight, damn it! Bury it all and fight!*

His pistol wavered in his less-trained hand. He cursed himself for not practicing more with his left as he took aim at his friend. Phong twisted and writhed in his direction. He steadied his sights as best he could and slowly squeezed the trigger. The bullet impacted right between Phong's eyes, pulling chunks of bone with it. The sockets cracked and caved the flesh in slightly. Blood oozed from his eye and dripped down his body. Phong stood there for a moment—would he charge again? Even now? Then, the body went limp and fell to the ground.

Waaaa…

From around the corner, a hail of bullets was followed by Ghost, Sinner, Bleak, and Kapaow. It really was a pleasure to see them all together again. Perhaps they'd help find the baby. Ghost was the first to approach him.

"Chinny!" he yelled. "Something's going wrong. It's like everyone's losing their minds! We feel it too, but it's worse for the other guys! What do we do? Chinny! What do we do!

Chinny listened to the baby crying, his mouth cracked open to reply.

Only laughter escaped.

CHAPTER 30
KAPAOW

"Why do you call them tree fairies, Grandpa?"

"Well, a long time ago, your great, great, great grandfather saw one."

"Really?"

"Yes, and when he saw one, the manner in which it appeared to him was as if it came to life right before his eyes. It was as if it grew out of the ground from among the trees themselves and stepped forward."

"Did they become friends?"

"No, dear boy. They did not."

"Why not?"

"Do you remember Feather Head? Your pet chicken?"

"Yes." He hung his head low.

"Oh, do not look sad, my boy. It is all right. Even now you feel remorse, yet when we were starving, you still ate your dear friend. Now, you eat chicken all the time. The tree fairies are not our friends, and they never will be. Not because they all do not want to be, but because when they want something, they will have it, and if needed, they will devour us."

"I'm scared, Grandpa."

"So am I."

* * *

It all makes sense now.

It was just one of them, one of the tree fairies. Perhaps a scout? He, she… it… watched us. That was that feeling, those dark shadows in the corner of my eye from time to time. Turn, and no one was ever there, but it felt like someone was there. Someone or something was there. They guided the attack on my home, but the attack was just some kind of test. With that kind of power, why test it? Haven't they done this many times before? It makes no sense to toy with us like this. They must have been curious of what the Americans were capable of. That would explain why the attack's nature was so out of the ordinary. Perhaps it even explains why we had seen so much combat in such a short amount of time.

I suppose that is why, back home, I fired that shot into what appeared to be open air. I was tired of that feeling: the feeling of something always scratching at my will, my soul, beckoning me to submit to its desires. I was tired of always resisting, always struggling as I watched so many others succumb and survive while my family and friends resisted and died. I wanted to kill some of them, the real them, not their puppets. In a sense, their puppets were simply more victims. No, I wanted to kill one of them. Was that so wrong?

Perhaps it wasn't a question of right and wrong. Wasn't it Ghost who said that death was neither right nor wrong–only necessary? Perhaps… it was simply a question of winning and losing. Were they going to win, or were they going to lose? Kapaow had put a bullet in one of them. Of all the generations his family observed, documented, and planned, it amounted to a single gunshot wound, which may or may not have resulted in a single fatality. The enemy was so mighty that Kapaow could not decide if that was a loss or a success.

He needed to continue succeeding. That was all. Once Ghost saw the truth, he would believe Bleak and make Bleak's unfocused banter more logical to Chinny. Once Chinny believed in Bleak, they all would believe in Bleak. Then Sinner would demand a call for action, and Bleak would carry it out. He would force himself to focus and find a way to rally help to their side. Once help came, there would be too many men on the ground for *them* to hide. They would be exposed, and the process would start over again, until more and more knew what was really happening. More would be called to action, and finally Kapaow could rest knowing his people would survive. As he watched them all begin to lose their minds, he worried. Had Kim been right all along? Had he been wrong? It was such a fragile plan that relied on one simple thing:

Keeping them all alive.

CHAPTER 31
GHOST DOC

Hahahahaha
It couldn't be real.
Hahahahaha
Some sort of drug?
HAhaHahaHaha
Disease?
HAHAHAHAHAHAHA!

Ghost checked Chinny's pulse and compared it to his own to determine if he was having a reaction to something. Ghost surveyed the situation and contemplated the possibility of mass hysteria. Everyone was coming unhinged. Ghost counted the beats, and felt sick when he realized his own heart was beating much faster than Chinny's.

Ghost wanted to hit Chinny, to smack some sense into him. What were they supposed to do if the top guy couldn't keep it together? And why hadn't Chinny prepared them for this? None of them knew how to handle these crazy guys hopped up on drugs not going down. Shouldn't they know?

Well, we don't. That's your fault, Chinny. Your fault.

"Sit still, boss. I need to have a look at you." Ghost grabbed Chinny and forced him still.

Bleak was in a firefight with three men, Sinner was pumping round after round into anything that refused to go down. Why weren't they going down? Why were their own people attacking them? Kapaow was trying to get the flamethrower working. Crazy was protecting Ghost. *All Chinny's fault.*

He checked to see if anyone was looking. They were all too busy. Ghost could feel bits of Chinny's skin scraping off under his nails. He looked down at how he grasped Chinny's arm, blood started to trickle from below his fingernails as he dug his way into Chinny. Thoughts of doing worse crept into his mind. It was Chinny's fault, after all.

Clak! Clak! Clak! Zzzzmmm, zzmmPOP! Cunktoom, kapraow!

Ghost let go. He was right to be angry, but now wasn't the time. Ghost tried to duck his head while examining Chinny at the same time. He stopped to fire several shots with his pistol into two men that had made it past Crazy. Maybe it *was* a disease of some sort. Chinny didn't have any signs of narcotics or other drugs in his system that he could tell. Had to be a disease. Was Chinny sick?

"What's wrong with the boss man, Ghost?" Sinner said, sounding understandably nervous.

"I'm not sure yet!" Ghost chose to hold off on mentioning his disease theory, lest they shy away from helping to move Chinny.

Bleak was scared too. "Come on, Doc. Make it fast. Ya dig?"

What was Ghost supposed to do? He'd just watched a guy get his jaw ripped off by two men seemingly unaffected by gunfire. His brain was like pea soup with little bits of ham floating in it. They always used to tell him that in moments of panic, he'd revert back to his training. He was like a puppet on a string going through the motions while his brain was running and hiding. He needed to bury it. Maybe Chinny was right all along. Ghost buried his confusion and panic into the pit of his stomach and pretended like he knew what he was doing. Eventually, perhaps, he'd actually know what he was doing.

"Hey, Chinny! Can you hear me?"

"Of course I can hear you! How ya doin', mate?"

Ghost picked up Chinny's rifle and tried to hand it to him. "Chin? Can you use your weapon?" Ghost thought about that for a second. "*Without* shooting any of us?"

"It was an accident. I'm torn up over it. I'm sure. Not certain I can be counted on!"

"What?"

"Didn't ya see?" Chinny smiled at him, like he was mentioning a pretty bird on a branch or something. "I shot Phong."

Thoughts flickered through Ghost's mind; less than a second of time, but it felt like forever. The time he'd convinced the usher to let them in even though the theater was all out of seats and he and Phong had sat on the floor together. Or when Phong was about to kill someone for the first time and he'd hesitated–when Ghost had told him it'd be okay, had talked him through it. When Phong had pulled the trigger and Ghost had patted him on the shoulder. Everything in his body had told him to take the gun away from Phong, to spare him. Instead, he'd patted him on the shoulder.

Walk through the valley, as Ghost's father would always say, was about going through things instead of around them. Still, did he have enough strength to walk through Phong's death? It was so easy to get lost in the valley, to never make it through.

How do I walk through, Dad?

It was the one question he never asked the man.

Ghost tried to breathe as some part of him waited to feel Chinny's hand on his shoulder, to tell him to keep going, to bury it and fight on, but he wasn't there. It was like the entire world had turned to ash. Ghost watched Chinny's head bob around as he explained what he'd done. Just a bash with a rock and there'd be justice. Chinny didn't really care about the Yards anyway. Curiosity caused Ghost's eyes to scan for the right size rock.

"What the fuck you doin'?" Bleak screamed in Ghost's ear, startling him.

"He shot Phong."

"What?" Bleak was either shocked or just couldn't hear him. Ghost didn't care which.

"Tried to shoot myself too, but I'll have to get back to that later. There's a baby around here somewhere," Chinny added.

"What the fuck he just say?" Bleak asked even louder, shoving Ghost. "Fix him up, Ghost!" Bleak commanded, as if he was even in charge. "I said fix him up or I'll fix *you* up, goddamn it!"

"*You* fix him," Ghost replied. Bleak could take a long walk off a short pier.

"I—" Bleak stopped to fire a few rounds, "—can't. That's what *you're* for, dummy."

For a moment, he made eye contact with Kapaow, who looked upset. In spite of everything the man had been through, it was a rare sight. It wasn't just sadness, or fear. No. It was strange. It looked like disappointment.

"NO! No FUCKIN' way! NO FUCKIN' WAY! NOOOO! NOOO!" Sin had lost it, too.

Sin's head was shaking, his hands were quivering… all he could do was point. What did he see? Was he hallucinating? Ghost looked closer. There were people running back and forth in one vibrating mass. He squinted, trying to focus more. On the ground there was a Yard soldier screaming for help. Ghost stood to get a better look. There was an NVA. He was… *biting* the Yard to death. Ghost fell to the ground.

What the heck was happening?

"Ha ha."

He felt the air escape, the vibration in his throat, but couldn't believe the sound. Had he just laughed? It was cold all of a sudden, hard to breathe. He must have been losing it, too. He looked over at Chinny, who kept turning his ear about and saying that he was shocked that no one else had heard the baby. They must have been exposed to some sort of hallucinogen. There were men in barroom-brawl fistfights, other guys attacking with bayonets without any result. Retreating. Everyone was slowly retreating.

"Ha! Ha! Ha!"

Luong and Zhang came running by with an RPG they must have picked up along the way. Luong, a surprisingly pudgy teen considering his speed, knelt down, took aim at the crowd of attackers, and fired the rocket-propelled grenade right into the middle of things. Bodies didn't exactly fly all over the place. More like they hopped up and then tipped over. As unimpressive as it looked, a good chunk of them were not getting back up.

One Tango charged right for Luong. That attack was quickly stopped by a three-shot burst from Zhang, who was guarding him while he reloaded. The attacker fell dead only inches from them. Without warning, it moved. The body that had been shot three times in the heart and lung area got up and bit a horrible chunk right out of Luong's leg.

He fell to the ground and Sinner landed two clean blasts from his shotgun in the side of the attacker. He... *it*... lost the use of its right arm. It kept pulling itself up with its left, biting chunks out of the poor kid in a trail right up his body.

Bleak emptied an entire magazine into it. Bleak screamed—or cried, it was hard to tell—as he emptied another. Chunks flew off in every direction until there was nothing left to bite or claw with. Finally, it went limp. Zhang said something that sounded like it may have been profound if Ghost knew the language. Luong pulled down on the barrel of his friend's weapon until it pointed at his head.

Zhang held his hand over Luong and said some final words, then fired into his skull. When he fired again, Ghost saw that he had shot out both of his friend's eyes. He had never heard of the ritual, never seen anything like it. It made no sense. Zhang ran off, back into the fight.

Crazy took a grazing hit to the shoulder. The bandages were out and wrapped around the wound in question without thought. Crazy patted him on the arm, smiled, and shot a few rounds over his shoulder.

Ghost tried not to get lost in his own hysteria, struggled to keep himself connected to everyone else. "This place is getting overrun, guys. We gotta get Chinny somewhere easier to defend. Bleak! What do we do? Bleak?" What was his problem? "Bleak! Come on, man! What do we do?" Bleak seemed to be hyperventilating. He was supposed to be the one in charge. Ghost was getting frustrated, but couldn't seem to think of a plan of action himself. *"Bleak!"*

"Chinny, what do we do?" Bleak pleaded.

"We search for the baby," Chinny said with certainty.

"Shit… all right… uh… grab him," Bleak said. "Uh… we're gonna keep moving up, up towards that wall. Yeah. There's a machine gun nest towards the end there. We'll make that the Alamo. Uh, shit…" Bleak took a few deep breaths. "Shotguns and M60s, hand grenades and Bloopers. Fuck everything else."

"Yeah, I hear ya on that! I can't be sure, but I think they changed the twist rate on them Tyco Toys. Those rounds don't do—"

"Later, Sin. Tell us later!" Ghost yelled.

"Leaps and bounds, two by two. We're *taking* that zone. You hear me? That's where we're going! That's what we're doing! That spot's ours! You hear me?" Bleak yelled like a man that actually knew what he was doing. Everyone nodded. "Let's go get ours!" They all barked in agreement.

They'd come together, Ghost wasn't alone in it. He started to feel less amused and more terrified. That was *good.* Perhaps he was coming back to his senses somehow. Ghost strung his arm under Chinny's and hoisted him up. He picked up Chinny's M16. It wasn't one of the weapons they'd agreed on, but he couldn't carry an M60 or a shotgun in one hand and fire it effectively. Sin slung Ghost's shotgun over his shoulder and they moved.

As they made their way to the left wall and followed it up to meet with the rest of the Yards, Zhang walked up to them. Ghost went to scream for him to follow them, but that was only for a split second. Then he saw the oozing stump of a shoulder that once had an arm attached and the exposed rib cage from explosives-related trauma. Organs and intestines were slowly, slowly, trailing out of the open spaces in his flesh. His eyes were facing them, but he wasn't really looking *at* them. He almost looked the way a spider looked at its prey–blankly, coldly.

"You stay back!" Sinner yelled, but Zhang charged. "I'm sorry!" Sinner blasted him in the chest with the shotgun… but he was still standing. Sinner shot him again. All that happened was he stepped back a little, and then made another attempt to charge. Finally, Sinner shot him in the head and when his skull shattered into pieces, his body collapsed. Bleak started screaming hysterically.

"Didn't I tell you? I *knew* this shit wasn't right. Where'd all the bodies go? You can't just walk around like that with your guts spillin' out like nothin's wrong! Where'd the bodies go! They been fuckin' gettin' up and walkin' *away*!"

"Shut up, ya stupid nigger. You didn't say nothing about people not dying. You said ghost soldiers, so don't go actin' like you knew this shit all along," Sinner barked.

"Fuck you, honkey! Clear the left side. We'll head up that way," Bleak snarled back.

"On it!" Sinner complied.

Don't lose yourself, Ghost. Hold on. You can do it. Hold on...

It felt like he was holding a tiny weight with an outstretched arm. How long could he hold it, really? How long? He felt exhausted already. The hail of shotgun blasts and M60s chugging and Blooper bombs blowing was enough of a melody to make music to accompany a children's fairy tale. Perhaps not the subject matter, but he could almost hear its melody. Although, Ghost considered, children's fairytales had some pretty gory stuff–the real ones, anyway.

Ghost sat down and thought back to that old book he'd read in the library as a kid. In it, Sleeping Beauty was just some comatose underage girl that was raped by a pervert, got pregnant, and then gave birth to twins, all while she was still asleep. In one old version of *Cinderella*, the wicked stepsisters tried so hard to fit into the glass slipper they hacked off their own toes.

zzzzzKAPRAOW!

A few bullets impacted around him and ricocheted off some metal, making a rather distracting noise. Ghost laid himself on the ground and stared at the sky to help try and concentrate.

Where was I? Oh, yes.

The woodsman never came to save Little Red Riding Hood with a pair of scissors. The wolf fed Red pieces of her grandmother before eating her too.

"Get off the dirt you sorry sack of shit!" some Green Beret yelled. "AAAHH!" Something knocked him on the ground. Ghost watched as the man wrestled with someone who looked like he was already dead. The man looked at Ghost and cursed him for being a coward. Ghost *was* a coward. That was always his problem. Maybe his mother was right for not wanting him to go to Vietnam. Then again, maybe his dad was right for encouraging him.

Another Thing climbed on top of Ghost. He pushed it back, but couldn't remember if being bitten was a good or bad thing. He just kept thinking about his dad. Life was so unfair, and cancer was such an unfair thing. He was strong, his dad. He was brave—the bravest. Why couldn't he be more like him? He remembered being so scared the day he left for boot camp. His dad had grabbed him and said, *Son, I'm gonna tell you something: it may not make sense now, but you remember it, okay? Ya promise me.* Ghost promised. *It's like we're all born on the top of one mountain, but we're meant for the top of another. The valley in between is what separates a boy from being a man. Now, walking through the valley might beat ya up something good. It might kill ya, but even if there's only a slight chance you'll break through and climb, and if you're lucky one day make it to the peak of where you truly belong, boy, that's living. Staying where God put ya to start, well, that's living dead. Ya understand? Ya gotta walk through, son. Walk through.*

That was the last time Ghost saw him.

Ghost shook his head. What the heck was he doing? He'd come back to his senses. He fired his pistol into the Thing's face but somehow it kept clawing at him. Blood sprayed all over Ghost. He tasted it as he pushed it off him. He emptied the magazine. It struggled for a moment and then–as if deciding to–collapsed. He sprang up and ran after the guys.

Walk through, Ghost. You can handle it.

They dove behind cover. When he looked up, he saw that jerk who stole Chinny's dog was on the comms crying and screaming and pleading for evac. Good. Ghost didn't really want to be stuck there much longer. He helped Chinny down and handed him a rifle, picked up an M60, and laid the barrel across the top of some sandbags and fired ferociously, doing his best to control the recoil.

"Come and get that you rice pickin' sons a bitches!" Sinner yelled. Ghost tried his best not to laugh and failed. The laughter wasn't funny. It was… something else. It scared him, and yet he laughed more. It almost felt like he was laughing at himself, like *he* was the joke. Like they were *all* in the joke, and it was just so gosh darn funny. It hurt, but he couldn't stop laughing. The people died, and then rose up. They became Things and they just kept coming. His thoughts bounced around. It was jarring… it was funny.

"Hey, did you know the Pied Piper was actually a pedophile that drugged the kids, and raped and drowned them, one by one? Who'd a thunk it, right?" Ghost laughed. A voice in the back of his mind told him he was suffering from some form of hysteria.

That part tried to reel him in, tried to diagnose him. Maybe if he had gone to medical school like his mother had wanted, instead of joining the service, he'd know right away what was wrong. Then again, maybe his team would have died a long time ago without him. *Get back to basics, Ghost. Focus. Breathe.*

Sinner stopped and looked at the jerk crying on the comms. He sniffed the air. "Well, you picked a fine time for that, didn't you, Lord? Ghost! Cover me. I gotta do something." *There you go, focus on that, do your job, focus.* Ghost fired into the crowd of approaching Things. "AAAWWWW shit." Sinner screamed.

Oh no! Had Sinner been hit? No. He was just kind of curled over.

"Whoa, man. Did you just punch yourself in the nuts?" Bleak asked Sinner, a question that seemed really odd under the current circumstances.

"I promised God if he made that pussy cry like a little bitch I'd punch myself in the nuts, and I keep my promises. Don't worry about that shit. Just shoot." Sinner was back in the fight.

"We're being attacked by our own people! What the fuck is going on?" a soldier cried right before being tackled.

"Don't think, just fight!" Chinny called to everyone. "If it's trying to kill you, it's the enemy!" They all barked in agreement.

So they fought, but the better they did against the enemy, the better the enemy seemed to fight. It was as if they were getting faster. He fired long strings of lead in slicing motions, severing limbs and lopping off heads. The sight made him ill, so very ill, and so very angry. The people that should have been dead rose up.

No. Keep it together, Ghost. Remember Dad. Remember what he said. Just because it's scary, we can't look away. We gotta walk through.

"Evac's coming. Go, go!" they heard someone yell. They fought their way toward the far side of the base, but it was slow going at best.

Popping and sizzling noises emanated from all around as their enemies dropped to the ground.

Hey, that rhymes, doesn't it? No! Come on, Ghost. Remember what Dad would always say about… about… the valley? Right. Something about a valley.

Ghost felt like his mind was just a stack of photos spread out on the ground, and someone was slowly flipping them over, one by one, so he couldn't see them anymore. "Hey, Sin! Popping and sizzling all around! The enemy's dropping to the ground! HA HA

HA!" It was like two different people in his head, one trying to keep it together and another tearing it all apart. Maybe if he stabbed himself in the face and chest and arms and legs he could blend in with the Things and get away... or maybe just mingle around a little bit.

"HA HA HA! That's pretty good!" Sinner complimented his poem.

In the back of his mind, a little voice was telling him to stop, but it was just so much fun to keep on going. Maybe the hysteria was just how it started. Maybe soon they'd turn into them and it wouldn't be so lonely. That'd be nice. Whatever it was must have gotten to Chinny first. The pictures continued to be covered up with black. He struggled to collect what remained.

"Hey, man. You want me to shoot you?" asked Sinner.

Suddenly, Ghost forgot what he was thinking about and instead turned his attention to how thoughtful and swell Sinner really was. He'd never noticed before. "Yeah. That'd be great."

"BLOODY HELL! It's the baby! I told you it was here!" Chinny yelled.

"Good for you, Chin. Ya found it!" Ghost yelled. The urge to stop was withering away.

Someone grabbed Ghost by the arm, hard. It was Bleak. He dragged him behind cover and gathered up the other guys. "Sit the fuck down! Sin! Shoot *that* way you fuckin' inbred doughboy mothafucka! Ghost! What the fuck is wrong with you?"

Ghost thought for a moment. "Ummmm ... you know that fairytale *The Girl Without Hands*? Originally it was about a girl who mutilates herself so she'll be so ugly her father will stop raping her."

He spent a while thinking, thinking about how much more awful the world is than what gets written down on paper. A few Yards came over and checked on him. He felt so drained, so lost. He felt something drape across his chest. They'd tied a pouch around his neck and suddenly, Ghost felt a few black papers get taken away. Still lost, but ever so slightly getting something back. Was it related? It couldn't be. Still, curiosity urged him to open the pouch. He emptied it into his hand.

It was just a bunch of rocks.

CHAPTER 32

SINNER

The dead bodies moved.
They *moved*.
He'd shaken it off. A target was a target. Didn't matter what it was, so long as it was neutralized. Still, the dead bodies moving made him feel... frail... inadequate. He needed his brothers, the men he knew he could count on. He *needed* them.

Sinner didn't take too kindly to the Yards being the front line. He needed them, too. The Yards were losing it, but nowhere near the way he or the rest of the team was. Somehow, Ghost was pulling it together, but that wasn't enough. *Get motivated, Sin.* The Yards had formed a defensive perimeter around them. Ghost got grazed on his shoulder. Kapaow's cousin took seven rounds to the chest. Bleak caught shrapnel from a mortar round in his cheek. Kim's dad lost both of his legs and continued to shoot as his blood poured into the dirt.

Whatever you want, Lord. But if my say matters, I'd like not to die today.

Bleak came running and yanked the last shotgun off his shoulder. Side by side they fired on the enemy. Bleak yelled to Kapaow to find more guns. Sinner nudged himself over a little bit behind Bleak and used the coon as cover. Shooting those bastards in the body just stunned them for a second. A shotgun blast to the head made them drop like Annabelle Smith's panties on a warm summer night.

The Crazy Mont monkey boy was hacking and flipping in ways Sinner never thought humanly possible. He had to be careful not to clip the bastard. He slapped away the hands of one of the Dead Bodies Moving and gouged its eyes out with his thumbs, quickly backing away from it before it could grab him. It made the fucker ragdoll to the ground.

So it ain't so much the head as it is the eyes.

The only hesitation Sinner felt toward poking their eyes out was how much that ooze reminded him of chili, and boy... he sure loved his chili. He'd hate to ruin such a fine meal with gross memories. Of course, he already had the memory of Crazy thumb-fucking the DBM skulls so... *dang.*

DBMs, that was good. He'd have to tell the guys about that later.

"Feast your eyeballs on *this* fuckers!" Sinner attached a bayonet when he'd run out of ammo. He thrust, just like in boot camp so long ago, again and again. *Kill! Kill! Kill!* they had him yell, over and over again. He stabbed deep into the skull of one DBM and yanked the bayonet back out before thrusting again, only to miss and instead rip its cheek clean off with a couple of teeth to boot. That scraping sound of metal on tooth always made him cringe something fierce. He thrust again, this time hitting home and stabbing the other eye. What the shit? The fucker was still moving! What the fuck was going on? "How the fuck do you die, bitch?"

Sinner never backed down from a fight. That's why he got along with Chinny. They both agreed: best way to kill some bitches was to fight some bitches, not run and hide from bitches. He stomached the stealthy patrols and silent observation that Chinny preferred in peace time, but if the shit hit the fan, "move up" was their slogan.

Only Sinner took a step back. Shooting them worked, but it didn't. Shooting them in the head worked, too… but also didn't. Stabbing the eyes out was working better still… and yet not working enough. How could he win when nothing worked enough? He took another step back. His stomach and the edges of his ears burned like watching an entire classroom laughing at him. He wanted to stand firm, but his feet kept stepping back.

Suddenly, a thick goo shot out onto the DBMs, like seed from a giant's willy. Sinner frantically scanned the area, trying to figure what was going on. Kapaow had a flame thrower on his back, but the piece of shit igniter coil thingy wasn't doing its job.

"Kapaow! FIRE! YA NEED FIRE!"

Kapaow looked over at him with his head cocked to the side like a dog looking at two bulls humping. After a moment's thought, he figured out what Sinner meant and smiled. He stuck the barrel down into a fire that was still cooking on one of the bunkers and pulled the trigger.

"NO! NOT LIKE THAT! AWWW, SHIT!"

Kapaow damn near set himself on fire, but he backed away from the mess he just made of the structure and turned his flaming stream toward the DBMs. Thankfully, he only set the back half of the crowd on fire, but boy did he cook them good. Shot until that whole thing went empty. The dead, now on fire, kept moving.

Sinner felt his back hit a wall of sandbags. Not only had he retreated as far as he could, but he'd hunched down and began to cower. He looked around to see if anyone noticed, but they were too focused to see. Now everybody had DBMs trying to bite them to death, no ammo, and a horde of flaming DBMs in the back that with a touch could kill or disfigure. Right when Sinner figured it was at its worst, it got even worse.

"Party's not ovah, mate!" He looked up at Chinny. The Aussie bastard actually looked happy as he hacked off the head of a DBM. Chinny hacked at its knees like a lumberjack, then turned and hoisted Sinner to his feet. It was nice and all, but they were doomed as doomed could be.

"Oi!" Chinny's yell startled Sinner. "When you're sittin' at a fiery card table with your mates in the depths uh hell with hands full of razor blade poker cards and the Devil's dealin', what kinda death story ya want, friend? When they're all yabbin' off about how one of 'em fell down some stairs or another died with a needle in his vein or got killed by a crazy hooker, where ya gonna be, mate? Ace on the top of the fuckin' deck fightin' off the very dogs of hell Satan sent to get ya in the first place!" Chinny wasn't very good at speeches.

The crazy fuck had lost it, smiling, the glint of burning DBMs reflecting into his eyes, lighting up his teeth. That's when it hit him. Even if they had to die, Chinny wanted them to do it right. It wasn't all about victory. It was about self-respect. Sinner took Chinny's hand and lifted himself back into the fight. Sinner took a deep breath of freedom and realized, as if he already didn't know, that he wasn't alone.

There was a thing about men and giving each other a nod before the end. It said everything that needed to be said. Men competed viciously in everything from who could eat the fastest, to who could kill the most, and even whose ideas were right and wrong. When it came time to give the nod, it meant, all competition aside: *I approve of you. It's been an honor. Thank you for being you.* It said everything a man could ever hope to say, and it said it better than any words he could spit out. So no words were spoken.

Together, they fought.

CHAPTER 33

CHINNY

"I think I hear the evac coming!" Bleak screamed. "We gotta move!"

"Set up a defensive line. Let them drag the wounded out. We'll cover them!" Chinny barked.

"Almost everyone *is* over there. Let's go!"

"They ain't gonna leave without us!" Sinner assured them.

"We can only move as fast as the wounded!" Ghost added.

"AAAAAHHHHH!" Chinny screamed as he hacked with his machete and taunted the enemy. "Live all ya want, fucks! Where ya gonna go without your arms and legs? Who ya gonna bite with no fuckin' teeth, yeah?" He laughed. Total body dismemberment, albeit difficult, was *working*.

Like a madman he took limbs from bodies and laughed at what was left. He stepped on one's head and smashed its top row of teeth down what was once its throat but was now a pulped pool of crushed flesh and dangling sinew. "DISMEMBER THEM! DISMEMBER THEM! That's right, boys. RIP 'EM APART!

More of their mates had fallen under the teeth, strangulation, and scorching Things. They tried to pull someone off of Xtung. Even with missing pieces, it still had enough strength to squeeze Xtung's neck so hard they couldn't pry him free and fight the horde back at the same time. When Xtung went limp, despite Ghost clawing to free him, the Things carried his body away. Chinny tried to think of a good farewell, but then Xtung came back too, and he gave up on the effort.

There was no time for questions. No theories, no investigation. Just slaughtering. Their semi-circle of machete-wielding defenders began to constrict. Their numbers dwindled. Even if they fought off the majority of the Things, they'd be done in by the fiery ones.

He hacked off a leg and landed a firm kick to a Thing's chest. He lunged as it fell to the ground and stabbed it with his piece of rubbish knife right through the eye. He stood up to stab the other eye, but slipped and landed face-first on the ragged optic hole. A hand grabbed his ankle so hard he feared it might crush.

There, at his foot, was the headless form of a Thing. How the fuck was it still moving? He hobbled up and hacked off the grasping arm at the wrist. Then he hacked the other arm at the elbow. He moved and hacked it off at the knees. He chopped its jaw off most of the way and let it dangle by a piece of skin. He cleaved its hips open and blood poured out like a dam had broken within its body.

Fuck the half measures. Fuck the professionalism. If the Yanks could be primates and make it to evac, Chinny and the boys could be brutes and make it out alive as well. He swung the machete the way he used to swing a hammer back at the village. He moved with stamina and agility gained from spending hours chasing down Yard children who didn't want to take their medicine. His rotator cuff was strong thanks to lifting up Cadeo all the time.

"No! Where the fuck are they going?" Bleak screamed.

Chinny saw the evac… already leaving. He almost collapsed. They'd taken too long to get to the rally point. It turned long enough to lay down a hail of bullets. It certainly helped, but it lasted only a few seconds. Then their chance of escape flew away.

There wasn't time for regrets, though there were many. He turned his attention back to the battle. His punishment would be dealt soon. Death couldn't come easily, otherwise it wouldn't be a punishment at all. A few Things charged him. He chopped off hands and ears, heads and fingers, legs and feet, until even his machete was lost in the frenzy. He shuffled back. Bleak shuffled back. Ghost fell over one of the wounded.

Chinny felt that all-too-familiar sensation of eyes watching him. Off in the distance, bobbing up and down over the horizon of the crowd, were two glints of white attached to a face, but there was something different about this one. Two more followed at its sides, pushing through the crowd. They were unique from the rest, but the Blue-Eyed one even more so. Looking straight ahead, he appeared clear and focused.

Yeah, Old Blue Eyes. You'll be the one, won't ya? About bloody time.

He picked up a piece of rebar and used it as a spear, stabbing and gouging until it became too slippery to hold. The dusty sand they had walked on at the start of the mission was now thick crimson mud. Kapaow had no weapon at all, but continued to gouge out eyes with his thumbs. He glistened red from his fingers to his elbows.

Chinny's lungs hurt, his throat hurt, worn from so many breaths in such a short time. He was beginning to get clumsy.

Meanwhile, the Things seemed to be increasingly agile. They weren't falling over the other bodies as much, leaving him less and less time to rest between waves. It was like the more they stopped, the better they got. How?

One of the Things snatched his weapon away. That was the first time that'd happened. He dodged as the Thing swung it at him. He shifted back, crouched down, and lunged, slamming into its rib cage like a rugby forward. He managed to launch that one in the air a bit before it landed just past the pile of squirming, somewhat-dead bodies. It struggled to get to its feet. After a few moments of slipping in the mud, it went limp. He shot a glance back–Blue Eyes was getting closer.

Another lunged, faster than expected, but not fast enough. Chinny shuffled in and stomped on its foot, burying it into the mud and holding it in place. He rotated his hand and grabbed hold of its wrist. Bending its hand until it locked, he twisted it, causing the entire body to rotate away from him. He struck its now-locked arm, dislocating the elbow.

"Where's the evac?" Sinner screamed.

Chinny twisted the loose appendage into the air, further separating the joint, turned and yanked until the shoulder dislocated as well. It was the odd sound of someone knocking on a door, underwater, while tearing a piece of canvas. He pulled on the flopping arm and made the Thing face the crowd. Back to back, he reached up to grab its flopping head. Its dry lips felt like a lizard's kiss, tacky and sticky, as they slid across his skin. He could feel its teeth coming closer.

"They *fuckin'* left us!" Bleak howled.

He hopped up and grabbed it by the chin. On his way down to the ground, he yanked hard over his shoulder. As soon as he had reached his lowest crouch possible, he jumped back into the air, which turned the body into a whip. The wet pop told him he had successfully broken its neck. He released and it flopped onto the ground. He stepped over it, stomping on its knee as hard as he could. Sure, it was still moving. Chinny wished it the best of luck on getting up and rejoining the fight. He gave it a wink as he passed by.

He lunged straight for the next one's leg and took it down. He placed his knee on the base of its neck and wrapped both hands around its forehead, yanking back as hard as he could. Three *click-clack-clunks* thumped through his arms as he felt the vertebrae separate. He pulled its arms behind its back and crossed them over, stomped on the lower back, and stood tall, raising the arms so awkwardly the shoulders dislocated. The Thing kicked around, but that was all.

Three more overpowered and knocked him to the ground. Old Blue Eyes was about ten meters out and drawing closer. Sinner rushed over to help pull them off, but was knocked aside by Blue Eyes. Chinny had imagined this all happening differently, holding off the Things and buying the men enough time to escape until he was overrun. Survival was in their nature. It was their training that taught them to survive as a *team*. They wanted to help Chinny survive. Now he'd have to try and drown out their screams with his own. The Things began to move in unison, like Spartan soldiers in a phalanx. Chinny looked to the others, but none knew what to make of it. What the fucking hell was going on?

"Push harder! Still alive!" Chinny howled.

"Still alive! We can fight!" the men replied.

There's nothing left to do but fight, Chinny. Fight until you die!

Strangely, Old Blue Eyes pulled the things off of him. Chinny scrambled back to his feet. He was a tall one as he looked down at Chinny. Chinny paused long enough to crack a smile.

It was like sprinting head first into a brick wall. Blue Eyes hit him once and he instantly fell to the ground. Two other Things moved into position on either side of him. While it sounded as if their bones were snapping and tearing as they moved, they were fast, faster than Chinny. Why were they special? They grabbed his arms and held him down while Old Blue Eyes began to choke him. With the strength of his grip, death wasn't far off.

The one thing he had forgotten about in all this glory was that thing they say: about how a person's life flashes before their eyes. Now, that fact suddenly occurred to him, and the thought was most unsettling. He began to jerk and twist. He tried to block it out. He stared at those blue eyes, tried to keep his mind in the present. It was the blue eyes that ruined it. Something about them started to bring back memories. It was a floodgate opening that he would die to close. Over and over he faced a rush of misery and thought he'd survived the worse, only to face even more painful memories.

Then the image of a door overpowered all other thoughts. The sound of a woman humming from behind it. What was this? The black holes in his mind were like eyes opening, mouths pouring blood into his soul. He would have screamed and begged for it to stop had he been able to breathe. His chest twitched and bucked, begging for air. It was so painful. He drew closer to the door and began to tremble. What was it? Why was it coming to him now? All that was certain was that he wanted nothing to do with it.

Make it go away. Make it end. Make it stop. I just want it to stop. Please. *It should have been me, goddamn it. Let it be me now!*

Those eyes, those dead blue eyes, stared into him. They weren't meandering like the others. They were focused. A death-grip still fixed to Chinny's neck, its eyes slowly crept to one side. Both of Blue Eye's mates turned their attention to the same thing. *Hey! I'm right here! Do it!* Chinny would have screamed, had he been able to breathe.

One of Blue Eyes' subordinates lifted his hand and examined his wrist. It touched his Yard bracelet. They all inspected the bracelet. Old Blue Eyes' bloody face drew close. There was no breath, only the rank smell of corroded copper piping. The tinny taste of it dripped in his mouth.

Its lips brushed against his cheek, chapped and dry, scraping against him like some disease-ridden leper. He felt queasy. He could see feet shuffling past him as they began to close in on the wounded. He heard their screams and hoped he'd die first. Ghost was screaming. Chinny's vision faded—a blurry black ring slowly constricting around the image of this Blue Eyed Thing.

A piece of its lip was missing. The skin blistered and swelled where its right eyebrow was scorched off. Its nose was gone, just a bony hole that trickled blood. Its eyes were wide open, too wide, like they were forced open. Its jaw hung open, a face frozen in terror as it stared into Chinny's dying eyes. It all faded to black. It wasn't suicide. He fought to the bitter end and he'd died.

It was about bloody time.

CHAPTER 34
CHINNY

Light.
A circle that appeared to be formed from glass floated above him. It cascaded white light over him and a portion of the landscape. He scanned the darkness around him. No heavenly gates, and surprisingly, no fire and brimstone. Where was he?

Cold.
Perhaps it was not freezing, but it was cold enough to be just shy of tolerable. The air had the appropriate amount of chill to make him to shiver. It was a damp sort of cold, and soon it'd be down to his bones.

Black.
Though there was light. He looked around and saw that everything appeared to be dyed a rich, deep black. He couldn't tell where the blackness ended. The ground was the same one he'd been strangled on, yet when he dug his hands into the bloody mud and let it ooze between his fingers and dry to his skin, it was black as night. Everything was as he'd left it, only black.

Surreal.
His men were motionless on the ground, their arms posed like statues fighting off attackers that were no longer present. Their mouths were opened wide and their eyes showed both rage and fear. They were wearing black uniforms instead of the olive-drab, and their faces were painted black instead of the same green. Their eyes still showed white, but the white shined luminescent, like that of a full moon.

Empty.
The air felt empty. Empty of sound, of motion—the space all around him felt hollow for what seemed like miles. His breath echoed through the cavernous dark. The only sounds were those he created, yet he couldn't hear his heartbeat or the sound of his stomach churning. It was as if everything inside him had stopped.

Movement.
He flinched. His muscles were so sore he was not sure if he could defend himself against anything, much less what lurked in the dark. When he detected movement in his peripheral and

turned sharply toward the source, all he saw was an endless horizon of black. Movement again, by the men. Yet upon inspection he was certain that they were indeed still frozen in time. He couldn't feel his heart racing, but it should have been. He couldn't feel his pulse quicken, but he knew it had.

His instincts cried out for his senses to take notice of… what? He couldn't tell. Yet still he knew it was there: something unseen, yet all encompassing. What was it? A chill flooded his body as the air became ice cold. He'd felt it before, time and time again, yet never gave it voice.

Fuck! Something fluttered past his shoulder!

Around and around his eyes went. He couldn't feel his lungs expand and contract, he couldn't feel his heart thumping in his chest. He couldn't feel his stomach turning over on itself or his throat run dry. All he felt was cold. He was lost in the numbness. Panic bashed into his skull like a sledgehammer.

Slop, slop, flop, plop

What was that noise? A horse? Smaller. Goat? Tiny, gentle little pitter-patters off in the distance, softer than hooves. Bear cub? Growing steadier. A monkey? Straighter. Human? At the farthest point he could see a shape, nothing more than a faint outline. It swayed back and forth. Two lights flickered on either side… no, not lights. They were hands, alternating into and out of the light above. Then hands, arms and shoulders flickered as a head became visible, and finally the entire figure. It was a boy, maybe ten years old, staring at the ground as he slowly crept forward. His mop of hair, so black it looked artificial, blocked his face.

Slop, slop, slop… slop

His footsteps sloshed through the black mud. The sound of him walking doubled and tripled as it echoed through the emptiness. Chinny's gut told him the boy wasn't supposed to be there, and if he *was* there, then something was wrong. Horribly wrong. Still, he couldn't help but want to talk to the boy, help him.

"How cold *is* it?" Chinny smiled, but there was no response as the boy crept even closer. "I say it's pretty cold, yeah?" No response. The chill raked across his skin and made the hairs on his neck stand on end. "It is quite cold in here. Wouldn't you agree?"

The boy's footsteps ceased, such that he stood an arm's length away. Now Chinny didn't know what to say. His own breathing shortened. He could hear the air rip past his throat, but did not feel it entering his lungs. He wanted to reach out and touch the boy.

Maybe some friendly contact would snap him out of whatever catatonic state he was in, yet his hands remained still. His heart should have thumped louder, but didn't. The boy's feet were black up past his ankles, black bruises all over his arms and neck. His pointer and middle fingers on each hand were twisted and blackened by what was no doubt internal damage. Chinny had seen similar injuries before, albeit not quite as severe. Did his face share the same treatment? Somehow, Chinny already knew the answer.

Relax. It's just fear, mate. Reach out.

Chinny reached out to move the boy's hair away and get a look at the state of his face. His hand crept closer and closer. The sound of his breath had vanished. It was a vacuum. No sound, no thought. Just some light and a battered little boy staring at the ground. Chinny's hand grew closer. The boy's hair moved slightly from his touch, but Chinny could not feel any of it.

"NO!" a voice boomed from all around him, making the ground shake and the air tremble like an earthquake and a tornado colliding on him. The air was speaking. *Deep breaths, Chin… steady. Breathe in. Two, three, four. Out. Two, three, and four. Calm.*

Silence.

A strange noise broke through the emptiness. Some sort of slimy clicking, like running a spoon through macaroni and cheese. Chinny looked closer. The noise was coming from somewhere near the boy. He scanned the area. Something glimmered on the ground in front of him—and moved. He strained to see.

It was a drop of black. It glistened and stood out among the rest of the blackened mud. He dipped his finger in it, examined it, and smeared it across his thumb. More liquid splashed into the black mud. The drips became faster and pooled, dark and glistening red on top of black. Chinny followed the trail only to see it disappear behind the boy's black hair.

The boy moved closer, and the trail of blood began to drip on Chinny's boots. It snaked between the creases of his pant legs and soaked through. His was sticking to his body. The blood soaked into his shirt and made tapping noises on its buttons. The drips began to drop faster and faster until it became a steady, thin stream. His clothing seemed to constrict around him. When it reached his neck, it was only then he realized the blood was ice-cold. Chinny's breath stopped.

The boy hovered over Chinny, shivering. His feet appeared frozen in the black ground. His body leaned all of its weight on his shins and the bones creaked under the pressure. Finally, his head tilted upward. The blood gushed. His eyes were open, but a river poured from underneath the lids and over his irises and pupils. When it got in Chinny's eyes it stung like salt. The boy tried to speak, but blood gushed too fast from his mouth to form words.

"What?" Chinny begged.

The boy stopped moving, frozen in time like his team. It was then that he saw another child off in the distance...watching him. He was strange for the situation, immaculate and bright. He wore a green robe of sorts. He looked like a student observing a lesson with rather deep contemplation. He wasn't afraid at all. Chinny looked at the bloody boy, frozen, Chinny was terrified.

"Something very valuable indeed." This other boy spoke as if someone were next to him, but he was alone. Then, he regarded Chinny directly. "We have no time to investigate further. But make no mistake, Brooklyn; you are indeed still alive. What I've seen is quite valuable. So when you come back, you must win. Do you understand? Forget what we told you before. You must win now."

Then he was gone, and the bloody child began to stir again, it began to claw at Chinny. Again, the air spoke. "NO!" The world trembled. "You are *not* dead, Brooklyn... *they* are not dead." The boy pointed to the men. "Brooklyn... there is still time... still a chance!"

The boy closed his eyes tightly and shook his head violently. He opened his mouth wide. He screamed. It sounded like pigs being slaughtered and it echoed through Chinny's mind. The boy snapped his head down and opened his eyes... they were no longer covered in blood... they were blue.

"WAKE UP!"

CHAPTER 35
CHINNY

It seemed as if time hadn't passed. Suddenly the pressure started to trickle out of his brain. Breath came back into his lungs. His arms were released. The two subordinates went limp on the ground. For a moment, he had dreamed, and something felt so significant about it. *Like* a dream, the more he thought about it, the more it slipped away from him.

He was free, *alive,* but not comforted by it. He was so close. Now all he felt was rage. He punched it in the face until his knuckles bled. Either he'd rip it to pieces or it'd finish the fucking job. He punched it just under the ear again and again until he heard the pop of the jaw dislocating.

He clawed over its eyes and felt the gelatinous film shave off under his fingernails. He reached into its bullet holes and tore at the skin. He pushed the entire body up as high as he could and tossed it to the side. He picked up a rock and bashed at its head, but it wouldn't move. It just kept making bloody eye contact, scrapes on its corneas and all, watching him. He wasn't going to be judged by a fucking dead man.

Suddenly, it went limp. The one to his left rose up again... but this one stared at him the same exact way, a different face with the same expression. It nodded... it gave *the* nod. It turned and... strutted. It moved the way Bleak would when he was angry or about to do something stupid. It reached down and grabbed one of the Things that was piling on top of the men, pulled it off, and flung it into the flaming Things, knocking some down. It was strong, perhaps stronger than a man, or as strong as a man experiencing a fit of adrenaline.

Shwunk

It was the sound of the entire horde of Things coming to a stiff halt. The men were at a loss. None knew what to make of it. This one–this odd Thing, if one could even coin such a term– continued to toss the motionless corpses to the side. Finally, the men were uncovered. They all had bruises in the shapes of mouths and blood dripping where skin broke. It grabbed the piece of metal they clutched and lifted them all up at the same time.

When the trees stopped swaying, and the birds and the bugs and monkeys and all living things fell silent, a man knew that something terrible was about to happen. Yet, somehow, Chinny's gut told him this was different. Whatever was happening was something the world had never seen before. Mother Nature herself was in awe … and that was more frightening to Chinny than the Devil and God combined. He didn't breathe. All Chinny could hear was the steady thump of his heartbeat echoing through the valley. It lasted what could have easily been an eternity.

Khhhhhhhhaaaaaaaaaaaaaaa

The horde exhaled in unison. It was a tortured moan riddled with the wispy and hollow sounds like the voice of a lifetime spent screaming from torture. Chinny had stopped trying to make sense of it. Now, it was simply about seizing opportunity. He clapped his hands as loud as he could to snap the men out of their dumbfounded gaze.

"Weapons!" Chinny cried out. No time to think, just fight.

They all scrambled to find… *anything*.

The long exhale had ended at the same time they found their machetes and knives either on the ground or in the eye sockets of the enemy. Silence. Their friendly Thing raised its arm and pointed for the jungle, looking over its shoulder.

After a second of stunned confusion, Chinny managed words. "What? Us?" Chinny asked, to which it nodded. If there was a chance to save his men… he had to take it.

"If you can stand, stand!" Chinny growled. Kapaow translated.

Some stood. Some did not.

"Ghost, get them up! Pair them off with those who can stand." Chinny commanded.

Chinny tilted his head to the side. His neck cracked. It sounded eerily similar to the sound of the Things moving. He exhaled. Bleak, Sinner, Kapaow, and Crazy came close and stood beside him. Their bodies were beaten, but there was more to them than flesh. Their will could never die, and they would fight even when their bodies failed.

"Is that thing fuckin' helping us?" Bleak yelled.

Chinny lunged forward and pierced the air with a wicked battle cry. His machete swung cleanly through bone as he fought alongside this dead creature that somehow wanted to help them. The men followed suit, what else could they do?

Together, they took a step to the side, fought more, and then stepped to the side again. Chinny looked at the other two things,

Old Blue Eyes and the other subordinate, just laying there like discarded chicken gizzards. Then he looked at the one standing, fighting with them. It moved like Old Blue Eyes, but wasn't Old Blue Eyes. There wasn't any time to ponder it further, but still, it was strange. He'd talk to Ghost about it later… if there was a later.

They each hacked away at their target's joints. Meanwhile their new, strange, *dead* ally smashed the Things using his fists like meat hammers. He looked like a man having a tough time ripping open a lobster. The Friendly Thing watched them fighting. It started to dislocate joints and eventually picked up a machete as well. It matched them as best it could, but what had made it suddenly turn and help them?

They stepped to the side.

"We're doing it!" Bleak yelled.

"Don't celebrate yet. We're not done."

They needed to win this battle head on. There was no other way. Then they could extract the wounded. Kapaow turned and ran off. He wouldn't abandon them. Not now. Chinny wasn't sure what he was doing. He just hoped he did it quickly.

The things began to maneuver, to flank. It wasn't a mindless wall of death anymore. It seemed intelligent. They were surrounded now. They weren't mindless. It was Chinny who had lost his mind.

As some of them fell to the ground, their muscles and connective tissues perhaps dissolving in the heat, they caught parts of the base on fire. He watched the regular Things stepping into the flames. Once they'd ignited, they continued in the same circular path the others had, like a noose tightening around them.

"AAAAHHHHH!"

Fiery Things moved in behind them. They didn't bite, didn't grab or claw. They just fell on top of the wounded. Even as the Yards were set ablaze and screamed in agony they gouged at the eyes, punched and clawed. It didn't matter. They were gone, and the noose was getting tighter.

"Sinner! Bleak!" Chinny roared. *"About face!"* He screamed with all his might. They turned as one and used whatever they could to push the fiery Things back and keep them at bay. The Fiery Things closed in. Chinny could feel the heat licking at his face.

Shplop.

The Thing Chinny faced had suddenly stopped when a great big blob of mud slammed square in its chest, dousing the fire in that particular area. The Crazy Mont hurled himself through the air and landed a mighty kick where the fire had been extinguished. His feet came back unburned—clever. The blow sent the Thing tumbling back, the fire destroying the muscles that would help it get back up. It went limp. Chinny started to move.

Fear is all that stops you, Chin. Deep breaths. You can do this. You can do this. Deep breaths.

The Crazy Mont flung mud in the eyes of every Thing, flaming or not. It didn't stop the attacks, but it slowed them down. As the blazing Things collided with the others, the amount of fiery bastards greatly increased. They flung mud as quickly as they could, and yet they were too slow. Behind them, in front of them, to their sides, Things walked. Some crawled as their flesh withered away, while others dragged themselves, their lips burned off long ago and their wretched teeth showing through the fire.

Zzthwump-Craow... zzthwump-Craow!

Kapaow had circled around. He posted on a hill and opened fire, from far enough that the hits were seen before heard. It was all pink mist and flaming bits as he chewed a hole through their ranks. Those that still had heads broke from the group and turned their attention toward Kapaow. The fat dripping off of their bodies left a trail of burning footprints as they walked up the hill. Some took too long and dropped, taken by the fire.

The Friendly Thing slammed into an enemy so hard it knocked over ten or more on its way down. It seemed to enjoy this method, since it continued to slam into them. The men followed behind and gouged out the eyes with rifle barrels and chunks of twisted metal. They were going to escape the circle.

"Come on, mates! It's the last push!" Chinny dialed back his vanity in time to execute another beheading. "Bleak! Sprint up there and see if you can't find some more weapons! Help Kapaow before he gets overrun!"

"On it!"

There *had* been hope all along. A battle was a battle. It didn't matter if the enemy was unexpected. Find the weak point and strike. That's exactly what they'd done. While they crushed the enemy in front, the enemy behind was running out of time. Consumed by fire, they were dropping again and again. Not much longer now.

"HEP! HEP ME!" a Yard screamed. Chinny couldn't see who it was. All he saw was a Thing pummeling something with the butt of a discarded rifle. The screaming stopped abruptly.

Chinny was seized from behind and felt teeth digging at his neck. He struggled to break free. Ghost was screaming for help, but Chinny couldn't tell what was happening to him. Another set of hands grabbed Chinny by the legs and dragged him to the ground.

Enough of this shite!

Chinny bit the Things back. He dug his teeth and tasted the copper and felt the flesh brush against his gums and stretch, rubbery against his lips as *he* ripped chunks out of *them.*

"E'rybody get the FUCK down!"

They skidded about, slipping in the mud as they fell back behind the sandbags. Chinny rolled around and flailed about wildly until he finally managed to break free. An RPG howled into the center of the horde. The Friendly Thing just stood there, looking perplexed as shrapnel tore through him, but his eyes and limbs and fingers and toes remained intact.

Bleak came sprinting down the hill with AK-47s dangling off both shoulders. He stopped every few steps to take aim at a fiery one. Sometimes the top section of skull would pop off, other times it was the back of the skull. A few shots were so perfectly aimed the bone gave out almost equally in every direction. It was fireworks, shooting off into the air.

Bleak fought his way back into formation and handed everyone an AK. The rest of the men opened fire while Chinny walked around to the ones that had fallen and put a round in each of their joints.

Stay alive till the end of time, ya twats, but you're still gettin' buried here.

Somehow, Chinny and his men had survived.

He checked the hillsides and listened for incoming threats. He jogged up to the men and was damn near tackled by Kapaow in a celebratory hug that picked him up off the ground and almost destroyed his spinal cord. The other men came over and picked Chinny up like the hero of a rugby game. What had *he* done? *They* did most of the work while he was off losing his mind.

"Bloody hell, Pao. *Ugh.* Let me go!" For whatever reason, he laughed.

They had won. Abandoned and alone, left for dead, *aided* by the dead, and they had actually *won.* As much as Chinny had thought this would be the day he got what he deserved, he couldn't deny how winning against such impossible odds felt. He didn't fight it. He accepted the sensation. He looked at Kapaow, who motioned with his finger his usual sign commanding Chinny to smile. *Alright, brother, you win.* Chinny smiled, Kapaow smiled back.

It felt good.

CHAPTER 36
KAPAOW

I was right. Chinny and his team are strong enough to resist the tree fairies. They are the ones.

Kapaow smiled. They had held it together when the dead revealed themselves. The only outsiders to survive such a thing. Granted, they had some unexpected help, but regardless, they'd survived it. Of course, the extra help they received seemed to overshadow everything.

"Where are you? Where are you *really?*" Kapaow said in his own tongue, barely even looking at the corpse standing before him.

He knew they understood many languages, like him. He figured if one was out there, it must have been too cautious to show itself. He looked around before returning his attention to the corpse.

"It's okay. I won't hurt you. I promise. You helped us. There has to be a reason for that, right? You can come out. I don't think the body you are controlling is capable of talking. In fact, I don't think I've ever seen a body talk. If we're going to communicate, you need to come out."

Kapaow looked around again. Chinny was standing next to him, staring at the Thing. Kapaow hugged Chinny momentously. He, of course, wrestled free and walked away. Kapaow didn't care. This was a good sign. Help was within his grasp. They had made contact; the one thing Kapaow had wanted. Actually, it was the *one* thing his people had wanted for the past couple thousand years.

"What took you so long?" Kapaow asked the body playfully before looking around again, hoping to see someone moving in the trees, watching them, *anything* to indicate the Tree Fairy's presence.

He saw nothing. He tried to think of what to say, or what to do that would make it comfortable enough to come out. His grandfather had said they looked human, albeit slightly off but very close. Close enough that a human could fall in love with one and few would be the wiser.

He turned back to the body with his usual smile, genuinely feeling happy. He was usually happy. Even when he was angry it was just a temporary deviation from happiness, to which he would always return. This time, in the middle of a horrid scene, was something beautiful: hope. He saw the good and let it overshadow the bad.

More NVA and VC would be coming. Perhaps now was the time to tell Chinny and the boys what was really going on here. Suddenly, an image of them overreacting popped into his mind.

The Thing was staring at the rest of the team instead of looking at him. Kapaow felt the pit of his stomach begin to sag, the weight of sadness pulling it toward the ground. He looked at the men. "You're not here for me or my people, are you?" He looked to the body, its eyes glassy and vacant. It slowly–very subtly, so only Kapaow could see–shook its head no. "You have your own problems, and you need their help for the same reasons I do." A slight smile, perhaps a look of surprise, twitched onto the Thing's face. Its controller was surprised Kapaow had deduced so much in the blink of an eye. "I am clever, friend. All of my people are clever."

Tree fairies were evil creatures, but maybe it was just their society that was evil. Not very different from humans, was it? What if some of them were rebels? What if this one helped Kapaow and his friends because it thought that they could help fight the evil in their own people? It would explain the subtle tug-of-war they had been experiencing in their minds. A strong power was driving them mad, but perhaps this rebel was softening the blows, making it easier for them to overcome it. Of course, the stones helped to block the influence slightly. He checked to make sure he still had his, which were laced around his neck.

They would have to be careful, just like Kapaow and his people had been careful. They would have to be cautious of how they spoke and behaved. Defiance was a delicate thing. Kapaow could not be too direct or risk breaking the delicate bond of trust. He made these assumptions, and a part of him waited for Kim to challenge him, but she wasn't there. In hindsight, leaving her without as much knowledge as possible was foolish. Who knew if Kapaow would make it back? He should have prepared her better. Why had he felt so compelled to keep her out of it? Who would keep the village on track in his absence?

The Thing extended its hand, which shocked Kapaow to say the least. He reached out and felt a gritty, slithering texture as dried bits of skin poked out through blood-soaked patches.

"So you'll try and help me, too?" Kapaow asked, and the corpse continued to smile.

This was the chance he'd been waiting for.

"You guys," he said. "You guys, come here. Come closer. I have to tell you something about this body that moves. I couldn't tell you before, you understand? How would you have believed me? I know you weren't sent here to save my people. I'm not a fool. But we have done more than just fight side by side. We have lived together, laughed together."

He looked to Chinny.

"If we continue, we have the chance to love together and become a family. We can stick together through this battle and overcome what lies ahead. We can return home, and maybe, just maybe, find a way to save our family for years to come. This being here is the key. You understand?"

Kapaow spoke with fire and passion. The men gathered around couldn't take their eyes off of him. "This body that should be lying dead on the floor is not what will help us. It is only a tool of the being that will help us. Somewhere close, perhaps far–I am not certain–a being *controls* this body. Beings like it are what have driven us mad at times. They create mass hysteria, pin us in two sided debates against each other. They make us, all of us, everyone in the world, squabble over nothing so that we cannot see them standing right next to us. I believe some of these beings are different, however. They want to fight what controls us as much as we do. I believe that is why this one helped us. There are probably more who will help us as well. This dead body that moves will be our emissary into their world. It is fighting against other beings with similar abilities that want to see us fall. This battle is *proof* we can defeat them." He looked at the standing corpse. "Together. Join me and we will bring peace to this land!"

They all smiled.

The dead body smiled.

Kapaow smiled.

This was their chance.

CHAPTER 37
CHINNY

"Ghost, you understand a fuckin' word Kapaow is saying?" Chinny watched Kapaow yabber on like a bloody moron for what felt like five minutes.

"I understand some of it. I'm still getting a hang of the language, ya know? Something about coming together and fighting. I guess he's praying or something? I don't know."

"Well, does he know he ain't speakin' no English?" Sinner asked.

"I'm sure he does. Like I said, probably praying. Just smile and make him happy so we don't offend him." They all embraced him in a group hug.

Once that nonsense was done, he found a pair of binoculars and began scanning the area. The men searched for supplies while Chinny tried to see when another wave would come. From time to time, he turned his attention away to observe Ghost as he looked at the different bodies. In some cases, even after being dismembered, eyes continued to move within skulls and watch them.

Chinny knelt down at one point to gouge out the eyes of one that wouldn't stop staring. It felt different to do harm when adrenaline was not part of the equation. The rubbery resistance, the tearing sound like ripping rawhide leather as he dug into the cornea. It was the kind of sensation he could not help but grit his teeth at. Sick as it was, it was worse when he felt the sudden pop and the vile liquid spilled out.

He turned his attention back to Ghost, hoping for something other than bewilderment. The Thing that had helped them… the *Friendly,* was very much alive, though it very much should not have been. Ghost was staring at its chest, waiting for it to take a breath. They all fell silent as they waited for its chest to heave, yet the moment never came.

They couldn't have been through all this to have no solid intel worth using. They needed to know something. Yet, the questions were becoming quite redundant. How was it possible? How were these Things still alive? How could they be alive without breathing? How were any actions possible if the bodily tissues were dying without oxygen? What was it? Why had it helped them? Could it be trusted?

"We need to go home," Ghost surmised.

"The mission is—"

"The mission's over!" Sinner interrupted Chinny. "We're done. They left us here to die."

"They did not just leave us. They laid down covering fire and killed quite a few before taking off with those they rescued, mate. We'd have done the same."

"No we wouldn't have!" Bleak stepped in. "You know how I know? Cuz we *didn't*. We stayed and fought, protected them while they all fuckin' ran away. It's cuz they're Montagnards, ain't it? Yeah. Ya dig? That's *exactly* what that shit's about. Don't nobody care about no black man gettin' left to die. Don't nobody care about no Yard *neither*. Fuck these honkies man. I'm done."

"Oh, enough of that. There were plenty of times they had our backs. We were just too busy with our heads up our arses to bloody notice." Chinny was rather ashamed he had not gotten his men to safety and was too tired to hide it.

How did the Yanks succeed where he failed? There was no point in staying, and yet somehow that was exactly what happened. Why? More questions for a pile without answers. They all looked at him, waiting for a better answer in regards to their next actions. He needed comms. He needed to make contact with the higher ups and find out what to do next. He wanted to be told what to do.

"Bleak, quit fuckin' off and ring somebody up."

"No."

Chinny was quite surprised. He couldn't remember the last time Bleak ever said no in an assertive manner. "Get on the fuckin' radio!" Chinny growled through his teeth with even more assertion than Bleak could offer.

"N-no... no... we're goin' home. I tell ya right now." Bleak turned to the rest of the men. Even The Friendly paid attention. "They left us for dead. Ain't nobody comin' back. If we dead, we off the books baby. We can do whatever the fuck we want. Ya dig? I thought this was what I wanted. A career. Prove all the white folks wrong. Now that I'm here, I don't care about them. I want to do some shit that matters. That ain't what these cats is about. Feel me? Stickin' with the Yards; that matters. I *ain't* gon' sit around and watch them get killed off until all that survives is a bunch of damn *slaves*. The Yards want to fight. I'm gonna help them. I'm going back."

Chinny looked at the smoldering destruction all around the base. Over the course of the entire fight they had "killed" roughly a hundred men. The problem was: they kept getting back up. It was probably the equivalent to eight hundred kills by the time they were abandoned by the evac. Maybe one-thousand to eleven-hundred total kill equivalents including the fight after it left.

"That it, then? Fight the good fight, carry out our own missions? Fuck what we swore when we became soldiers and just take care of these people?" Everyone nodded. "Well…" As Chinny was about to speak the words, he realized this battle had changed him and his view of things. "I suppose you're right." Everyone gasped. "Oh, piss off ya bloody sheepshaggers. Bleak's right… we're free. We can do whatever we want… problem is… there ain't much we can do for them without backing. So either we go and live with them and fight with them, *scrounge* with them, perhaps even *starve* with them, or we make ourselves known, get back in the game, kick some arse and maybe, just maybe, get someone higher up to notice that these Montagnards are more than just a local asset."

"Or," Bleak started, "we stay off the books for now. Relocate the village to a safer place. *Then* make ourselves known. We keep in contact with the village the whole way, but don't let anybody know where it is. That way, no attention gets drawn to it. We make sure we keep the pressure on and drive the enemy away from their village. If, along the way, we can get somebody's ear, then all the better. At least this way they're isolated from all this instead of being pushed into the thick of it. We already got too many killed bringing them into this fight."

"We fight," both Kapaow and Crazy protested.

"No one's saying you won't. We're talking about the rest of the village–the ones who can't fight. The men we left with them won't be enough for very long if they get attacked. Right now, the NVA and VC, they want all Yards dead. We need to stop them, or give them such an ass kicking they don't have the time for genocide. Besides, they *are* the mission, Chinny, and we haven't been given an order to abort."

"Say we do this. What's the plan? I sure as bloody hell don't have one," Chinny challenged.

"Remember those red circles and the X on the map piece? Kapaow and Crazy know all those spots. We stop waiting for bullshit orders that leave us walking in circles all day and we start hitting those places hard. We can confiscate what we need to keep it up, free people as we go, recruit others as we need. First we move the village and make sure it's safe, then we kick some ass and make sure its future is safe."

"But back home our radio's broken," Ghost reminded them. "How will we contact them to let them know we're coming?"

"Maybe we speak me friend. He go," Kapaow assured them.

"The guy with the little fruit things?" Bleak asked, and Kapaow nodded.

"If we manage a way to get a hold of him, tell that gook bastard to bring a basket *full* of them."

"Sin, *shut* your... bloody... anyway..." Chinny sighed for a moment and considered Bleak's idea. "Well..." Chinny sighed. What did he really have to lose? "It's a long trip back without a helicopter to pick us up."

"Other Yards will help us. Like Kapaow said: maybe we even find a radio. I know Kapaow's friend has one at his village. They just don't know how to use it. Even if we just steal one and make a quick call, even if everybody hears it, we'll just speak vaguely enough so nobody'll know where we're going or what we're doing. We can have them send a few guys to meet us at a place based on things we've done there instead of describing actual locations. By the time we get home, everyone will be packed up and ready to move. We'll have help. I mean, shit, Chinny. Most of what we done here so far is thanks to the Yards, not the military. Those assholes can't even send us the right resupply. The Yards know how to hide, fight, and survive up in here. You said yourself. Americans are too loud and too interested in blowing shit up to make a difference. Why did you even bother to say that unless you hoped to make a difference, Chin?" Bleak countered.

What was Chinny after, really? Did he want death, or did he just want to rest? Wouldn't this be a rest for his soul? To do something that felt right for a change?

"Bleak, I admire ya, right? Ya just don't see the bigger picture. Yeah, I want to do some good. It'd be nice. Even if we find a radio, get help, go back and save the day, it's *just* a day, Bleak. We can't save these people forever."

"Then we'll *find* a way," they all said to Chinny.

"Bloody hell... I suppose the Yards were our official mission when you think of it, yeah? Fine. We search for a way. I'll die for that. Just know eventually we're going to need bigger help, mate. We'll hide the Yards, then we make our presence known."

"I no hide!" Kapaow screamed, almost crying. "I fight! We fight! Have to! Have to!"

"Easy. Christ mate, calm the fuck down. Yeah. I mean women and children, fuckin' hell. We're gonna fight, mate, I promise. Okay? Not like there's any avoiding it. Look where we are."

"We stay together. No split. *Ever!*" Kapaow insisted. What the bloody hell had gotten into him? "Fight as one! Must!"

"Look, we'll..." Chinny had to lie to calm him down. "We'll figure out a way, yeah? I promise. We just need to... to make them want to help. We figure out how to make it advantageous for them, and they will." That, actually, wasn't quite a lie, was it? That's what it all came down to in the end. If it was profitable, it was worthwhile. What was advantageous about saving the Yards?

Other than the fact that they were great people, good people who deserved better, he couldn't think of much. Who knew? Maybe they would. Maybe Bleak would figure it out. Perhaps if Bleak and Ghost could start seeing eye-to-eye on things instead of doubting each other so much they could formulate a way all on their own.

So that was it then. He was finally going to make an attempt at doing something simply because it was right. *Here goes nothing.* He tried to fight off the feelings of doubt that crept up in his gullet. This was possible, and even if it wasn't, the attempt would be worth it. If Bleak could see that obsessing over a small detail like the Yards held him back from making a bigger impact on the total picture, maybe he'd learn to let it go. Either way, win or lose, it was a win provided that Bleak survived. If they went back and reported, who knew if they'd be redeployed on different assignments? Chinny needed to stick with him and keep him alive until he was truly ready to lead. As hard as he was on Bleak, he felt for the boy. Chinny wasn't ready to lead when they threw it in his lap, either.

"Ghost."

"Yeah, boss?"

Chinny wiped the sweat off his face. When he looked at his hand, it was red. "What is this thing? Any ideas? Tell me ya got a theory or something." Chinny's words were worn, his voice ragged. He was more than tired and they could hear it.

"I... he's... it's ..."

"Look, mate. I'm scared, too. Don't think because I got a blank expression that means I'm not completely lost and still losing it, yeah? Take a breath. Think it through. We already know what Bleak thinks of it all. What do you think?"

"Well… it's… not the enemy, right? He helped us? Kapaow seems familiar with him somehow. Maybe… I don't know." Ghost seemed hesitant to say something.

"What is it, mate? Come on."

"It's just… I don't know if Bleak was totally wrong anymore. All of this, if you really study history, it's kind of in all of our cultures, isn't it?" Ghost said. "I don't just mean like every culture has ghosts and goblins. I mean *every* culture has some history of the dead rising up. The real historical writings all describe them as recently brought back and only temporarily employed."

"Employed?" Chinny asked.

"Well, I mean, in the stories there's always some other person or power controlling the dead. That's obviously not what this is, but who knows? Maybe the stories were just people's interpretation of it. They're all slightly different, but the one thing they all have in common is the dead come back to fight. Who's to say *that* many different cultures didn't agree on it because it was actually true? Then again, maybe we're all just hallucinating off of some undocumented trippy green frog. I mean, I really don't know. We're in nonsensical territory now. Pretty much anything could be true. If you're asking for a guess, maybe dead people can come back to life, just only in a very specific and limited way."

"Well, what do we do?" Sinner asked, his voice quivering.

"No worry… not all bad." Kapaow was the only one who sounded certain.

"Not all bad, yeah. This one helped us. Maybe there's more? Come to think of it… on a slightly different topic: why didn't you go crazy like the rest of us, Kapaow? I was so caught up in the fight I didn't have time to think about it, but none of the Yards were losing it all that much," Ghost realized.

Kapaow held up the pouch full of stones that dangled around his neck. The men stared at it, then at Kapaow, who smiled a big idiot smile. Then Kapaow's smile left as he turned and began to walk away. The Friendly had left and was walking toward the jungle, slowly getting smaller and smaller. Kapaow was following him.

"You think we should follow it?" Ghost asked.

"Kapaow's doing it," Bleak said.

"Yeah, but Kapaow's a damn slant-eye. What the fuck does a slant-eye know about following dead people?"

Everyone turned and stared at Sinner as if to say, *Was that really necessary?* He shrugged as if to say, *What? I got poop on my face or something?* Or whatever stupid, bizarre saying he felt like popping off with at the moment.

Chinny listened for any sounds in the distance, but didn't hear a thing. He looked over at the Friendly as it beckoned, crooking its finger. *Follow me.* Kapaow beckoned as well. Chinny took a deep breath to try and squelch the awkward mix of emotions and butterflies that swirled about in the pit of his stomach.

"How about a compromise? We work our way home, sure, but we stay the hell away from that thing," Chinny grumbled to himself.

"Heard that." Bleak smiled and patted Chinny on the back.

"All right. Fair's fair. Let's get the wounded up on their feet. We're going t—"

ZZZZZzzzzzzzzzzPOP!

CHAPTER 38

CHINNY

"Contact! Sniper! One o'clock! Tree line! Two-hundred-fifty yards! Fire for effect!" The screaming designations came out of Sinner's mouth before the echo from the sniper's shot, which had barely missed Chinny's head, subsided. The second wave was coming.

The message was for Kapaow, who normally would've already had his M79 grenade launcher out and doping the wind before firing. Instead, Kapaow shrugged at Sinner, who cursed out some racial slur or another. Kapaow chucked a small rock the diameter of a half-dollar and bounced it off Sinner's head.

"Bleak?" Sinner ignored the strike upside his head.

"I got nothing, man," Bleak complained.

"The Dragunov, goddamn it!"

"That thing's a piece a shit. Anybody see my M14? Or a Springfield? Or an M1?"

"Oh, for shit sakes, coon. Just grab the damn rifle—it's right there!"

Bleak submitted.

"Multiple targets on the horizon, Chinny. We gotta go," Sinner said. "Bleak, fuck the shot. We sprint for that there tree line, we're gone. That sniper can suck on his own testicles."

"NOT WITHOUT THE WOUNDED, SINNER!" Ghost screamed.

"I know that! Shut the fuck up!" Sinner roared back.

Chinny looked over at the Friendly. "Keep your heads on straight, yeah? Bleak, get us some cover fire. We make it for the tree line. Whatever the closest point is."

Bleak fired while Sinner scanned the area. "Closest spot's by that Thing. Let's just move up slow and make our way over there." Sinner pointed to a spot a few hundred meters away from it.

"Agreed." Chinny responded. "Bleak, covering fire!"

"GO!"

Chinny moved, hesitating for a moment to glance at the Friendly, still beckoning. He felt his anger all the way in his teeth. Chinny grabbed Hieu, who was wounded. Sinner followed, grabbing another injured Yard. Kapaow managed two, while

Crazy had trouble with one. The extra weight of the hobbling wounded was a burden on all of them. Chinny fired at distant targets. They did not go down, which worried him because either they were not dying or he was missing. Bleak moved up to their position and fired while they moved again.

Chinny stumbled, the weight of Hieu throwing him off balance. The mud was useless for traction. They were all falling over themselves, gasping for air, burning from the inside out as the oxygen they drew in could not satisfy the amount required. Chinny looked out where they had planned to run, only a few hundred extra meters, yet in their current state if felt like a few extra kilometers.

Bleak fired with the Dragunov. Random AK-47 fire rolled over the hills as more enemies began to pour in. How could there possibly be *another* attack after such a long hold? He looked up to see *it* motioning its ragged finger. *Follow me.* He looked at their rally point. Too far. Looked back at it. *Follow me.*

They pushed forward again. Hieu stumbled and knocked Chinny off balance. He tried to get back up, but Hieu slipped again and knocked him down a second time. Chinny was frustrated. All he wanted to do was stand, but again and again he fell. At one point, it felt like Hieu was doing more harm than good, forcing him into the mud.

Mud and gravel pelted his face. The rounds were impacting closer than desired, kicking up muck all around him. He put his eyes on the goal, dragged Hieu's weak body to its feet, and together they marched. Poor Hieu was getting tired, leaning more and more of his weight against him, stumbling, sliding onto Chinny and pulling him down. He decided to drag Hieu whether he was walking or not, tripping or not. They were going to get to their rally point. He stopped shooting back and put his eyes on the rally point. They fell again, rounds hit over top of them. He began to crawl, his eyes fixed on the goal. Hieu dragging behind him. The Friendly crooked its finger. *Follow me.*

He was exhausted, weak, suffocating. If he could just get down there with the trees as cover, things would be okay. The jungle would be like throwing a blanket over his head to cope with fear. Yet, that sort of comfort was all Chinny could think about. Sloppy, bloody mud was dripping down his neck and under his shirt. He felt it trickle over his stomach and the grit of it stick to his skin. More oozed onto his head and trickled down his ear, trailing along his neck and joining the path of muck already working its way into the waistband of his Daks. Just then, it began to rain.

Crazy Mont was having a difficult time of it. His small stature made it near impossible to carry a man more than a few feet before grounding himself. Now the rain would make it even harder. They were all tired. He knelt down next to Crazy.

"Ya gonna make it?" Crazy's eyes were as wide as saucers. "What's wrong?" Crazy wasn't looking at Chinny... it was something behind him. Chinny turned... and stopped.

Bullets stabbed the air.

Explosions erupted from the ground.

Chinny knelt down.

He'd just gotten done with the impossible. As if that wasn't enough, he had to deal with this now. Chinny sat on his arse next to Crazy. He looked at some of Hieu's teeth showing bright. He watched his men begin to lose hope and crumple below cover. Chinny breathed. At this point, it was all he knew how to do.

He hadn't realized what had happened. He'd allowed his own panic to make him focus on one thing so much he missed everything else. He was a seasoned veteran, some might say, but he made a rookie mistake. He hadn't slipped, Hieu had pushed him down. He wasn't too weak to lift Hieu back up. He...

Hieu...

He...

Hieu held Chinny down.

Chinny buried what he saw, deep down, but it kept bubbling back up. Was he running out of room to bury things? He tried to face it, to get rid of it. He couldn't bear it. Chinny tried to choke back a conflicting sense of relief. It was like a part of his mind had no decency. A part so cruel it would be slightly relieved at the thought of not having to carry the extra weight to the tree line. Fear was all it was. Right now, there was a battle inside Chinny's mind: the desire to be punished versus the instinct to survive. Chinny remained seated as the men continued on to safety.

He laid the boy against the sandbags, sat next to him, and tried to think of a prayer. *Heavenly... I bring this... out of the depths I...* He sat with Hieu. Words wouldn't mean anything anyway. Crazy attempted to drag him from his spot, but Chinny wouldn't have it. Crazy yelled for Kapaow, but the men were too far. Chinny told Crazy to go, that it'd be okay, that he wanted them to make it. The problem was: the gunfire and explosions made nonsense of everything he said. Finally, Crazy left. *Well done, mate.*

He thought about Phong and how if he hadn't panicked he'd have known what he was shooting at instead of just reacting to movement. He thought about Cadeo and how, if he hadn't been so weak, he'd rather be hated than missed by someone he cared about. The boy would never have cried.

Had he been a man, he wouldn't have done what he did during his first tour in Malaya. Had he been a man, he'd have stood up to that prick and never have felt the need to enlist in the military in the first place. Had he not left Victoria... It wasn't one mistake, it wasn't ten, it wasn't a thousand. It was an entire life of running. Time and again he was given another chance when that wasn't what he needed. All he wanted was to feel like something in the world made sense. That *something* was right.

The sky began to darken. It rumbled and barked as the rain started to fall. The sky grew blacker as lightning sliced through the clouds. The earth was scorched and smoldering. Embers were picked up in the wind and swept away. Ash touched his face and he breathed in the smoke that wafted off the dead.

Chunks of his cover became secondary missiles that chipped away at his skin. He breathed. He looked to the tree line and saw his men with still so much more ground to cover. They had turned and were yelling for him to come. He smiled and waved them on. A chunk of something gave him a bump on the nog and tossed him to the floor. He lay down, relaxed, looked up at the show from all the lightning in the sky. When was the last time he'd enjoyed nature instead of cursing it for making his job more difficult?

Hhhagk!

He dragged... he was *being* dragged... by his shirt collar. *Bloody hell?* Kapaow... that fuckin' twat ran back into the line of fire. Chinny wrestled back and forth and tried to break his hold. A fist collided with his jaw and he lost his desire to struggle. Chinny ran out of breath... so he let himself be dragged. *Bloody hell.*

"What do we do?" Bleak screamed.

Chinny looked at their rally point, two hundred meters away. Then, he looked at the Friendly still waiting at a spot only fifty meters away. Slowly his eyes focused, and he swore he saw it smiling–*Follow me.* Chinny pointed at it.

Bleak looked back at the Friendly, looked at the men, then back at the Friendly. He searched for another way. Bleak caught a fragment of something in his eye and dropped down as low as he could, blinking again and again. Ghost was running out of bandages for all the wounds. Chinny inspected his own. A few had clotted up well enough to stop the bleeding, though they'd probably get infected at some point. Bleak struggled to clear his eyes. Finally, he kept the eye closed and spoke.

"Okay, let's go!"

Kapaow reached for Chinny, who pushed his hand away. Kapaow punched him in the stomach so hard he vomited a little inside his mouth. After being punched two more times, Chinny was forcefully dragged. Kapaow roughly tossed him to the ground within the tree line.

"You *stop* running!" he screamed, and kicked him while he was down. "You live! You alive! Undahstand? You alive!" He kicked him again. "You live! So be alive! Be alive! No more berry. Dig 'em mop. No give up! No time. Okay? No time!" He went to kick him again, but gave up in frustration and walked away.

Chinny had never seen Kapaow behave that way. He turned to see he had landed next to a few dead bodies. A closer look revealed that the bodies were Americans. It was then he realized the Friendly had dragged them there. It was actually thinking beyond simple functions for survival. It was reasoning. The invading NVA would assume they'd hit what they were shooting at when they found the bodies all facing the jungle, as if they'd almost made their escape only to be cut down. He looked up at the Friendly as it began to walk backward, a seemingly complex thing. It crooked its finger. *Follow me.*

Kapaow was right. He couldn't give up, and it wasn't what he truly wanted. He needed to keep his wits about him, especially now that all the strange things were happening. He couldn't lose sight of it. Bleak needed to get to the point he could truly handle himself. Only then could Chinny rest.

What are you? How are you? Why are you?

Chinny followed.

CHAPTER 39
GHOST DOC

They hiked for hours. Only a small part of his mind had the energy to try and figure it all out. Things had become black and white in his exhaustion. If it wasn't trying to kill them, it was a friend. They could deal with the rest later. As for staying with the Yards–maybe it was a pipe dream. Still, Ghost always knew he'd do something good, unusually good, by coming to Vietnam. Saving an entire race of people sounded pretty good.

As the rain pummeled him, Ghost struggled to read the map, until finally he saw it. The similar gradient lines, the *exact* same gradient lines. He looked at a cluster of sectors. All the gradient lines were the same from one square to the next. He hadn't noticed that the lines didn't connect. They were so fine and the map was so poorly made, it wasn't a section they needed until now. It almost looked as if someone got lazy and just copied squares to fill in a gap instead of getting the necessary information. Regardless of the excuses, they were smack dab in the middle of terrain that didn't match the map anymore.

He motioned to Chinny to move everyone up. He needed to talk to them. The Friendly came up to him and stared him in the eyes. Like two tarnished, graying marbles, dead and cold, it beckoned, *Follow me.* Ghost checked on the guys. They were all on guard, simply waiting for Ghost to indicate the next move. The Friendly beckoned, *Follow me.*

We're not following you. We've been going our own way this whole time. Don't get it twisted in your head.

Incorrect maps were more common than one might think; another thing that could get you killed in Vietnam. Ghost led them away from it. He marched them in a straight line and once it seemed like they'd made their way out of the bad sector on the map, he reoriented. Soon, they'd find their way back to the Yards. He couldn't wait to eat some good food again. For hours they hiked. He hiked until his feet were so sore he couldn't take another step. He sat down to rest.

The Friendly was there, waiting.

"Bloody hell?" Chinny stared at it for a long time, then shrugged it off in an out-of-character sort of way. "All right mates. Sun's about to come up. We'll rest by day."

"I can't sleep," Bleak said, staring at the Friendly sitting a little ways from them.

They all turned and looked at it. "Well, it hasn't attacked us..." Ghost said.

Ghost cringed as Chinny and the Friendly gazed into each other's eyes. There was something different about the Friendly now. Ghost couldn't quite place it. It seemed odd to say, but it was behaving like a different person all of a sudden.

"Shit don't make no sense." Bleak broke the tension in the air. "Right? I mean, at first it was like the headshots was workin', but then I hit this one creep right in the temple with a pistol round and the bitch just kept strangling me," Bleak said. "I gouged his eyes out, kept fuckin' stranglin' me. Finally I got away. It was like the thing was *still* tryin' to get me and then finally dropped dead. What kinda shit is that? My vote's on voodoo, ya dig? What else could it be?"

"He..." Kapaow spoke, but his voice was shaky, as if he were afraid. He looked at all of them with suspicious eyes. Had Kapaow begun not to trust them? "They no see you, but feel you. They no feel or see. They fall."

"They couldn't see us, so they dropped. Unless they were close enough to *feel* us. That's why we had to dismember the bodies. They won't stop until they aren't physically capable of killing us." Ghost couldn't believe the words coming out of his mouth, but it made sense. If he took what happened as fact and not hallucination, then Kapaow's explanation made sense.

"So what does that mean? That Kapaow knew this was going to happen and didn't tell us?" Chinny hissed through his teeth.

Kapaow's eyes widened. "No..." He looked around at them like they were all rabid and he wasn't quite sure if they would attack. "Me... me elder tell me... tell me stories. Me no... me no believe, think him just want scare me. Now I see." Kapaow sounded like he was formulating a lie, but at the same time, Ghost was beginning to doubt his own ability to have any idea what was going on. So he let it go.

Ghost's hands started to shake. Things starting to make sense should have helped him to calm down. It all being logical made it harder to believe he might wake up from it. It wasn't a nightmare. It was real.

"I…" Ghost was having trouble breathing. "I gotta go to the bathroom. *Don't* follow me. I'll be *fine.*" He left so fast he knew they'd be suspicious, but he was at the breaking point and needed space for a moment.

All he could think about was teeth chewing the flesh of people he knew and loved. He tried to forget it. Then he was reminded of the slimy, squishy, popping sensation he felt when he gouged the eyes out of a friend who'd come back to life to kill him. He attempted to bury it all, but instead it unearthed itself and surrounded him. He was completely surrounded. There had to have been something else he could have done to stop them from dying. All of them.

His vision blurred and his stomach tightened. He tried to hold back with all of his might. He fell to the ground and began to convulse. Tears poured from his eyes, down the bridge of his nose, down his cheeks. Their friends, their family members, had died, and nobody seemed to care. They all just moved on to the next thing, the next goal or mission. He cried, hard, and bit down on his hand to try and stop from whimpering.

Shcka, shcka, shcka

Someone was coming. Ghost wiped his eyes. His heart raced as he tried to pretend like he was doing something important. When he looked up, Sinner had come looking for him. Ghost tried to think of an excuse, but he was caught being weak, small, girly. He didn't know what to say. He didn't know what to do. His stomach burned from embarrassment. He was back in elementary school getting laughed at and picked on. What sort of ignorant, condescending insult was Sinner going to dish out now?

Sinner didn't laugh. As a matter of fact, he didn't say anything. He just turned around, knelt down, and covered Ghost. He waited there. Ghost listened to chirping and deep, muffled thuds softly erupting in the distance. No insults came. No mocking, no arguing, Sinner just protected him. Ghost gathered himself and wiped his face again. They always looked out for each other. All of them. How could he have ever forgotten that? They walked back quietly, no words needed. The rest of the guys' conversation gradually grew louder as they neared their camp.

"Same thing. One of 'em grabbed on me daks after I unloaded on him."

"What's a dak, boss?"

"Fuckin' trousers, mate."

"Oh, please. You talk that Aussie jibba jabba like people know what the fuck you sayin'."

"All right, ya twats. Right then. We can't really kill 'em. We can disable them, though." As they walked back, the guys were discussing methods for efficiently taking out the dead. "A Thing comes up your way, you put a round in every joint. Maybe Doc takes a closer look, dissects 'em or whatevah."

"I'm not… gonna do that … not even slightly." Everyone stared at Ghost like *he* was weird. "I'm not even poking one with a stick. It's just not happening."

The Crazy Mont said something that didn't sound like Vietnamese, or French, or even Polynesian for that matter. Kapaow raised his eyebrows approvingly and nodded his head. When he noticed everyone staring at him with confusion, he translated.

"Hips, hips, head," Kapaow said.

Everyone raised their eyebrows and nodded. "It makes sense," Ghost agreed. "It's simple. Shoot each side of the hips and you disable the joints there. Stops it from walking anymore. Then take out its skull and hope to get the eyes in the process. Just stay clear after that point so it doesn't grab you. Don't accidentally brush up against it or anything. If you can't beat the Risers, just disable them. I like it." Ghost was impressed.

"Were you gonna call 'em Risers? 'Cause I was thinking about callin' 'em Creeps." Bleak was seriously asking about what to name the Risers. *What a Melvin.*

"Well, yeah. I mean, they're dead… and then they *rise up.* Creeps doesn't really make any sense." Ghost tried to sound polite, but didn't.

"No, man. They *creepy.* Get it?"

"I was actually referring to them as Things myself," Chinny added.

"Yeah. Things ain't bad, boss. I guess that's better than Risers."

"Well, shit, ya'll. Why not just call 'em DBMs?" Sinner spat. "That's what I been callin' 'em. Sounds more militaristic. Ya know what I mean?"

"What's it stand for?" Ghost realized the answer to his own question. "Oh! Dead Body Moving, right?" he whispered with enthusiasm.

"There ya go, ha ha. Makes perfect sense, but it also sounds all jargon and abbreviated and confusing and shit, just the way the service likes it. Am I right?" They nodded.

"Doesn't DBM already stand for the Department of Budget Management?" Everyone looked at Ghost like he was a purple ham sandwich. "I'm just saying. Riser makes sense, too."

"Man, you see any budget management out here?" Bleak said. "Damn."

"Right, right, right. Okay then. Ya see a DBM–" Chinny tried to keep the conversation moving.

"D-Bams. Let's call 'em D-Bams. Two syllables instead of three."

"D-Bam. That's tight. I like that, Sin."

"Yeah, then we could be like D-B-M-S-O-S."

"What's that?" Ghost thought out loud. "Dead Bodies Moving, Shoot On Sight, right?"

"Ha, ha. Yep. We could be like, Da Bam Sauce, bitch! When we fuck somebody up. That's Da Bam Sauce right there." Sinner smiled… but Risers was still good, too.

Then Chinny said, "Okay." He stopped them and moved the conversation back on point. "So we have an idea how to stop them better. That's good. Let's think about getting back to the village, yeah? We're still a long way and low on… everything."

"Guys, look. This is going to sound crazy, but…" he hesitated.

"What, man? Come on, blood. Spit it out, Ghost," Bleak encouraged.

"Maybe we should trust him," he said, pointing at the DBM.

"Did I just hear you right? *Him?* Don't you mean *it?*" Chinny demanded.

"Look. He saved us. I didn't like it either, but he's still here and hasn't done anything bad. I'm only saying that maybe he deserves some respect for that."

"Yeah, Dingo. What? You want him to drink at a different water fountain now?" Sinner added.

"Hey. Why you think the DBM did it?" Bleak's question made everyone look its way.

"Well, people do things because they want something. That Thing, that DBM… I haven't the foggiest what it wants, but I'd assume it wants something," Chinny said.

"We should really name this guy." Ghost tried to sneak some humanity into the conversation. "How about Ralphie?" Ghost had a dog named Ralphie once. Not that this Thing was their pet, but it was loyal, and it was the first name that popped into his head.

"Fuck it. All in favor, those opposed. Done." Sinner didn't actually wait for anyone to vote.

Everyone got quiet, and Ghost spoke up at that point. "That was way more of a conversation than we should have been having out here in the open." Everyone seemed to realize it at the same time. "I think we're still in trouble from whatever's driving people crazy."

Suddenly, they were distracted when something strange happened.

Well… strang*er*.

CHAPTER 40
CHINNY

Ralphie convulsed slightly before seizing in place.
What? Are ya dead-er now, ya son of a bitch?
Chghk
Ralphie jerked back to life. He looked around like he'd forgotten where he was. He blinked as he took in the scenery and the people as if they were all new. He spent an unusual amount of time staring at Chinny. Ralphie-the-DBM's movements seemed more graceful now. He seemed to be smiling. Not the polite sort of smile, but a smile of someone sending flirtatious intent. Chinny almost vomited, though he couldn't tell if it was from the DBM or the ham and lima beans C ration he was eating.

Before he knew it, they were packing up again. It was dusk as they began to travel through the tangled jungle. In some areas the vegetation was so thick that they were forced back onto the trails. They broke from the trail as often as they could, however. Ralphie seized again. When he regained consciousness, he moved more slowly. He fell further and further toward the back of the team. His movements lacked the grace he had picked up earlier. Instead, he clomped along like an angry child. From time to time, he'd knock his fists together. Perhaps something remained of who the person was with their little fidgets and mannerisms.

"I hear some action goin' on up the trail." *Fuckin' hell!* Chinny's heart jumped as Bleak appeared next to him.

"What do ya make of it?" Chinny tried to sound calm. He'd been so focused on the DBM he'd lost track of his surroundings.

"Sounds like screams. Too far to tell. Could be a fuckin' pig for all I know. There's too much shit goin' on tonight. I got a bad feelin', though." Bleak's voice shook. Chinny tried not to look afraid, hoping to lead by example and show Bleak to not be afraid.

"Well, what do you want to do?" Chinny asked.

"I... I don't know... go around?"

"That a question or an answer?" Chinny preferred sounding angry to afraid.

"Damn, Chin. What it be like, blood?"

"Question or an answer, mate? Man the fuck up." Bleak appeared hurt. "We're too late. Don't ya get it? This is your fuckin' show, mate. It's gonna be all you soon."

"My mutha fuckin' show? Blood, you crazy, son. Fuck am I supposed to do in some shit where—where *dead* muthafuckas don't *die?*"

"Mate, this half-in, half-out shite ain't gonna fly, yeah? Yes, we're stuck in an unknown, but what does it matter? Did the mission suddenly change? Are we suddenly not going to do what we're going to do because things didn't work out the way we wanted them to? Fuck all, mate. That's it. We're at an impasse. Ya make the fuckin' call." Chinny felt awkward. Bleak didn't enjoy being cornered. But what else could he do?

"We should avoid contact," Bleak said, only half certain of himself.

"Intel's the standing order," Chinny replied almost immediately.

"We should… go check it out?"

"Look, mate. You want something, you say so. With *certainty*. How many times I gotta tell ya? Didn't they already teach you this?"

"You always ask me that. I told you already: it's *different* out here. Everything's *different.* I know how to lead people in a forest and a desert. There's all kinds of giant spiders and shit out here. Way worse than what they got back in the States."

Chinny slapped Bleak in the face, leaving Bleak speechless.

Chinny had a bad feeling, too. "Look. I was afraid when I got started," Chinny said, and part of him died when he said it. "I'm afraid now." Bleak stared at him with wide eyes. "I'll probably always be afraid." Chinny felt terrible as he spoke. "That shite Ghost is always spouting about being born on one mountain but meant for another? A man chooses to walk through the valley, while a boy chooses to hide out on his mountain. Understand? You're good, Bleak. A more fearsome soldier than most. But it's time to come down off your mountaintop, son."

"I'm just… what if we go around and it's a bunch of Montagnards getting slaughtered up there and we could have saved them?" Bleak's eyes were wet like a baby deer.

Chinny sighed. What was the right answer for that? "Well, Bleak. At this very moment, more Montagnards than you're willing to count have lost their lives in horrible, unimaginable ways. We can only do what we can do, mate."

Chinny watched Bleak stare up at the jungle and listened to the echoing screams. He tried to imagine what the boy was feeling as he listened to the screams that were in a language he didn't understand. Maybe it was Yards. Maybe it wasn't.

"All right," Bleak's voice quivered slightly. "Stay on mission. If we could call it in, we would, but we don't have the equipment." Bleak gritted his teeth and forced the words out. "Village first, then we can help other people. We're going around."

Chinny knew what Bleak was suffering. He'd suffered it himself so many times before. What was the right move? What were the consequences? What was the right answer? As Chinny observed Bleak moving out, his shoulders hung low on his frame. He knew what Bleak hadn't accepted yet. There was no right answer.

Thump

A Viet Cong stumbled out of the jungle, AK in hand, his face shocked at what he saw. Everyone froze. He must have gotten separated from his unit or something. It was easy to get turned around at night. Chinny's heart fell out of his sock he was so stunned.

Crunch.

Ralphie punched the bloke so hard in the face he hit the ground and started twitching. He was dead. Ralphie collapsed again right next to the body, the both of them face down in the mud. This time, he didn't get up. Instead, the other body stood up. It snapped and cracked, the behavior reminding Chinny of a glove being put on. It turned and looked at them and the words that escaped his mouth surprised him.

"Ralphie, is that you?" Chinny asked.

"I *told* ya'll mutha fuckas I knew what I was talkin' 'bout. Ghost soldiers, baby. Fuck ya'll. Come on. We movin' out before his buddies notice he's gone."

CHAPTER 41

BLEAK

"I'm tellin' you: it moved, man," Bleak said.

After walking for another few hours, Bleak noticed something strange with a dead body laid out on the side of a path.

"Bleak, foregoing the fact that you kinda-sorta knew what was goin' on 'round here 'fore ever'body else: I'm standing the fuck next to ya, partner. It ain't movin'."

"I said it moove-*duh*, like past tense. You ain't see it. I did."

"Kapaow, Ghost, Crazy, perimeter. What do ya got, mates?"

"Bleak thinks it moved."

"How crazy is that? Dead bodies are moving all around us, mate."

"Yeah, boss, but this one's rotten." Sinner's point was interesting.

"Ya think it matters?" Chinny wondered.

"Well how the fuck is it supposed to move if its muscles are all goo?"

"Hmmm … go take Ghost's place. Tell him I want to talk to him." Chinny stared at the corpse.

"What's up, boss?" Ghost asked when he walked up.

"Bleak thinks it moved."

"So? Everything's moving these days."

"Sinner doesn't think it makes any sense because if its muscles are goo, how did it move?"

"Hmmm… how much did it move?"

"Shoot. I don't know, blood. I saw the shit out the corner of my eye."

"Did it try to get up? Or did it just twitch?"

"Probably twitched."

"Hmmm…" Ghost thought for a moment before blurting out, "OH, BOY! Its eyes twitched a little. Ya think it's watching us?"

"Please. That Thing can't see us. Look at how milky its eyes are," Bleak pointed out.

"That's true …" Ghost agreed. "Maybe it's—"

Crunch!

The New-Ralphie stomped on its head and crushed it.

"Fuck you do that shit for? We was tryin' to figure some shit, man." Bleak punched it in the arm.

"Oh, man… it wasn't watching us… was it?" Ghost and New Ralphie shared a glance. "It *was* listening." They all scanned the jungle.

What else was tracking them?

CHAPTER 42
GHOST DOC

They walked through the dense foliage one meticulous step at a time, and he caught sight of a very strange formation coming into view–some sort of natural tower of rock with vegetation at the top. Of *course* it wasn't on the map. When it came into full view, he saw Ralphie was already standing at the foot of it. Ghost looked back for a second, swearing they'd left Ralphie behind a while ago. He was too tired to feel afraid.

As the cliff face came into view. He noted how jagged it was and the way the rock seemed to twist and writhe, like some tortured soul petrified in stone. The way the surface had eroded, it looked like screaming faces. Ghost imagined the gouges in the rock like eye sockets would make excellent handholds. The longer he stared at it, the less he noticed the rest of the team staring at it with him. It was like an epiphany.

"We're stuck in an entire country dead set on making us insane," Ghost concluded. "The enemy gives it to us. We get to the safety of a base and turn on a radio, only to find it waiting for us there. We even get it from our own people. Every direction we turn it's as if something is trying to wear us down. It wasn't until we'd already been beaten down pretty good that the full-blown insanity started. Whatever's messing with us, it probably doesn't need to work all that hard. We're not dead yet, though. We must be doing something right." He reached out. It felt good to touch the rock.

"Them in you head," Kapaow said. "Comenation, displin. Trust you instinct. Bweeve in you heart. Keep you on right path."

Ghost stared at the rock, stared at his hand touching the rock. He watched Kapaow's hand pull his away, felt him turn his face so they could look at each other. "You okay?" Kapaow asked.

"Yeah. I'm fine," Ghost replied. "I wonder what's at the top."

Together, they all stared up the face and wondered the same thing.

"Halved and quartered..." Ghost whispered, but no one responded. "People used to dismember the bodies of their enemies. That never made any sense to me growing up. Who would care if they saw a bunch of mangled bodies everywhere? A battle's a battle. Granted, teeth marks are pretty hard to explain… then again… it would make sense why so much ordnance gets used on points of failure…"

"Oh no…" Kapaow gasped. "You mean they touch you goobament?"

"They? Touch our government? I mean, if it is a *they*, I suppose anything's possible. It would certainly explain every stupid order that's ever been given in the history of warfare."

"Go Doc."

The rock was almost black, swirled with streaks of red, like blood mixed into charred wood. He felt a tingling sensation as he touched the stone, felt it through his whole body. Ghost felt… different… felt compelled to—

"Go Doc, me need to talk. I know beddy much more about what is it. You help me tell them," Kapaow whispered in Ghost's ear. Everyone else broke off and discussed various things amongst themselves, giving Ghost a chance to admire the rock.

Ralphie started to climb. Ghost watched him.

"Look at him go. Wow. I didn't think he could climb. Nice job, Ralphie." Ghost smiled.

"Go Doc."

"What is it, Kapaow?" Ghost asked. Ralphie looked at him, smiled an oozing smile, and motioned, *Follow me.*

"I not say before. You all not ready, jump in my throat."

"You mean…" Ghost could barely find the attention to listen to Kapaow. The rock was just so… fascinating. "…you mean, jump *down* your throat. We wouldn't do that, Kapaow. Whatever you need to say, just say it to everyone."

"Me tell you, you tell them, yes?"

"Sure."

"They tree fairy. I know, crazy, crazy. But no, beddy real. Long, long time we fight them. I teach you, you teach them. Dey beddy fox, you know?"

"Very fox? Oh, they're clever? Clever like a fox?"

"Yes, yes, Go Doc. They not strong, but danger much. Much, much danger. Hate human. Use us. Hurt us. Amuse us."

"You mean abuse us?"

"Yes. beddy bad, but hard to see. Me think dey here now. Some-a-time you see dem, side of eyes."

"Side of eyes? Oh, you can see the fairies in your peripheral vision sometimes? Man, that's so funny you say that. I swear, every once in a while I see someone standing *right* next to me, but I look and there's no one there." Ghost said without looking at Kapaow, without concerning himself much with the conversation. The rock was so smooth, but once his hand reached a hold it was a perfect little cup-shaped ledge… so easy to climb.

"Yes. You see dem, See dem all time but not always know. Dimiss it like crazy man."

"Yeah. I could see dismissing it. We're all so tired all the time. Heck, I just figured it was a shadow of something above me, or a cloud passing that played a trick on my eyes." Ghost's voice was growing fainter. He allowed it to happen. He didn't need to be loud to admire the rock.

"Yes, but you see dem dead fight, yes? You know me no crazy, yes?"

"No, Kapaow. I don't think you're crazy at all. I guess you were right to hesitate, though. If a few weeks ago you had told me that tree fairies existed, that they were evil and demented creatures that preyed on human life, that they were all around us and could influence our minds while raising the dead, I'd have said you were crazy, too. Now, after everything we've seen, I can't help but think of all the cultures I've studied and how hints have been there all along. The fairies must like to hide in plain sight. It probably takes less effort. I think of all the insane frenzies society has allowed itself to get caught up in throughout history. Witches, tulip mania. We've completely lost our minds whenever they wanted, huh?

"It's always been there, though, hasn't it? The Japanese had forest demons. Vikings mention Loki. Actually, now that I think about it, I remember when I was a little boy: I met a real live Indian. Not like in the movies. This guy was just a regular guy. He had jeans on. He told me a tale about a human-like creature that preyed on people, drove them mad, and could even raise the dead. Even our own fairytales used to be pretty horrific and involve people making foolish decisions, as if they were taken over by some sort of influence. It would make sense that what we're facing is nothing new; like searching for your keys when they're already in your hand. They're here. We just can't seem to bring ourselves to notice. Right?" Ghost turned to Kapaow and smiled.

"Yes!" Kapaow smiled back.

"I understand now, Kapaow. I'm sorry we made you feel like we wouldn't listen," Ghost said blankly.

"Yes! You tell them?"

"Sure, once we all get to the top. It's getting late. Don't want to climb in the dark, that's for sure. Don't worry, I'll… make them understand. I'll get Chinny to understand, and he'll get Bleak to understand."

They watched Ralphie, the way his movements seemed to tear at his joints, like things were dislocating and popping back into place.

Cli-clack, cli-clunk, cli-clack, cli-clunk.

"Someone coming," Kapaow said frantically.

Part of Ghost knew he should be scrambling for concealment and cover. He knew he shouldn't be standing in front of the cliff. Maybe he could hide at the top.

"Hey!" Kapaow whisper-yelled.

Crazy and Kapaow forced Ghost to the ground. He wanted to climb until he reached the top. He wanted to *live* at the top. Ghost stared at the cliff through the vegetation behind which they had hidden him. When he heard Kapaow talking in a dialect he didn't recognize, he figured it was safe to touch the face again. He heard Kapaow say something about a radio. Chinny and Sinner talked a little, talked about Ghost. He saw some hands waving in front of his face, but nothing interesting enough to make him want to look away.

"Where your luck?" Crazy asked in Ghost's ear.

He was referring to the stone jewelry the villagers loved to make. Ghost was pretty sure he hadn't taken his off, but when he felt around, it was gone.

I bet some of this cliff rock would make pretty jewelry.

"Luck help you fight them out you head, Go Doc. Where you luck?" Crazy had brought Kapaow over at some point to look at him. Ghost wasn't sure when.

He could chip some cliff rock off at the top for sure.

Ghost looked up and watched Ralphie climb. He tried to lift a finger and point. It was amazing that the Thing could climb. He reached out to point, but his arm didn't do what he asked it to. Instead, his hands grabbed the rock, even though it felt like his brain was asking to point. He reached out and touched the stone.

Ghost started to climb.

CHAPTER 43

KAPAOW

What do I do?

Some villagers had shown up. They acted like they knew Kapaow, but he didn't recognize them. Ghost was climbing, and the rest of the team was distracted. Was this coincidence? Or were they being attacked by the Tree Fairies again?

Kapaow closed his eyes and tried to speak to the souls of the Earth, to the souls of his ancestors and those of his family. When he spoke, the feelings that came back to him were garbled and chaotic, like a thousand people screaming different directions to an unknown destination he needed to reach.

He was starting to feel exhausted. It took so much, in so many different ways, to defy *them*. One had to take pristine care of their body, had to get enough sleep, had to conquer inner demons, had to reach out to others and be open, had to love, had to be everything, all the time. Kapaow, for so long, had thought he was very good at this. Now, his body was tired. He had not slept in a very long time, and it frightened him that such basic things could lead to the undoing of his efforts. But they were.

He looked at his stones in the pouch around his neck. They must only help to ease the effect on the mind, not obliterate it. Did it make sense to climb up and bring Ghost back down, or did it make sense to climb up and see where the corpse was leading them? The corpse knew where it was going, but Kapaow didn't, and he had trusted so many before to do right by his people, only to be abandoned at their most vulnerable moments.

I go up there, and maybe I find some kind of rebel tree fairy looking for allies. It is clear, though, that my own people are not its priority. Yet, I can't forget that perhaps my assumptions are incorrect. Perhaps he's not a rebel at all. Perhaps it's just a trap.

It couldn't be a trap. Could it? No. It made no sense. Why help when they were sure to die? It could have just left them there. But no, it fought for them. It guided them.

"Hello, friend," one of the strangers greeted Kapaow like an old friend, but Kapaow didn't recognize him.

"Hello… forgive me. I can't remember where we last met?" Kapaow knew they had never met, but did not want to appear rude.

"You do not remember your distant cousins, Ling Pao?" He knew Kapaow's real name. They must have met before. Kapaow never forgot a face, though. It seemed odd.

"Ah, of course," Kapaow lied, and smiled. The man approached and gave him a hug.

As Kapaow gave a warm embrace to a friend he supposed he never knew he had, the hug he received in return was… difficult to describe: cold, seething, as if anger were behind every pat on his back. The man's eyes were tense and wide; the way someone looked at a person who had angered them.

"I am sorry to have offended you, but I visit so many villages."

"No apologies needed, *Ling Pao*." The way he said his real name sounded almost mocking, but in such a subtle way that it was too faint to acknowledge openly or address directly. It made Kapaow uncomfortable.

"So what are the chances of you crossing paths with us on such an unlikely day?" Kapaow asked, hoping to coax as much information as possible without directly asking any questions that might reveal his own thoughts in the process. Who were these people?

"Not very likely at all. We are glad to be of help."

They aren't looking up.

It was true, that seemed rather odd, did it not, to never look up at two men climbing a cliff face? Especially when one was slowly dripping blood? Though, as Kapaow gazed up himself, hoping to draw their attention, he noted that they were far enough now that it simply looked like two men climbing. Perhaps they climbed all the time and were simply unimpressed and uninterested.

When he looked back to remark on their climbing skills, the man was still staring at him with that same strange, subtle… what? What was the emotion on his face, and why did he not smile?

"Help?" Kapaow asked.

"We have communications at our village. We can help you."

"We never requested–"

"Are you saying you don't want it?" the man challenged, a small smile forming on his face; polite. Somewhere in the background… it was as if he were mocking Kapaow.

"Yes, we need communication. It's just that–"

"We too had soldiers at our village… but they're gone now. We don't know how to use the equipment, but perhaps one of them does. We could use supplies as well. Not that we can't fend for ourselves, but medicine would be helpful."

So that was it. They were feeling betrayed at the moment, resentful, as Kapaow had soldiers that didn't abandon him. Now it made sense. "I am afraid they were likely called out to A Shau. That did not end well for most. They may not return."

"Oh…" The man… didn't seem surprised. "Well… we didn't feel they were all too helpful anyway. How have your efforts been with these Americans? Any more fruitful?"

Kapaow wasn't sure what to say to the man.

"Where's your friend going?" the man asked as he looked up at Ghost. "That doesn't look safe at all… you should probably go get him down, shouldn't you?"

The man spoke very plainly. There were no fluctuations in his voice, no signs of balanced emotions, or emotions at all for that matter. It made Kapaow feel uneasy. Was Kapaow just being silly, overly sensitive? Or was something wrong here? He was so tired.

I can't tell.

"Hey, you should probably help your friend, no?" the man repeated.

Something felt wrong about leaving Ghost to climb alone, yet something felt wrong about leaving Chinny as well. Ghost would make it to the top before he could catch up to him, yet Kapaow would catch up to him the fastest. Leaving Chinny with the rest of the team might not be all bad, but none of them could resist *them* the way that Kapaow could.

In the end, Ghost was more at risk being alone than the rest of the team was sticking together and waiting for them to return. Splitting up was never a good idea. It was as if the decision had been made *for* him by circumstance. Now he was funneled toward a specific path, incapable of choosing another. Was this fate, or was it the tree fairies, forest demons, Loki, whatever they were? Kapaow's attention was drawn higher, to the corpse climbing above, staring at him.

It smiled.

CHAPTER 44
CHINNY

"Bloody hell's he doing?" Chinny asked.

"Who?" Sinner asked.

Chinny pointed to the DBM and Ghost scaling the cliff face, trying not to tremble as he did. "Ghost, what the fuck are you doing, mate?" Ghost didn't respond. "Ghost!" Chinny yelled.

Everyone stared at him awkwardly; Chinny's voice had quivered. He struggled to bury his thoughts and focus on the task at hand. He tried to control his breathing, but felt as if he were falling, his heart collapsing inside his chest. His throat was dry. He'd had enough of the surprises and desperately wanted to get back to somewhere familiar.

Chinny's heart was pounding so loud in his ears that he could barely hear the blokes talking. A group of Yards had shown up, seemingly out of nowhere, and surprised the shite right out of Chinny. Thankfully, Kapaow had some relation to them, and they'd agreed to help them. It was odd. Chinny had difficulty trusting them. Not because he doubted Kapaow's bond with them. It was quite simply that he had grown accustomed to everything going tits-up whenever possible. Chances were this would be no different. Still, they couldn't just sit around waiting to die, could they?

He watched Ghost climb. How was the DBM able to climb so well? It paused to stare at Chinny, smiling a ragged and vacant smile, mocking him. Its knowing eyes, like it already knew all of his secrets... like it knew things about him that he'd buried so deep he'd forgotten they were there. He hated it.

The boys could handle themselves. Chinny just needed to get out of here for a bit and catch his breath.

That's all. You just need to escape for a little while, and then you can come back even better. That's it.

"We ain't got all day, boss."

"I hear you, Sinner. Kapaow, see if you can get up there and figure out what's wrong with him, yeah?"

"We all go. Stay together," Kapaow responded.

"No. You get him. The rest cover ya. You're the best climber. It's less risky if you go," Chinny demanded.

Kapaow shook his head. "Them say they have comms. We get Ghost. Then we go with them."

"Comms? Where?"

"Not too far. Too far without Ghost. We go for him, then go with them."

"All right. Well, you go get him. We'll wait," Chinny said. Kapaow hesitated for a moment, staring at Chinny with concerned eyes. What was his problem? "Just go get him, Kapaow."

Kapaow left, and it was only then that Chinny realized he had no way of communicating with the other Yards. One smiled at Chinny, big and wide and toothless. Chinny smiled back, and the little man patted him on the shoulder, right where he had an awful bruise from some of the debris that had come down on him at A Shau.

By the time Chinny looked up to check on Kapaow, he was already halfway up the wall. The man was fast. All this time of running and fighting, trying to escape, trying to make sense out of the DBMs, it was only now that Chinny tried to get his mind back on track as to what exactly it was they were doing. It was getting back to the village. It didn't feel like that was the goal, not lately, but yes… they needed to get back to–

"You can go, Chin. We got this, man. We'll be right behind you," Bleak said as he continued to call out holds to Kapaow on the wall.

No. We need to stick togeth–

One of the Yards tapped Chinny on his bruise again. He motioned to him that they should leave. Chinny nodded that he knew, but then pointed to Bleak as if to say–*Just as soon as they're done, mate.*

The man began speaking in his native tongue–something only Kapaow could translate, of course. Chinny nodded and smiled, hoping to keep up good diplomacy. There was no way he was going with them, unable to communicate.

Fog had rolled in and made it difficult to see very far, but he couldn't help but be distracted by something a few meters behind the little man. It was a woman, gazing at him gently from afar. Her features were soft, and yet there was a certain sense of power in the way she held herself. He looked into her eyes and expected her to look away. Her gaze remained fixed on him.

He felt weakened by her, and struggled to retain some sense of power in her presence. He tried to bury his guilt, bury his rage, bury everything that she might judge harshly. He tried to be more than what he was. They gazed into each other and everything else faded away from Chinny's concern.

The little man looked over his shoulder, and then looked back at Chinny as if he were a complete fool. The other Yards looked as well. Unsatisfied with what they saw, they looked back at him rather curiously. Chinny didn't know what to do, didn't know what to say. He just kept gazing at her. The longer he peered into her eyes the more he realized they were the most striking sort of green he'd ever seen. They almost seemed to shimmer.

She turned and walked away. "Come with us," she said without turning back. Her voice carried through the air powerfully, hypnotically. "The path leads directly to the village. Your men will find us easily, and it is only a short walk. Everything will be okay. Come with us." She turned back briefly, her shimmering eyes glowing through the fog. She was beautiful.

Chinny watched her, feeling as if something momentous were passing him by. Guilt crept from his gullet as he wondered if he'd been a fool for even thinking something had been shared in that moment. After a few seconds she turned and looked at him again. She crooked her finger as if to say, *Follow me*, and smiled an inviting smile. They shouldn't split up. They should stick together.

Chinny followed.

CHAPTER 45

BLEAK

"Where the fuck is that muthafucka fuckin' goin'?" Bleak didn't mean to sound so panicked, but didn't they already say they was gonna stick together? What the fuck?

"Damn... he couldn't have gotten far." Sinner waved his hand like it wasn't a big deal. "Take care of Ghost. He must be losing it," Sinner growled. "Keep everybody with ya in case you gotta catch his dumb ass. I'll go get Chinny and bring him back."

"Hurry up."

"Yeah, yeah."

Bleak had climbed before, but like most of the shit they put him through, the training version was nothing like the real deal The rock was dusty and stuck to the sweat on his hands, making the holds too slippery to grab. He didn't have any chalk to soak up the sweat. He dusted off his hands and latched on to a few holds. He slipped the edges of his boots into the little holds below and lifted himself up. He slipped off.

"Kapaow, get him. We wait," Crazy said.

Bleak nodded. He was just curious was all. The way the stone had eroded, it looked like millions of spiders sitting on top of each other, making one giant structure. He heard some scraping noises growing closer. He listened. It happened again. What the hell was that? He leaned in further and—

It *moved*.

It was a little pebble, rolling inside a crack. What the fuck was that? Was the rock going to break away? Was an earthquake coming? Would the guys fall? It turned and rolled around and then broke apart. Little splinters of it swung out. Bleak froze. He didn't breathe. He didn't blink.

Something slowly turned its attention to Bleak. He cringed. Those beady little black eyes that didn't move just looked at him like he wasn't shit. Those hairy legs that could climb all over his body, anywhere they wanted to go, and he couldn't stop it. Those fangs that could kill him with one bite or rot his flesh and make him ugly for the rest of his life. It was a spider that seemed to come *from* the rock. It stirred and wriggled its legs, flicking them across the stone.

The spider *JUMPED!* It landed on his neck and he felt its legs flicking and sliding up and down, those scratchy hairs digging into his skin. He gasped and let out a cry so loud he thought back to when he was a kid and woke up to cockroaches crawling all over his body. He was paralyzed.

GOD, please don't kill me. Please don't let it bite me. I don't want to die.

He felt its legs fluttering across his skin and felt his skin tighten all over his entire body, his neck hairs standing on end. It was all he could do to not scream out at the top of his lungs. It crawled over his ear as his hands kept missing it, moving toward his ear canal.

He shook it off, and as it fell, it spread its legs out wide and slowly floated to the ground. As soon as it landed it scurried off with a terrible speed.

"Crazy!" Bleak yelled.

Bleak froze. Over the whole cliff face it looked like the rocks were moving. Ghost climbed on, Ralphie climbed on. Crazy stared at Bleak. Bleak stared at the moving rocks. There was no way. It must have been hitting him, whatever had hit Ghost. He was losing it.

Just keep it together. You're losing it like Ghost, right? Stay focused. The shit ain't real. If it don't make sense, then it ain't real, ya dig? It ain't real.

If he was losing his mind, it wasn't like at A Shau. This was worse Maybe it was real? How could it be real?

Rocks and pebbles and boulders began to break away. Dirt and debris fell from them and landed on the ground.

It ain't real, Bleak. If it were real, Crazy would freak out, too. So it can't be real. Right?

The ground began to move. Spiders of all different sizes were scurrying right for him.

They're not real.

The ground moved like water.

They're not real! Let 'em crawl on ya. You'll see. They can't hurt ya.

They closed the distance before he'd even had a chance to breathe.

Hold still, Bleak. Then you'll see it's not real. It can't be real.

Crazy walked toward him and right into the spiders. They crawled on him, but he didn't react.

See? He'd freak out if they were real!

The blood pumped inside Bleak so hard it felt like his skin would tear open and the blood would pour out. Then the spiders caught up to him.

They crawled up his boots. He felt them crawling underneath his pant legs and up the bare skin of his thigh. Bleak couldn't breathe, he couldn't think. He couldn't take the feeling of them crawling under his shirt. He saw a man covered in spiders reaching out to him.

Bleak ran.

CHAPTER 46
GHOST

It was so serene at the top. The sun was warm on Ghost's face, but the air wasn't as thick as it felt a moment ago–not as humid, not so unbearable and suffocating. It was calm and relatively quiet, with only the sounds of birds chirping and bugs buzzing. It was nice.

Kapaow was standing over him, asking him where his bracelet was. He held up his wrist where the brass bracelet dangled. Kapaow shook his head and asked about his other bracelet, the one with stones. Ghost didn't know what he was talking about.

A few feet away, Ralphie stood, staring. Ghost had been holding the map, they had been choosing where to go, yet still the Thing beckoned, *Follow me*. Perhaps they had always been following it; they simply hadn't realized or hadn't accepted the fact. Was it such a bad thing, in the end? Ralphie had always led them to safety, hadn't he?

Ghost pointed toward Ralphie, urging Kapaow to watch while he pulled back some vines that covered a mound of earth. Kapaow helped Ghost to his feet and together they drew closer. There was no dirt behind the vines, just a cavernous black hole. He stared at the darkness, and felt lost in it, drawn to it, sedated by it. Suddenly, the outline of a face formed within the black. It drew closer and closer until he could see its eyes. They were the most vivid blue he had ever seen. The longer he looked, the more the blue seemed to… move. It was like looking at the ocean concentrated into an iris, swaying and flexing, shimmering–hypnotizing. Ghost thought of Chinny, and for a moment the fog cleared from his mind.

"A boy with blue eyes…" Ghost whispered to himself.

The boy calmly regarded Ralphie for a moment, who reached into a tattered pocket and handed the boy some stone jewelry like what Kapaow had been asking about. Had those belonged to Ghost? The boy inspected the stones briefly—his eyes regarded Ghost in the most peculiar way.

"Most injuries in this war occur from shrapnel, correct?"

Ghost flinched. The voice seemed to come from all around him. The boy looked in Ghost's eyes, but his lips did not move. It felt like Ghost's skull vibrated the sounds of words through his teeth.

"Your *flak jackets,* as you call them, protect you from the shrapnel, but little else. Regard the stones with as much value. They can protect against less direct, yet more common dangers, but will hold less and less value as others like me become more… interested in you."

A memory popped into his mind: of him stuffing stones in Bleak's pocket, who quickly took charge of the situation at A Shau. The Yards never took off their stones and they'd lost their minds the least of any of them. It couldn't all be the stones, though. There had to be something more.

"Distractions, Jeffrey, doubt: they plague your intellect. It is why I arranged for you to be here without the other members of your team. The level and severity of your doubt is of course by our design. I need you to learn clarity now, however. I will need your entire team for what must be done. I will need *you* most of all."

With that, the boy tossed the stones over the edge of the cliff. Turning back to Ralphie, he raised his arm, and Ralphie raised his own in a mirror image of the boy's. He smiled briefly, as if playing some sort of game. Then, like a bored cat, he waved his hand and the DBM collapsed to the ground.

Ghost felt dizzy. Not from losing his mind to some strange type of hysteria, not from drugs or poison. He was dizzy from trying to process too much information at once. For the first time in his life he wished he were a little more like Bleak. Bleak didn't need to sort through the information in a straight line. He could leap from A, skip most of the alphabet and somehow land smack-dab on Z with an intimidating accuracy.

"You hold great value, Jeffrey. I believe each of your team has a distinct role in our journey. Brooklyn especially. Very much the tip of the spear, that one. To be fair, much of your team is starting to open themselves. Memories, important memories, are being unearthed. Once exposed and faced, the true training can begin. Yet you are the catalyst, Jeffrey; the thing that leads to their willingness to change. Other components hold their value, yet *you* are what will bring it all to life."

The words felt as if they'd first come through Ghost's skull and then impacted the wrong side of his ear drums. He tried so hard to process what was happening, to understand it and determine what to do about it.

"My name is LamaNaCa-Ah Ma. Familiarity is likely to aid in the… adjustment process," the boy said, a sinister grin creeping across his face. "As we are already acquainted as such, you may continue to refer to me as… Ralphie."

Without ever moving his lips, the boy nodded as if the words rattling through Ghost's teeth were his own. On perhaps the hottest day he'd ever experienced in the 'Nam, Ghost shivered. His stomach ached, like something was chewing its way out.

"No, Jeffrey," Ralphie said tenderly, "it is not a parasite. It is not magic, ghosts, or extraterrestrial beings. Nor is it demons or anything else you or your team may have theorized. In truth, what you have faced since before setting foot in these lands is something far worse.

"For the first time, it appears I have encountered a strain of your kind that may possess the raw materials needed to distract my opponents." He pointed toward the darkness within the mound of earth covered in vines. "Your darkness makes you strong, if only you could slay the *inner* demons and break free. You will enter the darkness now." The boy who wanted to be called Ralphie disappeared into the darkness.

Kapaow tried to stop Ghost, but Ghost dragged Kapaow along. Was this his choice? As he entered the blackness, it felt too good to care. His movements felt like sleep walking, Ghost lost track of time. When they finally pierced through, he had to squint to let his eyes adjust to the light. It was so beautiful. There was sky inside somehow. It was bright and blue, not like the dreary gray outside.

They'd entered some kind of stone courtyard. It was constructed of stone, and the darker stones formed a circle on the ground where six more children sat, meditating. They were dressed in the same green robes as Ralphie. They breathed deeply, slowly, and controlled. They hissed as they exhaled and their breath surrounded Ghost, sending a chill up his spine.

Five of them sat closely with another posted about two feet apart from the others. Even though their eyes were closed, their heads turned to follow them as if they were watching him.

"Sit," the air commanded. The sudden harshness made Ghost feel awkward. "Please," the air followed, as the boy *Ralphie* smiled. Ralphie sat and crossed his legs, waiting for them to do the same.

Ghost and Kapaow both sat, crossed their legs, and draped their hands over their knees. They looked like mirror images of the boy. The other kids moved their heads back and forth, as if examining them, all without actually seeing them.

"You have questions. I will answer what I can and nothing more." Ralphie stared at Ghost.

At first Ghost hesitated, then slowly asked, "Are you controlling—"

"Yes, we bring back the dead. Though it is none of your concern *how*."

"Have you always been here or—"

"I cannot answer that."

Ghost figured they *had* always been around, somehow. He didn't know how. Maybe Bleak would have a theory on that. Still, his medieval times halved and quartered theory, a population obsessed with dismembering the dead, had to mean something. There were all kinds of folklore on the dead coming back and the measures taken to prevent it. Why would there be gaps, periods where the dead rising was not an issue?

"Where have all the bodies gone?" Ghost asked.

"Well," Ralphie smiled as the air boomed, "you truly are a clever one, are you not?" His smile faded. "I cannot tell you."

"What *can* you tell me?" Ghost didn't try too hard to hide his aggravation.

"Ultimately, I cannot guarantee you will see your beloved village again. Though I will promise you a chance to learn what is necessary to properly defend yourselves against the force you were not meant to survive against. Know that they will have likely adapted to the circumstances that saved you, and you will not be as lucky the next time."

"So why *did* we survive?"

"It is difficult to explain. I am not withholding information. I simply fear we do not have enough time to explain the process and motivations. What I can say quite simply is that my team and I are responsible."

"Okay, but *why?*"

"I chose you because I believed it would be the last thing our enemies would suspect," Ralphie responded.

"What are you?"

"I cannot answer that."

"HA! Fairy!" Kapaow clapped his hands and pointed at Ralphie.

Perhaps fairytales were just facts interpreted by people in a state of hysteria?

"They are quite unique, are they not?" Ralphie nodded approvingly in Kapaow's direction.

Ghost didn't like the way Ralphie referred to Kapaow like some piece of livestock. "Ha ha." Ghost chuckled lightly. "Ha ha ha ha." He laughed at Ralphie for being so rude to his friend. If Ralphie had any desire to gain favor with him, the last thing he should have done was mess with Kapaow in any way.

The sound of Ghost laughing seemed enough to make Kapaow laugh, too. Ghost began to laugh so hard his cheeks ached. Kapaow slapped his knee and pointed at Ralphie. Ralphie didn't seem to understand the joke. After a while it seemed like Ralphie had finally taken insult.

The boy looked around, like he'd seen a ghost, and backed into the little gap between the other boys. He sat down with them and closed his eyes. Ghost and Kapaow continued to laugh. The kids started to sway to-and-fro. It made him laugh more. A high pitched moan seeped out from their lungs, raspy and coarse, ear-splitting.

Ghost's vision started to blur. He felt a little sick, and yet he kept laughing. Something wasn't right. The part of him that was terrified became a smaller and smaller voice as he began to cough from laughing so hard. He felt his lungs tighten and his throat became raw. It grew more and more difficult to replenish his oxygen, but it was just so funny. His muscles started to burn. His hands began to cramp up. There was a sensation building inside him that felt so familiar–like someone holding on to his shoulders, but from inside his mind. Someone trying to drag him out of his own head. He hadn't really noticed it before, but the repetition, feeling it at A Shau, then feeling it now. Perhaps that feeling was Ralphie and his people?

Kapaow fell back as he laughed. He laughed harder. His arms stretched out. His head turned to the side, foam leaked from his mouth, and together they laughed. Kapaow looked like he was being pinned down by gravity.

Then, as if a switch turned off in Ghost's mind, he stopped laughing. A searing pain stabbed behind his eyes. Pressure built in his teeth so badly it felt like they were going to split open. His arm jerked forward, so hard his shoulder almost dislocated.

"AAAAAH!" Ghost screamed in agony.

What was happening? The pulses of pain forced his hand to move, jaggedly withdrawing his knife from its sheath. Ghost's bones snapped and twisted as he screamed. He moved into position over Kapaow, against his will. He raised his knife. It felt like something moved through his mind, flipping pages, looking for pieces of information. A part of his mind unlocked, the part that allowed him to completely understand what was about to happen to Kapaow. Ghost had become a prisoner.

"Come on. Yes, yes." Kapaow laughed, but his eyes showed only fear.

"Help me! Stop it!" Ghost screamed.

Ralphie and the other children's chanting began to sound like animals being beaten to death. The harder they chanted, the more his body ached, the more his joints tore away at themselves, pulses exploding inside him, forcing his body to plunge the knife lower and lower while he struggled to pull the knife away.

"NOOO! God! PLEASE! PLEASE GOD! NO! DON'T! PLEASE! PLEASE! PLEEEEAASE! PLEEAAASSSEEE!" Ghost pulled with everything he had. Still the knife lowered.

Kapaow stopped laughing. Stapled to the floor by some unseen force, he watched Ghost out of the corner of his eye. His breathing became labored. Ghost grew weaker and weaker. Other thoughts poured into his mind. He tried to bury it all, but it was like the more he buried, the weaker he got.

Puh Crk

The tip of the knife popped through Kapaow's skin. "AAAAAAAHHHHH!" Kapaow's scream just kept getting louder and louder.

All Ghost could do was fight as he was forced to listen to the cracking sound, like metal slicing through chicken legs. The knife continued to dig deeper. Kapaow spit and choked and gurgled, pain pouring out of his voice. The whole time he begged for it to stop. He begged in every language he knew.

The knife plunged deeper and deeper until it made a clinking sound and could go no further. Ghost felt his muscles spasm violently as he watched his arms tear the knife away, saw his hands were covered in his friend's–his *brother's*–blood.

Ghost shut down inside. Kapaow's head was suddenly able to move, and he looked into Ghost's eyes. He looked surprised, like he didn't believe Ghost would do it. Ghost didn't speak. He just ran away inside his mind, since he could not compel his legs to carry him anywhere. He watched his limbs stab the knife into Kapaow's chest again and again and again.

Then it was over, and Ghost collapsed. He regained full control of his body, but he was too weak to move. He lay in Kapaow's blood and cried like he'd never cried before. He felt someone at his side, putting a hand on his shoulder. It was Ralphie. Ghost was too weak to attack him out of anger, so he kept crying.

"I did not know… I am sorry," the air said.

You killed him.

"No. I tried to save you."

Me? Save Kapaow.

"We were… only capable of saving one."

Why? Why in God's name would you be so stupid and choose me instead of Kapaow?

"You are the key…" the boy sighed, but the air remained silent.

What happened?

"There is little time, my friend. I know you could feel me pulling back against the force that made you attack your friend. Some of my people are away on missions. Had they been here, we would have combined our abilities to stop the attack completely. I am spread too thin to properly resist our enemy. I need you and your men to help me with certain aspects of the resistance. I know this is a great deal to take in, but you have been sensing my presence for a very long time now. I have been watching over you."

What do I need to do?

"You are the only sensible thinker right now, so it needs to be you who chooses for yourself *and* for your men. If you agree to come under me and accept my training, it will be grueling, worse than the training you underwent to become the amazing soldiers you are today. You must know, though, that it will require going into a deep sleep for quite a while, in order for the mental conditioning to take effect.

"You will have to put complete trust in me to keep your bodies safe while we train your minds. The reward for such trust will be a better way to fight back instead of barely surviving." The boy looked at him, saw his disbelief. "I am sorry. I wish I had more time, but time is gone. All I can do now is leave the choice up to you, my friend. Stay and learn, or I will gladly put you back into the dark. But we will no longer be there to protect you. You will be all alone. The survival rate of soldiers without proper support is close to zero, my friend. Still, the choice is yours. I promise you this, though: if you hope to save what's left of your surrogate family, the hill tribe, you will come with me."

"I… I don't know…"

"I understand, but you still have to choose."

CHAPTER 47
KAPAOW

I'm still alive.

Ghost, help me! I'm still alive! Look for the flicker of life in my eyes. I'm still alive! Please! Put pressure on my wound, I'm still alive! Fight, Ghost! Fight! I'm here, you bastard! Look at me! Stop talking to them and think about the man lying next to you!

Damn you!

How can this happen? I fought, damn it! I fought! I gave it my all! I never stopped loving, I never stopped being open, even when I had reason to stop! Haven't I suffered enough! Haven't we? Why! Why? Why do we have to suffer? Why do I have to die like this? I was good, I am good! All the people I've helped, all the lives I've improved. The world is better because of me! Why do they shine while our light flickers? How is that right?

What else was I supposed to do? I'll do it! I've been listening this whole time. Just tell me what it's supposed to be! Anything you want, I'll do it! Answer me!

Answer me!

I'm cold.

Please don't leave me.

So this is what it's all come to then, huh? Were we supposed to just be slaves all along? That's not being alive. That's just existing. Existence without purpose, without joy, without love. What is that? I can't even grasp what that is. Why would you ever want that? How is misery easier?

Oh no.

That's what it was, wasn't it? Misery. When I grieved the loss of my family, and I put my hand to the ground and imagined myself going through their deaths, I stopped before my newborn son died. That's what this is, isn't it? Punishment for not truly letting go? Once I let myself avoid the pain and fear of one thing, I could avoid the pain and fear of another.

I could have told Chinny and the rest. I could have at any time. I was afraid. I was afraid of being alone, of being an outcast. I had already lost my family, and the village was just more reminders of that. So I went with Chinny and the team. I had to, to get away. To tell them the truth–that might have ended everything. And I might have been left alone in that jungle with nothing. And in that nothing I would have had nothing but my memories. And I would have remembered. I would have travelled back to my son's death. I would have gone through it and let go... and then what would I have?

What would I have?

I swear I didn't know that's what I was doing, I swear on my own soul I didn't know I was running, I didn't. It's so hard to be everything, so hard to face everything, to bear everything, I only slipped for a little while, why am I being punished?

Kapaow's muscles no longer flexed and contracted against his will. *They* had let go of him. They didn't need to hold him down anymore. They didn't need to force Ghost's hand anymore because there wasn't much left of Kapaow. *They* had won.

He had missed it all, yet it was all right in front of his face. Kapaow *knew* that carrying burdens without facing them created blind spots in a person's mind. Each blind spot took up space, leaving less and less room for their own humanity, until there *was* no humanity.

The Tree Fairies hid in those blind spots until they filled your mind, infected you until you became whatever they decided you would be, swayed like falling leaves in the wind, going wherever the current took you, much like an entire world looking away as Kapaow's people, the hill tribes, the true indigenous people of this land, were slaughtered; infected by *their* will.

The burdens of life were one of the keys. The bigger the burden, the bigger the blind spot, the harder it was to see anything else. He should have grieved the loss of his son completely. Instead, he had pulled away at the most painful moment. He should have never listened to Chinny when he told him to bury it.

Did that mean he was a complete failure? No. It couldn't. Perhaps if he had listened to Kim, none of this would have ever happened. If he had listened to Kim, however, nothing would have changed, either. The death of the tribes would be guaranteed. Knowing he could fail, knowing he could die, Kapaow had to try. He just lost sight of what was important along the way, and ran from his son's death, a blind spot big enough for the Tree Fairies to hide. More than that, he allowed his own fear to blind him to Chinny's needs. The man needed to be pushed toward the light. Kapaow should have tried harder, but fear begets fear, and along with the pain of his son, Kapaow had begun to fear failure. He was afraid he might fail with Chinny, so he didn't try completely.

Kapaow realized his final and perhaps ultimate mistake. In spite of his pride in balanced emotion and competence toward love, he had not truly mastered love at all. He had loved wholly until he had lost too much, and then he had pulled away. Now he saw that to truly love another, one had to love completely, even a loved one's passing. The concept seemed absurd, and yet as he began to drift further and further from life, it made more and more sense.

I should finish grieving the loss of my family now. To enjoy freedom for a moment before death.

He closed his eyes and felt the ground beneath him. He calmed his mind and let his anger fade away, putting it aside with many other feelings that blurred his inner vision. He continued to sift until all that was left was a deep, warm sensation with subtle tingling; the Earth's soul. Through the soul of the Earth, he began to travel in his mind, feeling the presence of everything. He would finish what he started and grieve his son.

He felt the blades of grass again and felt the laughter vibrating them. He travelled through the soul of the air until it touched the face of his newborn son, Go Doc. He waited, drifting about until he felt his son's soul allow him inside. He became his son.

He felt what his son felt as horror came to him. He suffered through the confusion again, the fear and overwhelming agony. He knew exactly what his son felt like, now that he too felt as if the entire world had decided it didn't like him anymore.

Kapaow dug his fingers into the earth as he felt time slow down, as he felt the explosion again, the shrapnel tear through him. His hands shook, his stomach turned. He felt his heart crushing inside him. Instead of pulling away, instead of screaming, he went back inside himself, to the place he had buried this moment, and he dug it up. He dug it up and embraced it. He felt his son die.

He felt the pain and understood now what his son felt as metal ripped through his flesh. He felt the fear, and understood, especially now as he felt the fear of his own death approaching. He felt the shame in not getting more out of life. He felt the loss. He felt cheated not being able to enjoy his family. He felt… he felt…

Clear.

Truly clear: a type of clarity that came as a shock, as if seeing the world for the first time. All that truly mattered became obvious, and all he had obsessed over seemed trivial. When he looked at the world around him, it *was* different than he had seen it only moments before.

His perspective changed. He had faced everything within himself and it opened his eyes completely. What he saw now was very different and very terrifying. There wasn't a cliff face at all. They had not climbed anywhere. They were lying on the ground at the foot of where the cliff had been. Chinny, Bleak, Crazy, and Sinner were all gone. Where had they gone? They were all supposed to stay close!

The boy with blue eyes was accompanied by many children. They sat in a large circle in deep meditation. Kapaow lay dying in the center of the circle as Ghost's tears trickled through the blood on his chest. Ghost talked to the boy with blue eyes, and in addition to the children, there was a man there. He looked human, but not quite, just as the boys looked quite close to human. It was just as his grandfather described: close enough to barely warrant a second look, but slightly off nonetheless.

The man was patting the boy on the shoulder, encouraging him, nodding in approval. After a moment of Kapaow staring, the man turned his attention toward him. More of his face came into view. There was a hideous scar up the side of his cheek that touched the corner of his eye, which was grayed and milky. The man smiled, pointed to the scar… and then pointed at Kapaow. He winked at Kapaow with his damaged eye and smiled a strange sort of smile that Kapaow had never seen before. It was a smile that wasn't a smile at all. It was a smile that said *"I got you."*

Then, Kapaow remembered that shot he took with his pistol, what seemed like ages ago, into thin air. He remembered the blood he and Chinny had found in the sand, and it occurred to Kapaow that at least some of this nightmare hadn't been about anything grandiose at all. It had been about revenge. He looked back up at the scarred man who continued to nod with that same smile.

"Mostly, this has nothing to do with you," the air seemed to vibrate around his ears making the sound of a voice within his mind. Was it the man speaking to him? Ghost seemed unable to hear it as he and the boy continued to talk. "I am teaching my son, as all fathers do. Teaching him how to herd the beasts of the world. Teaching him how to herd *you.*" The scarred man smiled. "Some say wars are about profits," he shrugged. "Profits herd people. It makes sense, and it is true, to some degree. Yet, for us, in many ways, wars are proving grounds. Displays of force and ability. They are status symbols, you see? We have many different types of status symbols, only one of which is turning the tides of war in our favor. Eliminating disobedient breeds; that's also a status symbol: a display of total competence in herding the livestock of the world. of maintaining complete control and total dominance.

"My boy," he patted the boy with blue eyes on the shoulder, "oh, I am very proud of my boy here for the things he's done with *you*. Especially for the things he is going to do with your people."

What? No! Ghost! Focus! See! Ghost! Chinny! Sinner! Bleak! Crazy! Help! Anyone! Help!

There were no good fairies. They were all evil, no matter what good they did. Their grand scheme had always been evil, and always would be evil. *Doom.* That was all Kapaow could feel as the man turned his attention back to Ghost and continued encouraging his boy. It was as if Kapaow had already ceased to exist. Why did this have to be the way he died, completely alone? He was a good person, the hill tribes were good people. They didn't deserve this. He felt himself drift uncontrollably. Too much blood lost.

Before I die, I'm going to finish this.

He continued to travel through the souls of the world. He decided to grieve his own death.

He felt the souls of his family, and the souls of all the world touching his skin. He felt a change in his state of mind. He shifted from his own perspective to all perspectives. He felt the stars, the sun, the Earth, the hearts of everyone. He felt the enemy. He felt their pain and their fear and their loss. He felt the way that pain blinded them, just as Kapaow had blinded himself by not facing his grief. He felt his friends. He felt his *best* friend: Chinny.

He felt Chinny's agony, and emptiness, and beneath it all, a yearning to connect again. He saw what had been destroying his friend from the inside out, and he was stunned by what Chinny felt. In spite of everything Kapaow had suffered, he had never suffered anything like that. That was why Chinny was the way he was. If Kapaow were able, he would have wept for the man. Suddenly, the desire for one last act of defiance presented itself.

Kapaow wondered, if he were truly connected to Chinny's soul at this moment: would Chinny feel his presence? If Kapaow believed he did, was he brave enough to communicate through the souls of the world and reach out to Chinny? He would never know if it worked, or if he had just been a fool, but what if he sent out a feeling, a warning, and Chinny received it somehow? What if?

Kapaow now fully grasped why his grandfather had pushed him so hard to conquer his inner demons. This was why fear had to be faced and not avoided. This was why he had to face the death of his own son, so he could be open enough to believe in a way toward victory, toward freedom, toward love. The difference between being a cold, mindless dead creature that did only as instructed, and a living, breathing free individual rested in these small victories.

He gathered up his feelings, focused them, concentrated them. He carried them through the grass, through the souls of the blood that stained the Earth until he felt Chinny's presence. Kapaow opened *himself* instead of trying to reach out to Chinny. He let his friend in, and he told him everything he had to say in a feeling. He had to believe that Chinny would figure it out, and the change would shift the outcome enough to save what was left of his people.

His entire body came to a calm and rested state. His eyes no longer moved, and Kapaow could swear he felt his friend's soul send something back. He felt the reply and understood that his friend had his own journey, and that faith was in letting the journey unfold as it needed. Kapaow let go, and as he faded, he felt it all: the universe, and his family… he felt his son. Kapaow let go as it all faded to black.

It's okay. I'm happy.

CHAPTER 48
CHINNY

"I tell ya, Chinny: I'm feelin' pretty good. Better than I have in a long while." Sinner smiled.

Chinny knew the feeling. It was almost out of place, like more of a good dream than a reality. Every bad thing in the world felt hazy, dulled. The sun was warm on Chinny's face. Everything was brighter now and the air wasn't as thick as it felt before; not as humid, not so unbearable and suffocating. It was calm and relatively quiet, with only the sounds of birds chirping and bugs buzzing. It was pleasant indeed.

"Feels strange, no?" Chinny pondered aloud.

"Yeah. Ya know what, though? I really feel like we're gonna be okay."

The woman with green eyes allowed her skin to brush up against Chinny's from time to time, and made him feel something he hadn't felt in quite a while. He looked into her eyes. The color seemed to sway, hypnotic, like emeralds glistening in the sun. She smiled. He smiled back at her—not a fake smile, not false-flirting to put up a guise for appearances. There was something about her. She radiated power. Her power made him feel less intimidated, like she was more than some delicate flower; like she could possibly survive him. The same way he could see into his enemy, he saw into her, and her soul was endless.

The Yards rejoiced and pointed to the distance when a small village came into view. For a moment, Chinny tried to remember how long they'd been hiking when the all-too-familiar sensation of watching eyes crept over his skin. He scanned the environment for any threats. After a few good looks, the only eyes he found were hers, gazing back into his. He took a deep breath and let it out. He gently reached up and plucked out a tiny bit of a leaf that had fallen into her hair. He could feel his cheeks turning red, but didn't care. She smiled.

The village grew closer, and he wondered about his own. He couldn't hate himself for leaving his own village. Orders were orders. They did what needed to be done. Chinny would make it right this time. They'd get on the radio, contact the village nearest their own, have them send word to their home, and get them to send help. Meanwhile, the rest of the team would meet them shortly at this place, where they'd likely have med supplies, food, a place to sleep, and most importantly, clean water. Then, once rested and resupplied, they'd rendezvous with their people and return home. They'd move the village somewhere new, somewhere harder to find. He'd do better there, the next time around. He wouldn't hold back as much. He'd visit with Cadeo and make amends. They'd forgive him. The Yards always did.

"The boys haven't caught up yet. Ya notice?" Chinny asked.

"We haven't been walking that long, I don't think. They're probably just being cautious."

"It'd be nice to have Kapaow here to translate."

"Eh, we're doing fine. These little bastards just need you to point and grunt and they pretty much get the drift. Besides–I'm sure they'll be here in a jiffy. Quicker we get the call in, quicker we get back home. We'll be fine. It ain't been all that long anyway, I don't think."

How long had they been hiking? Chinny couldn't quite remember whether it'd been ten minutes or ten hours. Though, since the sun still shone brightly in the sky, it could not have been terribly long. The sun seemed a bit… odd. It wasn't bad. It was merely a bit unfamiliar. The air seemed a bit odd as well: the jungle, the sounds.

Suddenly, he wondered if anyone at the village they were intending to contact even spoke English. Their team of Americans had been killed in a firefight. The enemy never found their village, but new soldiers were never sent, and the radio equipment had been left behind. They had communicated back and forth from time to time using the radios, but either Kapaow or Kim always did the talking. Now that their radio equipment was ruined and never got around to being replaced, their neighbors would have to relay the message. The problem was that Kapaow wasn't there to translate. They'd have to wait, so what was the point of–

She grabbed onto his arm, stopping him. She had decided to use him to balance herself while she adjusted her shoe. It seemed like such a strange thing to do. Part of him felt belittled by the action, yet another part enjoyed the fact that she'd chose him to lean on, that he was the sturdy thing she clung to. She brushed her hair over her ear and looked up at him with a smile from the corner of her eye. She looked embarrassed, or shy. It made him feel less shy toward her.

Somewhere in the back of his mind, he felt like there were things about their current situation that needed investigating. Her presence was so captivating, he couldn't steal his mind away long enough to determine what those things were. She smiled at him again. His stomach tingled like warm butterflies, and his skin tingled the way it used to before he'd gone completely numb over the years. He was coming back to life in her presence. Had he been staring at her for too long? He looked away.

They stopped at the foot of the village while the Yards entered. Perhaps everything was right about this. After all, they'd earned a bloody moment of peace, hadn't they? It was his gut instinct that was the problem, always screaming at him as if every corner and every person held danger. What could possibly go wrong with something good finally happening? He began to doubt the instinct, for if it had dragged him to Vietnam through kilometers of shite only to end up fighting an unthinkable enemy, perhaps his gut instinct wasn't worth a damn.

Together, Sinner and Chinny stared at the structures and people within the village. They smelled food cooking somewhere and enjoyed the pain of their hunger, because for the first time in a while, they knew it would be satisfied.

"I wonder if they make them little dollops of whatever with the crispy stuff on them," Sinner asked, more to himself than anyone else.

They hesitated to enter the village. He tried to search himself for a reason behind his body's actions. Then, suddenly, some sensation came over him. It swelled up in the pit of his stomach. It felt like he was dropping, only more epic than that—as if the whole world sank a few centimeters at once. There were so many thoughts racing through his mind at once, the feelings couldn't translate into anything. He just knew something had happened. He scanned the tree line. What was taking Kapaow so long?

She caught his eye again. Her smile. She bowed her head shyly, and crooked her finger. Follow me. Why did he let his gut ruin everything for him all the time? Some deep part of him insisted that his instincts were right, yet some other part of him was so tired of being unhappy.

He let his guard down when the village was attacked. He doubted Bleak about what was coming, when truthfully some part of him wanted to listen. Something needed to happen. He just couldn't figure out what.

He watched her slowly enter the village. She turned, with an alluring little smile on her face as she again gently crooked her finger, *Follow me.* Chinny nodded and smiled to her. As his stomach twisted again inside him, he began to follow her. Yes. He needed to figure it out, but right now he just wanted to enjoy a moment of peace.

Things were better, yet whether they were or weren't, he was going to enjoy them like they were. That's what Kapaow had always said, right? Smile. So, Chinny smiled. Everything would be fine. He felt *her* at his side and turned to smile at her. Out of the corner of his eye, he saw her smile. It seemed larger than what was natural. When he faced her… there was no one there. He turned and saw her walking through the gates into the village. He looked back–no one there.

Chinny hesitated for a moment. What was this feeling in his gut? He looked in Sinner's eyes and something seemed out of the ordinary with everything. For some strange reason, he thought of Kapaow. It was like seeing him for the first time. It was such a strange realization it was almost embarrassing.

Kapaow really is my friend, isn't he?

It was such a random thought, yet it was true. All this time, chasing intel, chasing orders, he was just avoiding the pain. Before they had left the village, the elder had told them all that when everything was buried, they needed to dig it all up again. He hadn't understood it, but now he had started to. Chinny had buried a lot, and because of it his judgment had been tainted, and many people had suffered. Cadeo, Kapaow, perhaps his own team. Perhaps Bleak especially.

Perhaps in this moment of calm, he had a chance to put things in perspective. No more waiting for orders. He understood it now. He didn't understand why he felt this sudden clarity, but that's what it was, wasn't it? Clarity. The Yards mattered, because good people mattered. Because you never left a man behind. Or a woman or a child for that matter. Those people had fought for them, were them, would always be them. The rest of the team was obviously on board, had been for some time. He looked at Sinner.

They were just waiting for me.

Normally, this would have pissed him off, the Yanks not thinking for themselves. For some strange reason he understood. It was hard being alone. It was hard going against the grain. It was hard not being accepted. The key was for the outcasts to unite. That was what they had all done, wasn't it? They were better than most, sure, but the bottom of the barrel as far as everyone else was concerned. They'd been slapped together into a haphazard unit and given unclear objectives: set up to fail. They hadn't failed, though. Instead, they saw past their differences, united, and won. That was all Kapaow ever wanted, wasn't it? A family, love... wanted Chinny to be his brother. So simple, and yet it only dawned on Chinny now. He felt it, though, for the first time in a long time: the possibility of a family. It felt good, like maybe it could work this time.

"When we make this call, when we get help, we'll see that the Yards get the real help they deserve, yeah?"

"Fuck yeah, boss. We've earned it, huh?" Sinner remarked.

"Earned what?"

"To feel like we done something good for a change. Some good to go with all the bad?"

Sinner was right, they *deserved* a moment of happiness. Kapaow had been trying to say that all along. Be happy. *Let* yourself be happy. Now, suddenly it was like the need to resist such a thing melted away and he got a glimpse of what his friend meant. *Kapaow is my friend, my.* His brother was trying to help him do more than just survive, but thrive. Perhaps... perhaps Chinny could be ready for that now. A true smile, a true laugh... perhaps a true *love.* Living again. Kapaow had taught him that, and now it'd sunk in. He'd go to Kapaow, he'd apologize. He'd let the bloke lead *him. Lead me toward that happiness, my brother.*

"Yeah, I'd say we've earned it, Sinner." Chinny smiled. He couldn't wait to tell Kapaow.

Things had finally worked out in their favor.

THE MONTAGNARDS ARE REAL.

The majority of their population has been annihilated. Today, Montagnard fighting men face a seemingly endless battle, where to lose means more than their own death. It means their wives and daughters will be chemically sterilized, and their families will be enslaved in work camps where they will stay until the day they die. The enemy they face never dies, and they are slowly being consumed by them.

The Montagnard people are one of few, if any, cultures who have faced attempts at genocide virtually alone and unsupported since 200 BC without giving up, nor is it likely that they ever will.

Many governments have promised the Montagnard people support. Each time Montagnard tribes accepted and fought with them, but once these governments' interests were secured, or political winds changed, the Montagnard people were abandoned once again to face an even more infuriated enemy. During America's involvement in the Vietnam War/Conflict, the Montagnards again agreed to fight in the hopes of gaining support for their people once and for all. They fought and died with American and Australian forces, and there are many American Special Forces that owe their very lives to the Montagnard people, who on many occasions sacrificed their own lives to save them.

When American soldiers were ordered to leave the Montagnard people behind and forget them, some refused, and instead set up an organization called Save the Montagnard People, Inc., which has rescued thousands of Montagnards from persecution. They continue to rescue hundreds more every year and give them food, shelter, clothing, as well as aid towards education and a chance at a future.

While they face far worse than the majority of people will ever endure, the most memorable trait American soldiers brought home about the Montagnard people was their limitless happiness. It was a happiness that, for some, pierced even the most war-torn hearts and changed their lives forever.

A portion of all sales of *Walk Through the Valley: The Hill Tribe* will be donated to Save the Montagnard People, Inc. (http://www.montagnards.org).

Coming Soon:

Walk Through the Valley
Origins: Calm Waters

Acknowledgements

Kyran Tompkins, for helping to tame the tornado
Eric Foster, Anne Marie Berger, Theresa Antonucci, Rudolph Rauch and many others for their honest input and proofreading
Tanya Stockton of Publishing Unleashed, who has no fiction department to represent me under, but saw enough potential to take me under her wing and offer guidance and support
Ludwin Cruz Design for the cover art
Felicia A. Sullivan for the editing and story input
Linda Tooch for the proofreading
Kody Boye for formatting

You, for taking the time to read this novel, which means a great deal to me.

Author Kephra Rubin has written articles, poetry and novels such as *Walk Through the Valley: The Hill Tribe*. A longtime fan of Vietnam War movies and Supernatural films, the decision to mix the two genres came as a natural choice. During the research phase, the book took on a life of its own as he interviewed veterans and learned of the little known Montagnard struggle against atrocities, including genocide, that rages on in the hills of Vietnam to this very day. A catharsis was experienced by both the author and the veterans, as painful and horrific truths laid the foundation for his work of fiction.

If you tactically acquired this copy and enjoyed it,
please consider purchasing a copy. The money you put
towards this book will actually help pay for
the production of the next book in the
Walk Through the Valley universe.
Also, a portion of the
proceeds will go to
benefit the
Save the Montagnard People, Inc.
Please visit the series website
for more information
and to buy your
own copy
now.

www.walkthroughthevalleynovels.com
-or-
www.wttvn.com

Thanks for reading
-Kephra

Made in the USA
Middletown, DE
05 April 2015